S.J. MARTIN

Byzantium

First published by Moonstorm Books 2023

Copyright © 2023 by S.J. Martin

All rights reserved. No part of this publication may be reproduced, stored or transmitted in any form or by any means, electronic, mechanical, photocopying, recording, scanning, or otherwise without written permission from the publisher. It is illegal to copy this book, post it to a website, or distribute it by any other means without permission.

This novel is entirely a work of fiction. The names, characters and incidents portrayed in it are the work of the author's imagination. Any resemblance to actual persons, living or dead, events or localities is entirely coincidental.

S.J. Martin asserts the moral right to be identified as the author of this work.

First edition

This book was professionally typeset on Reedsy. Find out more at reedsy.com

Contents

Chapter One	1
Chapter Two	10
Chapter Three	23
Chapter Four	33
Chapter Five	39
Chapter Six	49
Chapter Seven	61
Chapter Eight	71
Chapter Nine	81
Chapter Ten	95
Chapter Eleven	108
Chapter Twelve	119
Chapter Thirteen	125
Chapter Fourteen	133
Chapter Fifteen	144
Chapter Sixteen	157
Chapter Seventeen	165
Chapter Eighteen	171
Chapter Nineteen	182
Chapter Twenty	191
Chapter Twenty-One	201
Chapter Twenty-Two	213
Chapter Twenty-Three	222
Chapter Twenty-Four	232

Chapter Twenty-Five	239
Chapter Twenty-Six	247
Chapter Twenty-Seven	255
Chapter Twenty-Eight	264
Chapter Twenty-nine	274
Author Note	281
List of Characters	283
Glossary	285
Map	287
About the Author	288
Also by S.J. Martin	290

Chapter One

October 1100 – Constantinople

Georgio had been in the city for only a few hours when he decided to take a room, leaving his horse at one of the better inns near the walls. Handing his horse to an ostler, he carried his saddlebags into the inn. The innkeeper eyed this new arrival warily, for Georgio was in the full Horse Warrior regalia with his scarred, laced, leather doublet and trademark crossed swords on his back.

'How long are you staying?' he asked the tall warrior in front of him in a neither welcoming nor friendly tone.

'I'm not sure, but for several nights at least as I'm searching for a friend,' he replied with a smile that had little effect on the taciturn older man.

The innkeeper grunted in reluctant acceptance but then demanded payment upfront. Georgio, reaching for his saddlebags, straightened up and raised an eyebrow in surprise.

'Do you ask that of all your guests?'

The innkeeper put his hands on the table and snorted with disdain before replying.

'No, only the foreign strangers like yourself and shifty individuals who may be up to no good that I do not trust. We had many of those during the last crusade, leaving a lot of damage, and now they are considering starting another crusade to return to the Holy City. Madness, I tell you, pure madness and thousands more will die in the deserts.'

Georgio stared at him in dislike and thought about leaving to find another inn, but his horse would have now been untacked, and he was weary. He had little choice, so he took a silver coin from his purse, which the innkeeper raised to his mouth and dared to bite it, to check it was genuine. Georgio rolled his eyes in disbelief but followed the waiting serving girl up the stairs to a small room that looked out onto the high, dark, forbidding city walls beyond. He walked to a window; the shutters were wide open, and the odours of the midden and piss-pit behind the inn floated up from below. He stepped back, wrinkling his nose and shook his head, thinking how Conn would have had the man by the throat if he'd spoken to him like that. Georgio knew he may have earned the well-deserved reputation of a fearsome warrior in battle, but he tended to be easygoing unless challenged or threatened. While Conn often revelled in and enjoyed any confrontation and always emerged the winner.

The rather pretty serving girl was still standing inside the open door. Surely not waiting for a tip, he wondered, glancing at her, but then she smiled, raising her head and placing her hands on her hips. She now looked different from the girl downstairs, who had hardly raised her eyes before the innkeeper.

'I can provide extra services, if needed, during your stay here. A tall, handsome soldier like you, I would even give you a discount,' she said, grinning at him.

Georgio smiled and thanked her but declined the offer. Taking her gently by the shoulders, he propelled her out of

CHAPTER ONE

the room, closing the door firmly behind her. He sat on the bed and gratefully pulled off his dusty, high leather boots. He stood and placed them against the door as an early warning system and then lay down on the bed to rest his aching back and shoulders after a week of riding leagues every day and sleeping rough most nights since his stay in Thessalonica.

He closed his eyes and tried to sleep, but his thoughts churned around as he recalled the months of searching, following a thin, cold trail and only the odd clue as to where Conn was headed. He was fortunate that his friend was distinctive. Georgio was tall, but Conn was a hand taller and dressed as a Horse Warrior with the unusual crossed swords on his back; people in the towns and villages remembered that. He found, in a few places, that Conn had left mayhem and anger behind him with threats to kill him if they saw him again, so in those villages, Georgio made a hasty exit. It appeared that a grieving Conn Fitz Malvais was even quicker to anger, quicker to kill when threatened, and quick to swive a chieftain's willing, pretty wife while he was away hunting with his men.

While he lay there trying to sleep, Georgio admitted to himself that he was somewhat overwhelmed by the city's vast size, but he had been trained by the best, so he divided the city into four parts in his head. He would search each part in turn; if Conn were there, he would find him. The Horse Warrior would need a bed, so Georgio would try all the inns first.

The first day proved fruitless. He searched a better part of the city near his inn, but no one had seen a tall Horse Warrior. Even in October, the city was still hot, as the high, thick walls tended to keep the winds sweeping off the sea to a minimum. He returned to the inn that evening, hot, dusty and tired. He ate some food, washed and ventured out again, heading for the less salubrious establishments near the harbours, of which there were many.

He struck lucky at the third run-down alehouse; a scar-faced barkeeper remembered Conn.

'Yes, he was here, drunk and causing trouble two nights ago, but he paid well, so we let it pass. Usually, we would throw him out; the lads over there enjoy a bit of roughing up.'

Georgio turned and glanced at three sullen individuals sitting near the fire, who seemed to be weighing him up, probably assessing the weight of his purse. He suddenly realised his mistake of bringing a full purse to the streets at night, but he had not fancied leaving it in the Inn. Even the young pot collector, a thin, gangly lad, was shaking his head in comical dismay while watching the drama unfold. However, Georgio was not the type to be frightened off by a few ruffians.

'Do you know where he went or where he would be staying?' he asked, producing a coin. The barkeep quickly pocketed it but then shook his head, to Georgio's annoyance.

'No idea, never seen him before or after that night.'

Georgio grimaced in frustration as he headed for the door, but at least he knew he was on the right track; Malvais was here in the city. Meanwhile, the innkeeper grinned and nodded to the men near the fire; the pot boy sighed; another victim, he thought, shaking his head.

Georgio stood on the quayside for a while, staring at the low inn doorway, expecting to be followed, but there was no sign; perhaps they were deterred by the swords on his back, he thought, as he turned back to stare at the dark lapping waters behind him and the dozen or so fishing boats at anchor, lit by the bright moonlight. Suddenly, a hand touched his shoulder.

CHAPTER ONE

Georgio was surprised as he had not heard them approach; he whirled around, dagger drawn, dropping into a crouch to face his attackers. But it was the pot boy, tall with dark hair and eyes, a good-looking lad, who Georgio thought was about sixteen. The boy had stepped back in alarm, but the Horse Warrior sheathed his dagger.

'A good way to get killed, lad, sneaking up on people like that,' he exclaimed.

'I'm sorry, Kyrios, I did not think, as I was coming to help, but also to warn you.'

Georgio smiled at the use of the Greek word for lord; he, alongside Conn, had been knighted by King Peter of Aragon in his service, but he rarely used the title 'Lord.'

'This man you seek, he wears swords like this as well?' the boy asked, his head on one side.

'Yes, you saw him as well in the inn? Was he fighting?' asked Georgio, with a smile.

'No, I was not there that night, but I have seen him.'

'Where? Where did you see him?' demanded Georgio, stepping forward.

'Coming out of the gate at the barracks; he is a tall, broad-shouldered, impressive warrior. People's eyes are drawn to him, especially with these swords. He will be one of the mercenaries there. Our Emperor, Alexios Komnenos, is recruiting foreigners again for the war against the Seljuk Turks. I wanted to go and join, but my mother lives alone; I am her only son, and she refused to let me become a soldier like my father was,' he said woefully.

'You would also be too young,' pointed out Georgio, ignoring that both he and Conn were only sixteen when they rode off to the wars in Spain. He flipped the boy a coin for his information. The boy drew himself up to his full height.

'I am Darius, and I have my name day in a few weeks, and then I will be eighteen. Surely that is old enough.'

Georgio looked at the thin young man before him; he was sure he would see every rib if he lifted the thin, dirty tunic. He changed the subject, not wanting to offend the boy.

'So what was the warning?'

'Atreas and his men left by the inn's side door; they are waiting for you in the shadows to take your purse. They will probably cut your throat,' he announced in the matter-of-fact voice of a street urchin who has seen it all.

Georgio laughed and asked, 'Do you know where they are waiting?'

The boy nodded. 'They are getting set in their ways; they hide in the same doors and archways. It is the main thoroughfare for people to return to the city from here.'

'Is there any way of getting behind them?'

'You mean to get around them? To escape?'

'No, for me to come quietly up behind them and give them a taste of their own medicine', he explained, as the boy's eyes widened.

'I did say there were three of them, and these are well-armed, hard thieves from the wharves; few would take them on.'

Georgio shrugged, and the boy sighed at the foolishness of this warrior.

'If you are set on this, we must go over the rooves. I warn you it will be dangerous,' he exclaimed, to another snort of laughter from Georgio.

A short time later, Georgio softly dropped from a low roof into a dark, narrow, stinking alley running up from the harbour. He flattened himself against the wall, drawing his

CHAPTER ONE

long war dagger as the boy, Darius, dropped behind him but kept his distance, as instructed. The alley curved and widened, and Georgio could see the moonlight on the harbour waters through the arch at the end. It also showed the shapes of two men whispering to each other. However, he could not see the third man, which worried him as he crept slowly forward. His boots slid on the stinking refuse beneath his feet, and he knew he would have to be careful not to slip or slide when he took them on.

It was dark in the shadows, but fortunately for Georgio, the lone man standing in the doorway, just ahead of him, spat out into the alley. Georgio had been trained in stealth by the best warriors in the world, and he moved forward in silence. The man had craned forward, to watch his two friends, when Georgio slid in behind him; swiftly pulling his head back, he slit the robber's throat with only the slightest gurgle. Wide-eyed and excited at how easily this had been done, Darius slid behind him.

'Which one is Atreas?' whispered Georgio.

'The bigger, thick-set man on the left who is telling the weasel-faced one off for moaning.'

The two men were arguing as had taken far too long for the warrior with the full purse to appear, and the weasel wanted to return to the inn. Suddenly, there was the unmistakable sound of drawn steel close behind them, and both men reacted, reaching for their swords. Georgio slashed at the weasel's arm before his sword was out of its sheath. The man stood frozen, staring at where his hand had once been, as his sword clattered to the ground and blood flowed freely from his arm. He let out a strangled scream and ran, holding his arm to his chest.

This left the leader, Atreus, who quickly realised they had

taken on more than they expected, so he tried to bluster his way out, as he backed out of the alleyway towards the harbour. Atreas was no swordsman, as he relied on numbers and surprise in dark places. The Horse Warrior slowly and steadily followed him, sword in hand, out into the wider space, where they circled each other warily.

'You have killed and injured my men. Can we not now call a truce and go our separate ways,' he suggested, his brow now beaded with sweat, as he knew he was no match for this man.

'A truce suggests that we had engaged in a war, Atreas, but you set up a cowardly attack, an ambush, with three men onto a poor, unsuspecting stranger in your city.'

Realising that talking would not help, the robber assumed a resigned expression and then suddenly charged at the Horse Warrior, raising his sword high. Before the sword descended, Georgio had run him through as Darius stared open-mouthed at the speed and skill of this man, with the crumpled body of his attacker at his feet.

Georgio cleaned his sword on the dead man's tunic and turned to face the open-mouthed boy.

'Tell me, Darius, do you enjoy working at the inn?'

The young man shook his head.

'Good. For now, I will engage you as my servant and squire. This post might mollify your mother as you'll not exactly be fighting, well, not yet anyway.'

Darius was too overwhelmed to speak; he nodded enthusiastically as Georgio put two further silver coins in his hand.

'Your next three month's wages. Buy a decent tunic tomorrow; I cannot have my servant looking like a ragamuffin from the streets. You can give the rest to your mother and now for bed, for we have a busy day tomorrow when you will show me these barracks you spoke of tonight. Meet me at the inn by the eastern walls. My name is Georgio di Milan.'

Without further ado, Darius bowed to this knight and stepped over the dead body of Atreas without a backward glance. He trotted after the tall warrior, striding ahead, but could not keep the grin from his face as he clutched more money than he would usually see in a year to his chest.

Chapter Two

Early the next morning, Georgio was washed and dressed, ready to meet Darius at the arranged time. However, the boy was nowhere to be seen in the taproom or when he stepped outside the inn. Georgio did begin to wonder if he would ever see him again, or if the young man would disappear with the two silver coins he had foolishly paid him in advance. There was a bench outside the inn, and Georgio, crossing his long, booted legs, sat in the early morning sunshine, cleaning his bridle and waiting. He watched the bustle on the streets around him; the inn was at a crossroads near one of the gates, and hundreds of people were passing to and fro. Given his age, Georgio had always considered himself exceptionally well-travelled; now in his early twenties, he had seen sights and visited places that most men would never see. But that was before he reached Constantinople in the heart of the wealthy Byzantine Empire.

Georgio had been born in Milan, which he barely remembered, as his parents, who were poor weavers with seven children, had been forced to sell him to the monks when he was only six. This made his pathway through childhood difficult and, at times, torturous. This is where he met Conn; fortunately, they had been rescued, and as his family did not want him back, he was adopted by the Malvais family and taken to Brittany, where he had happily trained as a Horse Warrior.

Conn and Georgio's warlike career had taken them to Spain for several years to fight, in the forces of El Cid, in the Reconquista Wars against the Moors. As a mercenary, he had visited Leon, Toledo, Zaragoza and several other ancient and breathtaking cities in Spain. He had even spent a month with friends at the lavish French court of King Philip in Paris, with its marble floors and halls. But all of this was nothing compared to the sights of Constantinople, the great capital of the Eastern Roman Empire.

They said this city had been built to rival Rome, and Georgio could believe that, as he had ridden through the impressive stone entrances in the high defensive Theodosian walls the day before. The busy, teeming streets seemed to stretch forever inside the city as Georgio passed magnificent palaces and huge buildings with high, domed roofs, turrets, and towers. At one point, he had dismounted and stood inside the awe-inspiring domed Church of the Holy Wisdom, the seat of Nicholas III, the patriarch of the Eastern Orthodox Church. He continued exploring the city for hours until he eventually reached the city walls on the far side of the ancient harbour of Prosphorion. He had tied his horse to a rail and climbed the high wall surrounding the harbour. A brisk, salt-laden sea breeze had blown his curly dark hair from his face as he scanned what lay before and behind him.

Georgio realised why the city was easy to defend, as it was on a wide pointed peninsula between the Sea of Marmara to the west and the strait of the Golden Horn to the east. He had stared across the Bosphorus towards Asia Minor. He realised this was where Duke Robert of Normandy, Count Raymond of Toulouse and the other leaders of the First Crusade had crossed with their huge armies, heading south to take back the holy city of Jerusalem. He now knew that only a fraction of them returned alive.

Turning to gaze over the city's rooftops, he could see it was enormous, and Georgio had suddenly felt a sense of hopelessness, which was unusual. He had been searching for his friend, Conn Fitz Malvais, for months, but he had no idea how to find him in a city of this size without help. It had seemed a Herculean and daunting task, and that was if Conn was even still here in Constantinople.

Now, he thought he had found someone to help him but he grew tired of waiting outside the inn as he realised that young Darius was not coming; he was disappointed in the boy, and sighing, he stood up. It was now his task alone to find his friend. He wondered where to start, and the words of their mentor, Piers De Chatillon, echoed in his ears.

"If a man truly does not want to be found, he can remain lost forever."

It would be easy in a city this size to remain lost. Conn likely did not want to be found after the harrowing and tragic events they had been through; he was grieving and full of guilt, anger and sadness. However, Georgio was determined to find him, as he was not complete without Conn in his life. They were brothers in arms who had been through hell together. They had come out the other side, but neither had been left unscathed by the year's events. Now, however, he had a clue; Conn had been seen coming out of the barracks. Somewhat naively, he wondered how many barracks there could be in Constantinople as he strode off to begin his search.

CHAPTER TWO

There proved to be far more than he imagined, depending on the status of the soldiers and guards. Georgio soon found that Emperor Alexios had over a dozen large cohorts of men garrisoned in different parts of the city, some of them from distant parts sent by allies of the Emperor. Alexios cleverly kept them apart with their own serjeants and officers who spoke their language, but they all followed the Emperor's orders. He worked his way around the city and found that the guards, on almost every gate, regarded an armed Horse Warrior warily, while some were downright threatening. So much for the comradeship and solidarity amongst soldiers, he thought as he sat down wearily in the shade by one of the many fountains in the city.

It had now become too hot to tramp the streets, and realising he was hungry, he wandered to one of the many market food stalls. The array of food was tempting and smelt delicious. He tried rounds of pastry full of goat's cheese and folded parcels of meat, highly spiced, which made his mouth tingle, but he liked them and ate two more. Being far to the east on the Spice Road he was tasting foods he had never encountered before. It was there, in the shade of the late afternoon, that Darius found him napping under a tree.

'Kyrios, I have been looking for you everywhere; I had an urgent errand for my mother, but you had gone when I reached the inn. I checked that your horse was still there and then tried to find you,' he said with relief.

Georgio sat up and stretched but then narrowed his eyes at him.

'You were late on your first day in my employ. Imagine what would happen if warriors were late for battles, Darius.'

The incorrigible young man dared to grin.

'Then I imagine many lives might be saved.'

Georgio gently cuffed his head in admonishment, but he was pleased to see him; he needed his help in this city. Darius took Georgio to the barracks close to the Great Palace, where he had seen Conn emerging from the gates. Here, the guards were more encouraging as the older serjeant was called, and he looked the tall Horse Warrior up and down. He was clearly pleased by what he saw.

'Are you here to be recruited, to join the Emperor's army? We need more trained men of your sort,' he asked.

Georgio, not rising to the *'your sort'* comment, took it as a compliment and thanked the serjeant. Then he explained his quest and admitted that perhaps he might be recruited later when he had found his friend; this was said more to appease the serjeant as he had no idea of Conn's plans.

'Yes, we know of this Horse Warrior called Malvais. A ferocious fighter, few can stand against him. He was found and recruited by John Doukas himself,' he announced proudly.

Georgio could see that the serjeant expected a surprised response, and he did his best while looking to Darius for clarification.

'The great war hero and general, John Doukas, an honour indeed, Kyrios,' he said to Georgio, adopting a suitably awed expression.

'General!' exclaimed the affronted serjeant.

'John Doukas is no mere general; he is the Megas Doux!' he replied proudly.

Georgio raised a questioning eyebrow, never having heard the term.

'The Commander-in-Chief of the Byzantine navy and now also of the army in Anatolia, he is the brother-in-law of our emperor, Alexios Komnenos and has defeated the Turks in a dozen great battles,' the serjeant explained, exasperated at the foreigner.

The two men standing in the dust outside the barracks looked impressed by this man's accolades, but this was not why they were there.

'Can you possibly get a message to Conn Fitz Malvais that we are out here waiting to speak with him?' asked Georgio.

The serjeant nodded, bowed his head in salute, and left them. It seemed an eternity, and it must have been over an hour, for the sun was beginning to descend when a guard returned to say that they had looked everywhere, but Malvais was not in the barracks or on the training ground. Turning away in frustration, Georgio thanked the man, but then he turned back.

'Tell me, where do the mercenaries and soldiers from these barracks go to drink?'

The man grinned and pointed.

'There are long, narrow streets running up that hill to the east with many taverns, alehouses and stews full of the better whores. The knights tend to use those, but it can be dangerous once it gets dark, especially in the lower streets.'

Darius nodded. 'I know that area, but it is a good walk.'

Georgio sighed, having been on his feet all day.

'Everywhere in this city seems a long walk. Come, Darius, let us go; we may be lucky and find him in one of the inns there.'

Darius set off at a pace while describing the city, its streets and its sights as they went. 'This is the great Roman hippodrome where they held chariot races. Some say it would hold nearly a hundred thousand people. The Emperor Theodosius filled it with statues of heroes such as Heracles and huge bronze horses, most of which are still there. They say some of the giant obelisks came from the pharaohs of Egypt. You should visit it while you are here; the starting gates have four huge gilded horses on the top. They will take your breath away.'

Georgio could hear the pride in the boy's voice for his city but was also impressed by his knowledge and articulation. It made him curious about him.

'How do you know these things? Can you read, Darius?'

To his surprise, the boy nodded.

'When my father was alive, he would send me to the monks twice a week. We had money then, and as a second son, he wanted me to enter the Church, giving my family more status; the monks said I was bright and could go far as I had a fair hand for calligraphy and the illumination of the gospels. My father was a serjeant in the Emperor's army, and Gregori, my older brother, joined him there as soon as he was old enough. They fought together under the great John Doukas, but my father was killed in the long and bitter Battle of Ephesus some three years ago; Gregori was badly wounded as well. They brought him home, but he died of his wounds a few weeks later at the age of only eighteen. This is why my mother refuses to let me join. We received the army death payments, but that did not last long with rent and food, so I gave up the idea of the Church, said farewell to the monks and became the family breadwinner by finding jobs in the taverns; it helped that I could read and write so I could sort and deal with bills of lading and deliveries.'

Georgio put a hand on his shoulder in sympathy as they entered the streets that ran up the hill; dusk was beginning to fall, and lamps were being lit in windows in the narrow streets. However, the numerous street traders were not deterred, and street after street, the array of merchandise on the stalls entranced Georgio. He ran his fingers over fine bolts of silk and inhaled the heady aromas of herbs and spices, some he had never seen piled high. There were mounds of fruit and vegetables, with chickens, rabbits and even snakes stacked high in cages and baskets, while the smell from the numerous food stalls was enticing. The noise was sometimes almost deafening with the ringing blows of the small hammers and awls of the metalsmiths, who worked in brass and sometimes silver; the large decorated metal platters hanging for sale on the walls shone like beacons in the light from the sinking sun.

The streets were busy with people of all shapes, sizes and nationalities. He saw tall, blond, armed men who looked like the Rus from the north, with braided hair and long moustaches. They rubbed shoulders with Nubian servants escorting beautifully painted women, and he caught a glimpse of a cross-legged Chinaman, with his distinctive pigtail, as he wove intricately patterned baskets. Traders acted in amusing scenes to bring customers to their stalls with much laughter while calling out their wares. Musicians and drummers seemed everywhere, sometimes playing instruments Georgio had never seen before. These streets were also rife with thieves, but forewarned, Georgio kept a tight grip on his purse, backhanding away several barefoot children with small sharp knives, hoping to cut it from his belt. Despite that, he loved the cosmopolitan nation of Constantinople; it was one of the liveliest and most vibrant cities he had ever set foot in.

The further they went, the streets became darker and narrower, with fewer traders and the stench of the refuse and detritus underfoot rose as they visited several dubious establishments to no avail. The men there know of the Horse Warrior as he could sometimes be a troublemaker, but they had not seen him that night. As they climbed higher, the streets widened again, and larger houses and trees appeared. It seemed a slightly better area of the city, but it was still teeming with soldiers, and dark figures stood in doorways who would rob anyone in the blink of an eye. The crossed swords on Georgio's back seemed to deter them.

Finally, they reached a larger, well-kept establishment, with a sign hanging outside, announcing that this was *Le Cheval D'Or*, with a faded picture of what could once have been a rearing horse. Georgio laughed, peering at it as it swung in the slight breeze.

'I would lay odds that we'll find him in here.'

Darius looked puzzled as he could read and speak Latin but not old French. To the amusement of passers-by, Georgio found himself imitating riding a rearing horse while Darius laughed.

This inn was a better class of establishment; their feet did not slide on filthy rushes or stick to the wine and ale-splattered floor as they entered the large taproom that ran the full length of the building. It was full, with almost every table occupied; Georgio could see at a glance that many of the clientele were soldiers, although he noticed several well-dressed merchants or sea traders deep in conversation. Half a dozen serving girls were wending through the crowd while keeping up sassy banter with the men at the tables. A bench and a small table near a window became free, and Georgio moved to take it. He realised he was hungry, and to thank his young friend for his help, he ordered plentiful food and drinks for them both.

CHAPTER TWO

After a quick scan of the room, Georgio realised Conn was not there; he was distinctive and would easily stand out in a room, although that sometimes had disadvantages. Georgio was disappointed, but at least he knew Conn was here in the city, so it was only a matter of time before they tracked him down. This was the closest he had been yet to find him, so he did not even ask the owner, who seemed to be rushed off his feet. It was now approaching midnight, and standing, Darius mentioned one or two other places they could try before returning. As they approached the outside door, an older but still pretty serving woman ascended the staircase. She turned and smiled a welcome to Georgio.

'Another tall, handsome Horse Warrior. Would you like to come upstairs as well?' she asked.

She did not get the response she expected as Georgio, with a sharp intake of breath, reached out and, grabbing her wrist, pulled her down the two steps to stand in front of him.

'There is a Horse Warrior upstairs?' he asked.

Misunderstanding him, she pulled her wrist away and laughed at what she thought was his naiveté.

'Yes, but he might be very busy; he has two of my best girls with him.'

Without another word, Georgio pushed her to one side and took the stairs two at a time to the narrow, dark balcony above, which looked down onto the room below. This led to a windowless corridor with four doors, all on the same side. Torches flamed in holders on the walls. Georgio opened each door in turn, surprising several customers and receiving a foul-mouthed rant for his trouble. In the third, he received an invitation to join them, and finally, he reached the last door. Could she have been mistaken, he thought as he slowly turned the handle, with Darius hovering close behind him.

However, the door was suddenly pulled open, wrenching the handle from his hand. A buxom girl stood there clutching a leather pouch of coins. Georgio recognised the red leather purse immediately; it had the papal stamp on the side and was part of the payment Conn would have received for his last assignment with Piers De Chatillon.

Her eyes flew wide as she saw Georgio and Darius on the threshold, and she stepped back into the room. Looking past her, they could see a big corner room, probably the best in the inn, well furnished with a large bed. There were several candles, some of which had burnt down and were guttering, but there was still enough light to take in the surroundings. Having spent the last few years of his life in establishments like this, Darius knew exactly what was happening.

'Stripping him clean, are you?' he asked, confronting the whore who stepped back again and nervously glanced towards the bed.

Another naked girl swung her legs out of the bed, and sitting on the edge, she reached for her tunic and pulled it over her head. Meanwhile, Darius snatched the purse from the first girl's hand, who let out a squeal of rage but could do little against two sober, armed men. Untying the purse, Darius tipped several silver coins onto his hand and hissed through his teeth as he saw how much was in there.

'Taking him for a fortune, were you? Robbing a palace warrior, one of John Doukas' men. Should I shout that from the balcony to the men below and see what happens to you? They would swive you first and then lynch you from a beam,' he spat at her as she cowered back from him in alarm.

He took several of the smaller coins and dropped them at

her feet. Dropping to her haunches, she scrabbled for them before they dropped through the gaps in the boards, and her companion rushed to join her.

'That's more than you deserve. Now get out, both of you,' he yelled as they scurried past him.

Georgio stood, surprised, as he watched the easy-going young man turn into a different person in front of his eyes; suddenly, he wondered if Darius was also setting him up; he was alone in a strange city and had trusted the young man. However, Darius grinned at him and immediately handed him the purse.

'Have your back teeth out to sell as well, if they could,' he muttered, and then, glancing at the bed, asked, 'Is he alright?'

Georgio stared at the prone figure and slowly walked over to him while Darius picked up a candle and, bringing it closer, gave a low whistle.

'I have never seen anything like that before,' he exclaimed.

Conn lay face down on the bed; Georgio could see that he was breathing, so he was either drunk or drugged. He knew that whores would often drop something into the drinks of those worth robbing. However, what was unusual was that Conn was naked, for he had always kept on a thin linen tunic with any woman, as he did himself. Georgio had never known Conn to risk anyone seeing him naked, which worried him.

The full-length tattoo on Conn's back was there to see in all its colourful glory. It ran from the nape of his neck to the base of his spine. It was a large steel blue sword, but it had been turned into a crucifix, with a widened wooden cross guard, on which the crown of thorns rested. From this dripped seven large drops of blood to represent the Brotherhood of the Seven Warriors of Christ. Blue and yellow flames fanned his lower back from the blade's tip. The warrior monk who had inked this on their backs had explained that these were the flames of vengeance against the enemies of Christ, the infidels, the blasphemers against whom they would fight. He had taken days to complete this painful tattoo on the seven boys.

'What is it? What is it for?' whispered Darius.

Georgio grimaced but did not reply at first, for he also had the identical tattoo on his back.

'He had no choice. The Warrior Monks forced it upon us when we were boys. Taken, bought or, like Conn, stolen away from our families, and now we have to wear it as a badge and a reminder of those nightmare painful years for the rest of our lives.'

'Tattooed Warriors,' whispered Darius as Conn groaned and began to stir.

Chapter Three

October 1100 – Rouen

Sibylla of Conversano, an Italian beauty, wealthy heiress and newly married wife of Duke Robert of Normandy, watched her husband as he raged, roared and stormed up and down the chamber. She waited until he stopped by the mullioned window, his face red, his chest heaving with emotion, then she stood, walked over and put a hand on his arm.

'This may make you feel better in the short term, my lord, but you need to calm yourself and think through the possibilities the King's death and your younger brother's betrayal presents to us. Come with me.'

Robert met the serene face of his wife and let out the breath he had been holding. This had been a marriage of convenience at first; the only daughter of Count Geoffrey of Brindisi had brought Robert immense wealth, but after a few months, he found that he was falling in love with his young wife, Sibylla. She may only be twenty-two years old, but she had helped to manage her father's households and estates for years, and he discovered that not only had she been well educated as her father's only child, but she also had a wise and astute head on her young shoulders.

She led him to the steep stairs of the castle tower in Rouen.

It had been a bleak place, rarely used, but the views were outstanding, and it now boasted chairs, a table and a brazier placed in the round room to make it more comfortable. If she had thought this would calm him, she soon discovered her mistake; he was surprised and annoyed she had brought him here, and he stomped to the larger window, which looked out across the rooftops and streets of Rouen below, and threw open the latched wooden shutters. The city had originally been the capital of Normandy, but Robert's father, King William, had moved the capital to Caen, where he built an impressive fortress. However, once he came into the dukedom on his father's death, Robert returned the capital to Rouen to the delight of the city's burghers and merchants. It had now grown to a prosperous and wealthy port on the River Seine.

'Come and sit Sire; there will be a way to resolve this; we need to think it through,' she said softly.

'Can you see this window, Sibylla? This shuttered window,' said Robert, stony-faced as he turned to face her.

She nodded, not sure where this was heading, as she could see he was working himself into a fury again.

'My loyal brother, Henry, once threw a man to his death from this window. A young, wealthy wine merchant who, in alliance with my brother, William Rufus, fomented a rebellion against me here in Rouen, in my capital! And, while my nobles told me to flee to safety across the river, Henry was here in Rouen leading my troops and slaughtering the rebels, which is what I should have been doing. Then, with his own hands, he dragged the leader of the rebellion, Conan, up here and flung him to his death on the cobbles below. I was pleased at the time, partly relieved that it was over, but I should have realised then how ruthless Henry was and that underneath

CHAPTER THREE

that studious, clerkish mien, he longed for power and was, in fact, cleverly undermining me. I'm sure he and his men spread the rumour that I had run away.'

Sibylla said nothing; instead, she assumed a sympathetic expression, and indeed, she had great sympathy for him. For the second time in his life, he had been deprived of the throne of England. His younger brother, William Rufus, stole the crown at his father's death, and it happened again. While he was away, risking his life for years on the crusade to take back Jerusalem, his brother, Henry, stole the crown from under his nose.

'I presume you have realised the one great positive of the death of William Rufus?' she asked, coming to stand beside him at the window and placing her hand in his.

The rage was still too strong inside for him to think clearly, so he just blinked at her, unable to see anything positive about the death of William and his brother's betrayal.

'The vifgage!' she exclaimed. 'You do realise that the document you signed was with William Rufus personally. It was not with the King of England or with the English Treasury. When he drafted that agreement, the King's man, Ranulf Flambard, thought he was clever and protecting William Rufus. Now the King is dead, and I hear his treasurer, Flambard, is incarcerated in the Tower of London charged with embezzlement,' she stated in satisfaction.

Robert took Sibylla by the shoulders and gazed down at her, trying to grasp what she meant. He had signed the vifgage document in good faith before leaving for the crusade. He had mortgaged Normandy to William Rufus for ten thousand marks, a fortune that had enabled him to equip, feed and pay over a thousand of his knights and men to take with him on the crusade. He had no doubt, at the time, that with the plunder he would accumulate in the Middle East, he would easily pay off the vifgage and take his dukedom back from William Rufus. In fact, the plunder had been limited, and most of his money went on feeding and retaining the few hundred men he had left. The crusade had lasted for years, and thousands had perished in the heat, drought, dirt and disease in the deserts. His marriage to a wealthy heiress had saved him, and he now had the money to pay the vifgage.

Comprehension finally dawned, and he realised what she was saying, although his mind refused to accept it at first, and taking her hand, he pulled her around to face him.

'You are saying that I don't need to pay off the debt; surely that cannot be right, for we made oaths to keep to the agreement in front of the nobles and with the approval of the Papal Envoy, Piers De Chatillon.'

Sibylla sighed as she started to explain again.

'Yes, but your brother is dead, and the vifgage document died with him. So yes, you have the problem of Henry stealing your throne while we were returning home, but you now have the funds to right that wrong if you wish.'

Robert pulled her into his arms and, holding her tightly, he bent and kissed her eyes and lips; she laughed at him and pulled away.

'Come, I hear voices and bustle from below, and I imagine your supporters are arriving. You must go down and hear their views, for I imagine they will be as equally angry about this betrayal by your younger brother as you are.'

This was soon shown to be the case as some of the wealthiest and most powerful nobles awaited Duke Robert as he descended the stairs into the Great Hall. A great cheer of acclaim went up, and Robert Belleme, Earl of Shrewsbury, who held immense lands in England and Normandy, was the first to greet the Duke. Although a cruel, sadistic, and manipulative man, to give Belleme his due, he had supported Robert since his early rebellion against his father. Beside him stood William, the powerful Count of Mortain. Cousin to both Robert and Henry, he held all of Cornwall and the strategic castle of Pevensey, with a good harbour in the south of England. A raft of other nobles had also gathered in Rouen: William Warren II, Earl of Surrey, Eustace, the Count of Boulogne, Henry, the Count of Eu.

Casting his eyes over them, Robert realised that many of these men, or their fathers, had backed his failed rebellion of 1088 to seize the crown from William Rufus. Now, despite their losses and the punishments they received for that venture, they were back again at his side; such loyalty overwhelmed and inspired him.

Watching with satisfaction, Sibylla thought it was more than that. They had seen or heard that Henry's acclamation and coronation had been a hasty hole-in-the-corner affair, with only a fraction of the nobles to support his accession to the throne. Also, Duke Robert had far more to offer as he was a victorious crusader, the hero of Jerusalem. He was also the eldest son of King William, and Henry was now an oath-breaker; they had seen him with his hand on top of the holy relics as he had promised to pay homage to his brother, Robert, as the chosen heir to William Rufus. She could see that these nobles believed Duke Robert had a genuine grievance against Henry and were there to support him.

She watched in delight as they clasped arms with him. Many had fought alongside him, and several had been with him on the Crusades. She did not doubt that with such support, Robert could rout Henry and take back the throne of England, and then she would become his queen.

'Tell us your plans, Sire, and we'll begin to prepare; our men can be rallied in months. Apart from the Beaumont brothers, there are few who will support Henry's claim,' shouted William of Mortain.

'Sibylla and I are to travel to Mont St Michel in a few days, for I made a sacred vow in Jerusalem to give thanks in the abbey there if I came back alive to Normandy. However, I will purposefully travel through the Cotentin, the land Henry still thinks of as his. The nobles all cheered at this point until Belleme cleared his throat and strode to the front.

'Sire, I see that the Papal Envoy is noticeable by his absence. Piers De Chatillon is usually found at your side in troubled times. Is this an indication that the Pope supports Henry's claim? Because many of us here can attest that Chatillon spent many weeks in London, at the side of William Rufus, before the King's untimely and unexpected death.'

'I have sent a missive to Pope Paschal to ask for his support in this matter. My brother, Henry, has broken his oath. Therefore, his coronation should be declared null and void, and with the Church against him in England, Henry cannot remain on the throne. I have also sent a missive to Piers De Chatillon to ask for his wise council on this, as you say, Belleme; he has never failed me in the past. Meanwhile, I assure you that we will assemble a large fleet.'

'I have the large harbour of Treport; it is six leagues north of Dieppe and would be a shorter distance to cross the channel, Sire,' suggested Henry, Count of Eu.

'That sounds ideal, and we'll begin almost immediately.

CHAPTER THREE

Belleme, will you join Henry of Eu in establishing our base there? We now have almost unlimited funds for men, weapons and ships, and I will leave it in your capable hands.'

At this, another great cheer went up in the hall as there was a commotion at the back of the hall, the sounds of arrival and several men appeared in striking blue livery. The crowd parted like a wave as they slowly marched forward, escorting a diminutive hooded figure in their midst. Robert paled slightly as he stood with his wife, Sibylla, for he recognised the livery and knew who it was arriving. So did most of the assembled nobles, and the whispers began as elegant white hands lifted the hood from her blonde hair, which still surrounded her head like a halo and cascaded down her back in waves. It had always been her crowning glory. Her eyes met those of Duke Robert, and she smiled.

Due to the Crusades, he had not seen her for several years; she was older, and despite the smile on her face, she looked colder and harder than he remembered. But, there again, he had lived with the soft beauty of Sibylla at his side for the last nine months since his wedding. He finally found his voice as, putting out his hand, he raised her from the low bow she had sunk into. The large crowd of nobles watched, almost transfixed to see how he would deal with this arrival.

'Welcome, Countess, although I'm surprised you are here as I hear your husband, the Earl of Buckingham, has not only accepted the coronation of my treacherous brother but even had a hand in facilitating it.'

Agness de Ribemont, the long-time mistress of Duke Robert, gave him a sweet smile whilst ignoring the public slap in the face he had just delivered. She stepped closer to him, ignoring his wife beside him and the numerous nobles behind her.

'Sire, both you and I know that our long-term love for each other transcends these petty transgressions. Buckingham has always transferred his loyalty with the direction of the wind or depending on the generosity of his new patron. As you know, I have always despised him. I did my duty and gave him the son and heir he wanted. Now, I wash my hands of him, and my attention will be given to supporting the career of our handsome, successful son, Lord William of Tortosa.'

Sibylla had watched this calculated and manipulative play in front of her in silence, but now she gave a sharp intake of breath at this woman's audacity to publicly not only acknowledge her relationship as the mistress of her husband but to suggest that it would continue while championing their illegitimate son. Robert found himself caught once again as he stared into his mistress's large, unusual violet eyes; she had wrapped and held him tight in her coils for years. She may be older, but she was right; they had a joint interest in their son, not only that, she was one of the most exciting, albeit demanding lovers he had ever had. Suddenly, he felt a sharp nip on his forearm. Turning away from Agness, he found Sibylla's questioning but understandingly angry gaze on him.

'Countess, may I introduce my wife, Sibylla of Conversano? I assure you that we both welcome your support. Anything you can do to persuade the Earl to recognise the rightful heir to the English throne would be appreciated.'

Sibylla, whose eyes had never left the woman's face, saw the quick flush of anger on her cheeks; she gave Sibylla a vitriolic glance before she inclined her head in a quick bow before reluctantly moving away.

'Mio Dio! She truly hates me', she murmured to Robert, who ignored what she said and clapped his hands for wine

CHAPTER THREE

and refreshments to be brought.

The nobles settled onto the benches and chairs around the trestle tables while Sibylla suddenly felt a shadow at her side. It was Robert de Belleme, the Earl of Shrewsbury, who boldly ran a finger along the bare skin of her forearm, which made her shiver involuntarily.

'You have a true viper in your nest there, my lady. I suggest you stamp on it hard and cut off its head before it has time to strike. It would be best if you persuaded the Duke to remove the Countess of Buckingham from this court, for no good will come of her poisonous presence here, and she may do immeasurable harm,' he whispered.

Sibylla looked up into his dark eyes and realised she could have a powerful ally in Belleme, but she was not naïve; she had cut her teeth in the courts of Italy and could imagine what he wanted in return. For now, however, she would keep him on her hook, so she placed a hand on his and, smiling up into his face, thanked him for his warning before stepping off the dais to join Robert.

Belleme watched her go; her tall, graceful figure swayed through the tables as she smiled left and right, welcoming the Anglo-Norman lords. He smiled, for he was determined to have her in his bed before Yuletide.

Much further north, a few leagues southwest of Paris, Piers de Chatillon, Papal Envoy, a wealthy French lord and assassin, was in a quandary. He had received the missive from his friend,

Duke Robert, and had been about to leave for Rouen to be at his side when a new message arrived by pigeon from Rome. It was an order from the inexperienced Pope Pascal that he never expected to receive, an order not to go to Rouen or give support to Duke Robert yet. Instead, Chatillon was to await further developments and use the time and his informers to find out exactly who would support Robert in his planned war on his usurping brother in England.

Chatillon clenched his fist and slammed it down on the desk in frustration. This new Pope was erring on the side of caution. If Robert ever found out that the Pope had endorsed and helped to facilitate Henry's request to assassinate William Rufus, that could bring about their downfall. But if they did not support Duke Robert and he was ultimately successful in taking back the crown, he would never forgive them, and they would have lost any influence over him as the new King of England, which they had spent decades building.

Chapter Four

November 1100 - Palace of Westminster, London.
It was with great reluctance that Archbishop Anselm of Canterbury accepted the coronation of Henry Beauclerc as King of England. He had been in exile in France at the time, and the Bishop of London had been persuaded to conduct the ceremony in Westminster Abbey only days after the sudden death of King William Rufus.

'You were crowned with indecent haste, Sire, although I cannot fault the procedures which were correct. More surprisingly, it appears the Pope has been minded to accept your claim, although he is now reluctant to do so publically. I believe you made him promises to protect the Church in England. While you may propose candidates to fill the many empty senior positions, the Church will always retain the right to invest or sanctify them into the role,' explained Anselm.

Henry, standing at the window, managed to contain his annoyance as he gazed at the forested slopes running along the west banks of the Thames. He believed the King should have the right to choose and invest the bishops and archbishops, for these were often powerful positions in England and could be lucrative or used to reward or cement alliances. For now, however, he needed the support of both Archbishop Anselm and the Holy See in Rome, for he did not doubt that his brother, Duke Robert, would be planning to take the crown back.

'I think we need further discussion on this Archbishop, but there are more pressing tasks for now. To show my good faith to the Holy Father in Rome, I have reviewed the annual payments of Peter's Pence to the Holy See, which my brother ignored, and I will begin them again. Now, I need you to officiate at my marriage and the crowning of my Queen.'

'I must congratulate you, Sire, on your choice of a wife. Not only is Matilda born in the purple, the daughter of a reigning king and queen, but she is a direct descendant of Alfred the Great himself. However, I am unsure if I can conduct the ceremony unless you keep your word to the Pope. As Archbishop of Canterbury, I have the divine stewardship of England, and I cannot see how I can even stay in the country until you agree to Pope Paschal's conditions.'

Henry glared at the Archbishop, and without another word, he dismissed him, worried that his anger might erupt and he would say something he regretted. He paced back and forth for a while and then summoned his bride, who had been given a suite of rooms in the palace to prepare for their wedding. Matilda forewarned that the Archbishop of Canterbury had left, bowed to the King, and took the chair he was offering. Henry related the conversation with Anselm; he wanted to share the weight and issues of kingship with Matilda in the same way his father had done with his mother. Henry had watched his father, William, seeking the wise counsel of his mother on many occasions. Matilda saw the worried frown on Henry's face.

'I understand your concerns, Sire; you are undoubtedly

afraid that if Anselm leaves England, then as the senior English prelate, he may go to Rouen and crown your brother as king in your stead.'

Henry's pale face and quick nod confirmed her thinking.

'I suggest you propose a truce on this issue with Anselm until Easter. Promise him that all lands and revenues taken by Ranulf Flambard will be returned to the Archbishop of Canterbury immediately and that you will grant no investitures of bishops in this truce period. Meanwhile, a mission should be sent to Pope Paschal promoting a compromise in England between the Church and state.'

Henry dropped to one knee in front of her and, taking both of her hands in each of his, he kissed each one in turn.

'What a fortunate man I am to be marrying a woman with such a wise head on her shoulders,' he murmured.

His hands became bolder, and encircling her waist, he pulled her closer. She laughed and put both hands on his chest to keep him at bay. She was very aware of his prodigious sexual appetite, witnessed by the number of his bastards running freely around the palace. However, she was determined that she would remain a maid until their wedding night, as was right and proper in the eyes of the Church and the court.

'Now, Henry, let me go. I will come with you to visit Anselm while you make your proposal. I have a good relationship with him and think I can persuade him to carry out the ceremony. I'm sure he will enjoy the honour of crowning me himself.'

Henry smiled and pulled her close to him, kissing her deeply. She finally broke away, quite breathless but still pressed firmly against his body; she could feel how aroused he was.

'I look forward to the night when I can do more than only kiss you, Matilda,' he said. Taking her hand, he placed it on his hard manhood and held it there.

'As you can feel, I'm impatient to make love to you, and I know you will give me strong male heirs for the throne of England.'

Matilda blushed and dropped her eyes; although she had been protected and kept in a state of innocence since her early years, she was not naïve, and she knew what would happen when he bedded her. She was both excited and apprehensive. Watching the emotions play across her face, Henry laughed aloud. He was delighted with his choice of wife, a queen with an old English bloodline that would give his reign the legitimacy it needed.

The last few months had not been easy for him. He had a few powerful supporters, such as the Beaumont brothers, the Earls of Warwick, and Leicester. But his problems were twofold; most Anglo-Norman nobility were homage bound to his brother, Duke Robert. Also, he was much younger than his older brothers; he was not well known nor a knight at arms. He had not fought alongside them as Robert had; he had always been studious, hence the nickname they gave him, Beauclerc. This meant that the older, wealthier nobility did not know him, but they certainly knew his brother, Robert, the crusading hero who had taken back the holy city of Jerusalem. His marriage to Matilda of Wessex, the daughter of King Malcolm and Queen Margaret of Scotland, would help, so it had to go ahead as soon as possible.

November 1100 – Tower of London
Almost a league away from Westminster, on the northern bank of the River Thames, the stark walls of the great white tower of King William I reflected the last rays of the setting winter

sun. William had built the Tower of London to overawe the population of London, who could prove to be both rebellious and brutal. William wanted a castle to reflect the might and power of the Normans, and in that, he succeeded. When William Rufus, his son, came to power, he commissioned a massive outer wall to be built around the white tower, replacing the old wooden palisade fence that had stood for over a decade. The man tasked with overseeing this project now found that he was the first prisoner to be kept in the white tower. He leant against the sill of the mullioned window, watching the sunset with a sense of irony.

Ranulf Flambard, once the most powerful man in England, the influential chief minister of King William Rufus and recently appointed Prince Bishop of Durham, found himself imprisoned, accused of embezzlement by the new king and several bishops. Now, he awaited his fate at the hands of King Henry I, a prince of royal blood whom he admitted he had previously treated with contempt. He had belittled the young prince at every opportunity, but now, he thought bitterly how the worm had turned.

He whiled away the time at the window for several moments, wondering if Henry would execute or maim him as his father, William, had been wont to do. William always preferred to see his enemies alive and suffering, never thinking twice about taking their eyes or their hands before incarcerating them.

Flambard's other problem lay in his lack of allies and friends to speak up for him or come to his aid. He was low-born and seen as a self-important upstart, universally hated and despised by the nobility, the Church and even the middling classes. He had taxed the merchants and burghers of the city mercilessly for every penny he could get out of them. His only consolation was that King Henry had allowed a generous amount for his upkeep in the tower; two shillings a day had been allocated, a fortune to many. This kept him in the best of food and furnishings and allowed him to wine and dine with the Norman Constable of the Tower, Sir William de Mandeville.

Flambard, cunning and manipulative even in these dire circumstances, had discovered that not only was Mandeville ambitious, but he was avaricious. More importantly, he had detected a touch of awe at the status of his prisoner and also a wisp of sympathy that Flambard could possibly use. He wondered what was afoot in Rouen as he watched the sun finally sink. He had heard that Duke Robert had returned; surely, he would try to take the English throne back. Although never fond of praying unduly, despite his position as Prince Bishop of Durham, he suddenly felt inclined to drop to his knees and pray that Robert and his Norman lords would invade England before Henry had him executed or mutilated.

Chapter Five

November 1100 – Constantinople
It had taken almost all night for Conn to throw off the effects of the sleeping draft the whores had dosed him with. Georgio and Darius had tried to snatch what sleep they could, wrapped in their cloaks, on the hard floor. It had not been a restful night as Conn had thrashed around on the bed, mumbling and shouting occasionally, caught in the throes of some dark dream. Finally, in the early hours, he quietened and dropped into a deep, normal sleep, which allowed them with some relief to do the same. When Darius shook him awake and shouted, Georgio felt as if he had barely closed his eyes, and he sat up rubbing his tired eyes, which felt as if he had sand in them.

'He's gone! He was dressing when I woke, and he has left. He ignored anything I said, and when I put a hand out to stop him, he gave me a glare that would have curdled milk.'

Georgio stood up, still rubbing his eyes and glancing around the room. Darius was right; Conn's clothes were gone, but significantly, his leather doublet and crossed swords and harness were still there.

'He is coming back. Conn would never leave his swords behind. Stay here, Darius,' he yelled, as he raced down the stairs, hoping to catch up with his friend.

It was early morning, and fortunately, the streets were not crowded as Georgio raced downhill. Knowing him as he did, he reasoned that he would head for water, a public fountain or pump, where he could sluice off the sweat and smell of the whores from last night. Before long, he spotted Conn's tall figure striding off into the distance, but then he disappeared. Georgio ran while avoiding tradespeople with handbarrows and carts setting up their stalls. There was no sign of Conn ahead, but glancing to the left, down a long set of stairs that went steeply downhill, he glimpsed him some distance below, turning a corner. Georgio shouted his name; it echoed off the high walls, and Conn glanced back for a second but kept going.

Now, hearing the sound of waves as he descended, Georgio realised where his friend was going, and as he ran round the corner, he saw an alley leading to the sea. There was an ancient crumbling stone slipway that was used to pull the boats from the water or launch them. To the left were several old wooden boat sheds leaning precariously over the water. Several naked young boys played and swam in the shallows, protected from the rougher waves by the harbour walls. He watched as Conn, on the end of the low wall, peeled off his braies and, in only his linen shirt, dived into the deeper water, striking out for a small rocky outcrop further along the coast.

Georgio sat on a nearby wall and waited for what felt like an eternity as Conn dived and swam back and forth before pulling himself up onto the rocks. Then the Horse Warrior sat with his head in his hands; Georgio felt his sadness and despair, and his eyes filled with tears as he watched him. Conn had loved Marietta, and yet she had been murdered in front of

CHAPTER FIVE

their eyes and had died in his arms. Georgio knew how much he was hurting, but he could not stand by and let his friend drink himself into oblivion or watch him suffer alone; that way, self-destruction lay. Conn Fitz Malvais, knight and Horse Warrior, had often been distant, almost aloof, due to what happened to them in their childhood. Despite this, Georgio had experienced real comradeship with him and seen the affection on his friend's face. Conn may try to push him away, but they had fought side by side in Spain for years, and Georgio loved him like a brother. He could try to ignore or brush him off, but he was going nowhere.

Over an hour later, Conn finally re-entered the water and swam back. He shook the drops from his body and hair and pulled on his heavy linen braies. Several girls and women were now scrubbing clothes on the slipway, and they called out ribald comments on his physique and what they would like to do to him. Conn sent them a grin as he strode up the slipway, and they collapsed into giggles. However, his face hardened as he approached Georgio on the wall.

'Why did you have to follow me? Did you not realise I wanted to be left alone? No, you are always there, standing in my shadow, reminding me of a life and a time I want to forget.'

The words hurt Georgio, but he knew he was lashing out, so he did not reply at first; he just shrugged as Conn stood, hands on hips, glaring at him.

'Whether you like it or not, we have been together since we were six years old; you are like a brother to me, and I cannot abandon you as easily as you seem able to abandon me,' muttered Georgio.

Conn turned away, sighing, and stared across the water. He

would have liked to walk away, but it was not easy, as Georgio's words had resonated with him.

'I have signed up with John Doukas for the Emperor, and you may not be ready to do the same. I cannot go back to Europe yet, and if you decide to stay, I do not want to talk about what happened at the villa in Aggio. It is all in the past; this is my future and possibly yours if you wish. We are sellswords, Georgio; this is what we always said we would do, sell ourselves to the highest bidder, and the Emperor Alexios Komnenos is paying very well, far more than we earned in Spain.'

'Very well, Conn, I will stay in Byzantium for a while, but I will talk about our family in Morlaix, your father, uncle and stepmother, for they are my adoptive parents, and I love them dearly. I promise I will never mention the events in the villa unless you raise it. But I will remember, and I will pray for and honour the people who died there.'

At that point, Conn turned to look into Georgio's dark brown eyes, and he could see the pain and hurt there as well before he looked away.

'Let us go back to the inn, and then I will find you a bed in the barracks,' he said, setting off through the now crowded, noisy streets.

When they entered the room, Darius sprang up from the bed,

'You were so long I wondered if you were coming back,' he murmured to Georgio. Conn looked him up and down with a snort of derision.

'Is this yet another waif and stray you have picked up, Georgio?'

Stung by those words, Darius pulled himself to his full

height.

'My father and brother were warriors who gave their lives for the Emperor, so I'm no waif and stray, and one day soon, I will fight for Alexios Komnenos too.'

Georgio put a hand on the young man's shoulder.

'Darius was instrumental in saving my life last night; he is also a very knowledgeable and useful young man. I have hired him as our servant with the chance of becoming a squire, if he lives up to it; he'll see to all of our equipment and is good with horses.'

Conn reappraised the young man and reluctantly agreed.

'I presume you are Greek?'

'Yes, but not from Constantinople. My father was Laconian; his family came from Mystras on Mount Taygetus. He left there as a young man to fight for the Emperor and quickly rose to become a serjeant.'

Conn raised an eyebrow, 'Mystras, I know of that from my early lessons. It was part of Sparta, so your family does indeed have martial blood in your veins. Let us all hope you live up to it. Now we must go for I will be looked for, and the sun is high in the sky. Where is your horse, Georgio?'

'It is back at the inn. Darius knows where, so he can go and collect my horse and belongings and bring them to the barracks.'

They both stood before the great John Doukas himself a short time later. He may have been the Megas Doux and the Emperor's brother-in-law, but first and foremost, he was a military man. Whether on the decks of the ships he commanded or leading his men in the harsh deserts of Anatolia, he was always at the forefront of the action. This was no commander who stood on a hill in the distance; this was another El Cid, someone who fought beside and inspired his men. His large room they were in at the palace barracks was that of a man with little liking for luxury. There were few comforts for someone so high in the imperial family: a simple cot in the corner and hard chairs pulled around a small, empty fireplace. A large table stood in the window covered with maps and rolls of vellum; sharpened goose quills were laid neatly in a row beside a pot of ink. Shelves behind him held even more maps of the vast Byzantine Empire.

Georgio regarded the man sitting behind the desk with interest. He had nodded briefly as they entered but then continued writing. Georgio had expected someone older, probably battle-scarred and grizzled, to go with his fearsome reputation. They said that John Doukas rarely gave quarter and would slaughter a whole town or village if they defied him or refused to surrender. However, the man in front of him seemed surprisingly young. Georgio thought he was in his mid to late thirties, a dark, handsome man with a patrician Greek profile. He finally looked up at them and gave a cynical smile.

'It was an enjoyable night, was it, Malvais?' he asked in an unforgiving tone.

Conn stared straight ahead, inclined his head in guilt and shrugged, which resulted in the Megas Doux suddenly slamming his fist hard down onto the table. He seemed satisfied that both Horse Warriors jumped.

'I have no objection to any of my men enjoying the delights of this noble city, but I expect them to be here ready to ride out on patrol early the next morning. Your men have been sitting waiting for you for several hours, Malvais. Do you think that is acceptable?' Conn shook his head.

CHAPTER FIVE

'No, Sire, it is unacceptable and will not happen again. I am prepared to take any punishment you name to atone for my failure to attend.'

Georgio, who had stayed silent throughout, could see the injustice of this and, before Conn could stop him, blurted out….

'He was drugged, Sire; it was not his fault. If we had not found him, I dread to think what may have happened.'

John Doukas looked at this second Horse Warrior in astonishment, that the man had the audacity to speak without being directly addressed, leaving him temporarily lost for words.

'Who are you that you come into my headquarters uninvited and then show such lack of respect and discipline?' he yelled in a voice that would be heard on the opposite side of the parade ground.

Georgio, realising his mistake, bowed deeply.

'I am Georgio di Milan, and I fought alongside Malvais in the Reconquista wars in Spain. I apologise for my uncalled-for interruption, but I have always tried to right any injustice I see.'

John Doukas remained astonished at the outspoken young man before him, and then, shaking his head, he laughed harshly at the young Horse Warrior's effrontery.

'So, Malvais, you fell for the charms and tricks of the harlots of Constantinople, and did they leave you drugged, naked and penniless?'

'No, Sire, Georgio arrived in time, but I assure you it will not happen again.'

'It had better not, Malvais, for I have an important assignment for you, but first, you and your insolent friend can go to the quartermaster and obtain two spades. The new latrine pits need digging twenty paces to the west of the current ones, including a deep trench that needs to flow down to the river when it is sluiced. I would imagine it will take you at least until the sun sets; you can then get your idle men to help you lift and move the wooden structure that sits over the old ones to the new ones. Not a pleasant task, for you will be up to your knees in shit, but your men may forgive you in time. Tomorrow, you will report here at dawn ready to ride, and I will tell you where you are going.'

Dismissed, they went out onto the large training ground outside, where the sun was now beating down.

'Not an auspicious beginning to my career in the forces of the Byzantine Emperor,' muttered Georgio. He stopped and watched a wide-eyed Darius staring at the size of the barracks and palace buildings while leading his horse towards them.

'We have learnt the hard way, Georgio; discipline and professionalism are everything in our world, as we cannot make mistakes that can cost lives and today, in front of one of the greatest warriors of the east, we have let ourselves down,' he said, in disgust.

He gazed up at the hot sun as he pointed Darius toward the stable block and sighed, for he now had the unpleasant task of telling his men that they were also to suffer on his account. Conn had put the troop together a month ago; he was now putting them through a hard training schedule. There had been a lot of resentment initially, as many were cavalrymen. Now, he was trying to turn them into Horse Warriors with double swords on their backs. At first, he had to make an example, especially with Gracchus, a big, ugly man who resented being told how to ride or fight by a young foreigner. When Conn knocked him to the ground three times, and he saw his blade whirl from his hand, he conceded that the young Breton might be able to teach them something.

Georgio looked around the group of twenty-five men with interest; they were a mix of nationalities and all shapes and sizes, but he noticed they listened with rapt attention as Conn openly admitted that he had been rolled by a pair of whores. This occasioned much laughter and ribald comments and gestures. Conn then turned to Georgio.

'This is Georgio di Milan, my second in command, who has ridden at my side for a decade and is almost as good as me, but not quite.'

They laughed at that and greeted him warmly while Conn went on to describe the punishment issued by John Doukas. Most thought he had got off lightly; usually, he would have been flogged, but they took it in good stead that they had to lift and move the heavy, stinking wooden structure at the end. Georgio, Conn and an unhappy Darius then stripped down to loincloths and a knotted linen shirt to protect them from the sun and got to work digging the new trenches and pits. The sun beat down as they started to dig, and it was not long before they were sweating profusely. However, the rest of the men unexpectedly arrived with shovels and rigged a canvas sheet over them for shade. Georgio smiled, for it seemed Conn was already getting the loyalty he needed from his new men.

It was dark when they finished, and walking to the well, they poured buckets of water over each other to remove the muck and the stench. Unbeknownst to them, John Doukas had a meeting in the palace next door, and for a while, he had stood on a shaded balcony, a tall, dark figure looking down at Conn and his men working below; he could hear the banter and laughter. He was pleased by what he saw; he had always thought of himself as a good judge of men, and from the first moment of meeting Malvais, he knew he had found an outstanding warrior and leader.

Chapter Six

December 1100 – Constantinople
It was barely dawn the next morning when a surprisingly bright-eyed Darius shook Georgio awake and told him that Conn was already breaking his fast. Georgio threw back his thin blanket and swung his legs to the floor. He found his back was aching after so many hours of digging, so he stretched the muscles not used to the bending and lifting he had inflicted on them. Darius, who annoyingly seemed to have suffered no effects, grinned as Georgio grimaced as he dressed. Then he led him across the training ground to an impressive stone loggia on the far side. It had originally been part of the palace complex but had been integrated into the barracks, as space was needed for feeding the large numbers of men. It was open on all sides with carved and decorated stone arches, ideal for letting the cool breezes through in this climate. Georgio had seen these Roman buildings before in Toledo. Now, it was filled with dozens of trestle tables, and the buzz of conversation and the irresistible smell of food filled the air.

Georgio found Conn and slid onto the bench alongside him and his men, who welcomed Georgio already as one of their own.

'This is very impressive,' said Georgio, waving a hand at the delicately carved arches and mosaics.

'It was originally part of the Great Palace, which was the main residence of the Emperor and his family for generations, but Alexios still uses it as his main administration centre and for formal functions. I hear he spends most of his time at the smaller and more peaceful Blachernae Palace, out by the north-western walls,' he explained.

Georgio had hardly filled his platter and torn off a chunk of fresh, warm bread when Conn stood and announced,

'I go to meet John Doukas, who has the details of our assignment. I will share our destination when I know, but I believe we may be away for many weeks. Now, go and see to your horses and tack; I expect you to be ready to leave as soon as I return.

Georgio nearly choked as he wolfed down his food and tore off a leg of chicken to take with him as the rest of the Horse Warriors headed to the stables.

'I expect Conn has already seen to his horse,' he muttered to Darius, while still eating the chicken. Darius smiled and handed him a cup of breakfast ale to wash it down.

'Yes, I helped him, oiling the saddle and bridle while he groomed his horse from top to toe. He is certainly not afraid of hard work.'

'We are Breton Horse Warriors, Darius; rule number one is looking after your horse, and they are always fed and watered before you are. Then comes the grooming, checking and oiling of hooves in dry climates. As you will find out, if you do that well, your horse will look after you and even save your life on occasion.'

Conn stood again before John Doukas, but he waved the

CHAPTER SIX

Horse Warrior to a bench by the wall this time.

'I imagine you have already heard of another crusade heading our way.'

Conn nodded, 'From Lombardy, I believe.'

John Doukas sighed and leaned back in his chair.

'Pope Pascal has encouraged this, as there have been messages from the Kingdom of Jerusalem asking for reinforcements and assistance. As you know, the Seljuk Turks are our enemies here in Anatolia and the East. The further South you go, the more the tribes are different. When they reached Jerusalem, Duke Robert and Geoffrey of Bouillon faced large armies of Fatimids, an Arab Caliphate based mainly in Egypt but spreading widely over North Africa and into the Levant. Our Emperor, Alexios, negotiated an alliance with the Fatimids to help us fight the Seljuk Turks, which was successful at first, and we drove the Seljuks back, but the alliance was scattered to the winds when the Crusaders defeated the Fatimids at the Battle of Ascalon and took Jerusalem. We lost an important ally.'

'So good for Christianity, but it endangered the Byzantine Empire,' suggested Conn.

John Doukas nodded. 'But, we are trying to form more alliances to stop the Seljuk Turks from sweeping south. The Emperor refused to send troops to help the Kingdom of Jerusalem, so the Pope insisted that those European knights who never took the vow to free Jerusalem or, even worse, broke their vows, deserted and never reached the city must be part of the group to go back to Jerusalem, now, to give them the reinforcements they need.'

'I have heard that the successful knights and heroes of the First Crusade are already deriding this group by calling it the Crusade of the Faint-hearted,' said Conn, smiling but wondering what this task was to be. Was the Emperor thinking of turning them back?

'I gather from your tone, Sire, that the Emperor is not altogether pleased with the arrival of another crusade.'

'If Jerusalem needs reinforcements, they should have been sent in ships across the Mediterranean. Jerusalem has been supported by the Maritime Republics of Genoa and Venice since 1099. However, I think Pascal is trying to emulate his great predecessor, Pope Urban, by setting off another crusade, this time in his name. My informers tell me that, as with the first expedition, three large groups have set off from different parts of Europe. It is the first group that concerns me.'

'Is this the one from Lombardy?' asked Conn.

'It is led by the Archbishop of Milan, a great orator and influential man trying to make a name for himself to get a Cardinal's hat. With him, he is bringing a group of lesser Italian nobles whom I would call respected rather than exalted, none of any significance. The leaders are Count Albert of Biandrate and his brother Count Guibert of Parma, wealthy and powerful persons whom the Archbishop has inspired to set forth.

'Is that not a good thing that they have knights with them that are experienced in warfare?' he asked.

'It would be if it were not for the disorganised rabble they are bringing. My informers tell me they are over twenty thousand in number, but less than a quarter are soldiers. The numbers are made up of non-combatants, clerics, women, and children who were sold the vision of a pilgrimage to Jerusalem that would wipe their souls free of sin. More worryingly, the rest are made up of the inhabitants of the slums of Lombardy who

CHAPTER SIX

are out for loot and plunder.'

'That sounds like a recipe for disaster,' murmured Conn while Doukas inclined his head in agreement

'Alexios has graciously agreed to provision them at the behest of the Pope, but only on a promise of good behaviour. However, they seem to be an uncontrolled mob over whom the leaders have little influence. On the instructions of the Emperor, our armies have escorted them since they crossed the borders. We have now split them into three smaller groups so that we can provision them over winter, and exert more control. The camps are at Philippopolis in Bulgaria, Adrianople and on the coast at Rodosto. However, reports are coming in that they are pillaging the countryside, seizing livestock and fowl without paying, robbing the churches, and even desecrating ancient Greek shrines.'

Conn looked suitably shocked that a Christian crusading group would do this in the lands of Emperor Alexios.

'Have they been punished?' he asked in an incredulous tone.

'Some were caught and killed, others were flogged, but it was not quite the deterrent we expected, and there is a lot of resentment. I need you to ride out with your men and impose order on the camp at Rodosto, for it is too close to Constantinople for comfort. Albert, Count of Biandrate and his brother Guy of Parma are supposedly in charge, attempting and failing to keep control. Take your men and let the Emperor's displeasure be known; you have free rein, and do not be lenient with them, Malvais.'

Conn bowed and left, and he did not doubt what that order would mean. A short time later, he briefed his men, giving them an outline of the difficult task ahead. Then, they headed west for Rodosto along the coast on the Sea of Marmara. It was rough going in many places along the rocky coastal path, where many of the steep, scree-covered hills seemed to run down into the water, obliterating the narrow track. Having talked to several locals, Conn knew it would be a ride of over twenty leagues, but five more if they took the road further inland, so they would have a few nights on the slopes of the shore.

Georgio began to realise that Darius was a real Godsend, for he seemed to have the ability to find things in the rockiest and most remote places, including a full basket of chickens to roast on the spit, which he swore he paid for. Even Conn, who seemed only to tolerate their new servant, was impressed. However, Conn mellowed slightly more when he saw how his horse Diablo accepted Darius grooming him. Georgio was pleased, but amazed, as the horse matched his name and usually bit and kicked out at anyone who came near that he did not know.

Now, sitting around the campfire, the mountains looming behind them, Georgio watched as Darius sat hanging on every word of the past exploits, skirmishes and wars the men around the fire recounted. Georgio joined in with a few of his own hair-raising exploits in Spain, but Conn sat silently throughout, letting his men try to outdo each other in valour and danger. It was nights like this when there was true camaraderie around the campfires, and he saw his fighting men begin to come together as one unit. The next night, as the sun set, they topped a hill and stopped to look down on the wide bay before the coastal town of Rodosto. It was a beautiful place, and to the south of the small town, they could see the dozens of fires where the Crusaders had set up camp. As his men settled around the fire with their food, Conn explained in more detail why they were there and their role.

'So we are gaolers for these people, to keep them under control and contained, but you say many women and children are there,' commented Gracchus.

'Yes, but apart from being an inconvenience and highly likely to be slaughtered on the way to Jerusalem, they will probably prove to be no problem as long as they have shelter and food. There are approximately a thousand Lombard soldiers there. However, it isn't enough to keep these people in order, as the Archbishop of Milan has encouraged the dregs of the northern cities to join him. When he preached of stores of wealth, he meant the type to be found in heaven by carrying out acts of penance and pilgrimage. Some mistakenly took this to mean plunder and loot, which attracted the worst elements of the back streets of the Lombard towns. It is now our job to try and prevent them doing that, by the sword if necessary,' he replied.

The next morning, they rode into the streets of Rodosto, which were unnaturally quiet apart from a blacksmith forge, which Conn noticed seemed very busy with several artisans making weapons. Darius had been given the privilege of carrying the gonfalon, Emperor Alexis's large triangular double-tailed golden pennant, which drew attention. Before long, local people appeared from behind barred doors and shutters to welcome these representatives of the Emperor and demand that he defend them against the marauders camped on the outskirts of their town, who were ripping planks of wood from their houses to burn on their fires.

A large red-faced man planted himself in front of Conn's horse and refused to move unless the Commander listened to their woes and helped them. Diablo took exception to the man and semi-reared, striking out with his forelegs at what he perceived as an enemy. The man fell back into the dirt in shock and was helped to his feet by his friends.

'My horse takes exception to your attitude and tone of voice as I do! But I can hear and see your concern, so I will let it pass for now. I'm here on the instructions of the Megas Doux himself, John Doukas; we are sent to protect the people here and their livelihoods.'

The man seemed slightly mollified but was not done yet.

'I am the Steward of this town; I made representation to the leaders of the crusaders, Count Albert and his brother, about the damage being done and the thefts, especially of wood torn from our houses. More importantly, Rodosto is famous for its large cherry harvest, but they stole all the fruit and chopped down many mature trees in the orchard for firewood. This is our livelihood they are destroying, and the farmers are distraught. The fishing boats refuse to land here now as the renegades line the wooden quay to steal their catch. The leaders seemed to listen at first, but then their nephew, a vile, arrogant and disrespectful young man, had me chased and stoned from the camp to much laughter and derision. This is not how I expect the leaders of a holy crusade to treat the leader and spokesperson for the town.'

Conn was alarmed by what he heard, and he inclined his head in recognition of the man's complaints and promised that he was on his way to see these leaders and raise these wrongs; they would be compensated. The man and several other town notables bowed repeatedly in thanks.

They rode out of the town and not far along the rocky shoreline, before they came to the beginning of the Crusader's camp; Conn rode onto a slight rise and looked across the considerable camp, strung over a great distance. He could see what the troops of John Doukas had tried to do; by placing this large group here, they were easier to contain as they could only go forward or backward. They had the sea on one side and the rising mountain slopes on the other. Rodosto sat in a ring of steep hills, so it was a sheltered spot where there were several scrub-surrounded meadows on the lower slopes that the locals had cleared for their animals to graze. Most of those large meadows were now covered in an array of tents and makeshift shelters.

It was now late November, and the winter drizzle was arriving with much lower temperatures. Conn could understand the need for firewood, living as they were out under the skies, but he could see plenty of scrub and bushes all the way up the higher slopes that they could burn. Taking wood from the houses in the small town was an easy but lazy option. Slightly higher up the slopes, in the middle of the camp, were several larger tents and coloured pavilions flying the flags of Lombardy. Conn led his men through the camp, picking their way through the people, children, dogs, tethered goats, mules, horses and covered carts that people were sleeping in or under. Several rough canvas awnings were spread over bowed branches and weighed down with stones to keep the weather out.

They had been there less than a week, but already it looked and smelt like a midden. There was obviously no organisation, and people were digging holes to shit in beside the tents, where the children played, instead of building communal latrines further away. The sight of a martial troop of Horse Warriors on their large, well-groomed mounts, their signature crossed swords on their backs, triggered fear from many, who retreated into their shelters, as they approached, and they received resentful or angry looks and snarls from sullen men of all ages. They had been brought and kept there for the winter by Alexios, a man who was not their emperor or ruler, and they did not like it. Their leaders had promised them they would be in the safe and warmer city of Constantinople by now.

Conn dismounted below the largest pavilion, handing his horse to Darius. Diablo rolled his eyes and snapped at him, unsettled by the smells and loud noises of the camp. Darius circled him a few times and spoke softly, receiving a nod of approval from Conn. The first man Conn met was the captain of the Emperor's troops sent by John Doukas; he had seen the man once or twice in the barracks. He was a young but experienced soldier, now with a worried frown; they clasped arms in greeting.

'God's blood, I am pleased to see you, Malvais; the Megas Doux sent a message to say you were on your way. There is no way to hide that this situation is a living hell for them and us, and any control or support from their leaders is minimal, or they even overturn or go against our orders,' he explained in a low voice.

'Well met, Orontes. At first glance, I could see the problems; also, I met the town leaders. They appear to be on the verge of rebellion as they have brought in several extra blacksmiths making weapons, which is never good.'

Captain Orontes ran his hands through his dark hair with an exasperated sigh.

'The problem, Malvais, lies in how the groups were split; I'm told the large groups of clergy and clerics clung together like lemmings and raced to be in the first group, left behind in Bulgaria. They could see that the Archbishop had made a mistake, and they were witness to the first attacks of pillaging and violence, so they rushed to separate themselves from the rabble. The middling classes, the knights, minor lords and their families did the same and moved into the second group, so here we are in Rodosto with the remaining group, which contains the worst elements of the slums. Many of these men were renegades in the forests, deserters, or runaway thieves. They heard the Archbishop preaching in the squares and saw this as an escape from pursuit, with the added attraction of the wealth in the east.'

'How many men do you have here, Orontes?'

'About three hundred and fifty fit for duty, some were wounded in the first skirmishes and attacks. The problem lies in the fact that there are just not enough of us to hold a line across from the shore to the slopes, and they break through and attack the town at dusk or dawn when my men are often at their lowest ebb. I have them on six-hour shifts of duty, but they are weary and becoming somewhat disillusioned at their inability to stop the rabble, who are all armed and have no qualms at attacking the Emperor's men.'

'So where are the rest of the troops, the men brought by the Lombards? Surely you should just be reinforcing them?' asked Conn with a puzzled frown.

Orontes gave a snort of disdain.

'There seems to be little discipline amongst them; they do not take orders from us because we are not their commanders. They arrive for an hour or two and then wander off to sleep. I tell you, it is an impossible situation, Malvais.'

'Not anymore, Orontes, not anymore! Leave it to me. Show my men where they can bed down and graze their horses.'

'Of course, good luck with them in there; you will need it!' he said, indicating the largest pavilion and clasping arms with him again before striding off down the slope.

Conn stood for a moment, staring after him, while he gathered his thoughts to find a middle way. He knew that going in with a heavy hand wouldn't work. The words of John Doukas resonated, *"Respectable but not exalted nobles."* In other words, what he would call petty nobility trying to make a name for themselves and, as he had found in Spain, the worst possible types to deal with at times. He took a deep breath and strode towards the largest pavilion; there were four guards outside who regarded him with a wary and even belligerent stare.

'I am a commander of the forces of the Megas Doux, John Doukas and also the Emperor's representative here to meet with Count Albert of Biandrate, who I believe is the noble leader of this group of Crusaders,' he announced, making sure his voice was loud enough to carry over all the pavilions.

He stood, towering over them, meeting their now uncertain stare with a glare and waiting to see what response his slightly exaggerated status would bring.

Chapter Seven

Early December 1100 – Rodosto

Conn's announcement seemed to work on the guards, who straightened up, and the older one nodded in recognition of his rank and disappeared into the pavilion. Moments later, he returned with a younger man who seemed somewhat taken aback as he looked up at Conn. In full Horse Warrior regalia and at six foot four, Malvais was an impressive sight. He also had one of his men standing behind him, with the Emperor's royal gonfalon fluttering in the slight breeze from the sea.

Conn could see the uncertainty on the noble's face, as he had expected an older man, probably a cleric or official of the court. Conn raised an eyebrow at him as he waited. The silence continued, and the man coloured up.

'My uncle is within, and he will see you,' he said, before turning and re-entering the pavilion.

Conn bade his man plant the Emperor's gonfalon outside the entrance and guard it while he followed inside. It seemed stiflingly hot inside the tent as a large brazier was in the centre. A man in his fifties sat behind a table on the right-hand side, and a slightly younger one stood beside him. The petulant young noble had thrown himself into a chair. Both men regarded Conn with a similar surprised expression, but the eldest quickly recovered as he eyed the sealed scroll in Conn's hand.

'You are welcome, Commander. I am Count Albert of Biandrate; this is my brother, Count Guibert of Parma, and my nephew, Otto Altasparta, my sister's son,' he said, waving a hand at the younger man, who Conn thought was in his thirties. Conn bowed his head to all three.

'I bring greetings from the Emperor Alexios and John Doukas, the Megas Doux,' he announced. Stepping forward, he handed the scroll to the Count, who broke the seal and, after reading its contents, handed it to his brother Guibert.

'We were under the impression that we would be welcomed by the Emperor into Constantinople, not expected to wait here for several months. The Archbishop and the Pope will not be happy at how we have been treated.'

Conn gave them a measured stare before continuing.

'John Doukas has communicated with the Archbishop, who is at Adrianopolis. He has indicated that he is happy to overwinter here where there is shelter and, as promised, provisions will be provided. The winters here can be bleak as those in the First Crusade discovered, and out there in the deserts of Anatolia with little shelter and limited water supplies, you will lose thousands of your people. The Emperor considers that he has been generous in allowing you to cross his territory and provide you with food and water. After all, you are not here to fight for him; you are merely reinforcements making your way to the Kingdom of Jerusalem. Do you wish me to report that you are unhappy with what some would say has been a show of magnanimity, in allowing you free passage through his lands?' he asked, raising an eyebrow.

CHAPTER SEVEN

Conn saw the narrow glances pass between the two brothers; that was the last thing they wanted. However, before Count Albert could reply, his nephew, Otto Altasparta, was on his feet.

'You call these provisions? Meagre sacks of flour, fruit and vegetables that we would think twice before feeding to our pigs, and the sour wine which is almost undrinkable.'

Conn did not even deign to glance in his direction; watching the dismay on his uncle's face was enough.

'Be silent, Otto, you know not of what you speak,' he commanded, which did little to calm his nephew's anger.

'We agree to the Emperor's conditions, Commander, and please thank him for his generosity, but may I ask that we be allowed to do so in person?' he asked, hopefully.

'John Doukas asked me to invite you and your brother to attend the court for Yuletide, where you will be warmly welcomed.'

This mollified the Lombard counts, and Albert smiled.

'You seem very familiar to me. Can we have met before?'

Conn gave the usual tight smile before answering.

'No, but apparently, I am the image of my father at this age, Lord Luc De Malvais.'

'Of course, the Breton Horse Warriors,' he said, indicating Conn's leather-laced doublet and crossed swords. Both men's faces had paled.

'When we were much younger, we were both involved in the wars in Sicily, and we fought against your father. Nothing could withstand the ferocious attacks of the Horse Warriors. Otto's father was seriously wounded in that war; he lost his sword arm and never really recovered; he died five years later.'

Seeing Otto's face, Guibert jumped in.

'But that was nearly thirty years ago, and there have been many wars since; after all, we are knights who were trained in warfare and expected to risk our lives, as we do on this crusade to aid Jerusalem.'

Conn inclined his head in respect.

'Georgio, one of your compatriots from Milan, and I fought beside El Cid in the Reconquista wars in Spain, but now we serve John Doukas and the Emperor.'

The brothers looked suitably awed as Conn continued using every ounce of diplomacy he could muster.

'I have brought twenty of my men and have orders to remain here to assist you in keeping order. With your permission, I will arrange the camp on military lines, arrange for proper latrines to be dug near the sea and ensure that the provisions are allocated fairly. However, I'm sure that I do not need to remind you that any looting or pillaging from the local inhabitants will be met with swift justice. Although I'm sure you have been doing the same, I can imagine your difficulties with these numbers. I intend to liaise with the captain of your soldiers and take the weight of responsibility from your shoulders, especially while you spend a week or two in Constantinople.'

He could see that the two brothers were unsure about this as they did not wish to give up any authority. However, they also knew that he was right and that many of the rabble camped around them were not completely under their control. But the attraction of Constantinople and the famed Emperor's golden court outweighed their initial embarrassment, so they nodded and agreed. Their nephew, though, always hot-headed, was not so easily assuaged and leapt to his feet.

'No! This cannot be allowed. I am in charge of our troops,

and I am not handing that authority over to the son of a Horse Warrior, who probably took my father's arm from his shoulder!'

Count Albert closed his eyes for a few seconds in frustration as he realised that Otto did not understand they had little choice but to accede to the Emperor's orders. However, before he could remonstrate with his nephew, Conn turned on the young Lombard.

'You were in command of the soldiers when a mob from here raided the town, stole the cherry harvest, felled the trees for fuel, and looted the houses of the locals? What orders did you give your men to stop this happening? I have been told that you have a thousand trained troops, yet a mob of only a hundred ran amok and went unpunished as they ripped shutters and planks from houses to burn.'

Otto's face was now flame-coloured, and he fought for the words to answer these accusations. Having none, his hand went to his sword hilt.

'Otto!' shouted his uncle, standing and moving around the table. Conn had not moved a muscle as he kept a steady glare pinned on the nephew's face, who reluctantly flung himself away to stand, fists clenched at the far side of the pavilion.

Conn narrowed his eyes at him while ignoring the two older men.

'If you had done that in front of the Emperor's guard in Constantinople, they would have taken your hand from your wrist in seconds. I suggest you leave him in the camp, for you will all be sent packing in hours if he takes that belligerent attitude to the Emperor's court.'

With that, he bowed to the two older men and left. He emerged from the pavilion, shaking his head. Captain

Orontes, waiting for him, laughed at the expression on his face.

'Is that frustration I see there, Malvais?' he asked in a jovial tone.

'Only a small amount; I have received permission to take command of their forces despite the volatile objections of the nephew.'

Orontes gave a small whistle of appreciation that Malvais had succeeded where he had failed.

'Yes, Altasparta needs watching; I have my suspicions that he was leading, or encouraging, the raids on the town. Large rounds of local cheeses appeared in their pavilion the next day, and he laughed at me when I remonstrated that he or his troops had not tried to stop the raid.'

Conn stood, his hands on his hips, thinking about everything he had just heard.

'There is a large, long sandy beach down there in that first cove. We rode past it on the way in this morning.' Orontes nodded. 'Mid-afternoon, I want all of your men immaculately turned out in rows on the north side of the cove, infantry at the front and mounted cavalry behind. You may sit your horse in front of them. Meanwhile, I want to see all of the captains of the Lombard forces on that beach now.'

Orontes nodded and smiled; he knew what was coming and raced off to give the orders.

Conn stood on an outcrop of rock with Georgio beside him and waited for the captains to arrive, which they did in a laggardly manner. Finally, all ten were there, including a fat, older man sweating profusely. Some were laughing when they arrived, others were muttering in discontent. He waited until there was silence as he stared at them.

CHAPTER SEVEN

He then introduced himself.

'I am Lord Conn Fitz Malvais, leader of the Emperor's Horse Warriors, and from this moment, I have been given command of the camp, of you, and all your men; now line up.'

Shocked glances were exchanged between the captains, who would be the first to admit they had been having an easy time of it at Rodosto. Conn stepped down from the rocks and walked around them, looking them up and down; they were not a prepossessing sight; the tunics and doublets were stained or covered in dust. He pulled the sword from one man's scabbard and shook his head as he looked at ingrained dirt and rust near the hilt. The owner had the grace to lower his eyes in embarrassment as Conn slotted it back in. The wheezing captain at the end stared at him belligerently at first, his stomach straining the fastenings on his doublet. Conn repeatedly poked him hard in the stomach, forcing the man backwards.

'I expect my captains to be a model of smartness, their uniforms and livery clean, their weapons shining, their blades sharp and ready for action. I also expect my captains to be fit enough to fight alongside their men. I would lay a silver penny that you wouldn't be able to run to the end of the beach, never mind to fight off the Seljuk Turks. I'm aware that each of you is in charge of a hundred men, and I want you and your men lined up on this beach by mid-afternoon, in good order, with their weapons and equipment ready to be inspected. I want every man. Even the malingerers are to be here unless they are at death's door. Do you all understand?'

They nodded, and he dismissed them. He watched as they returned to camp, some with enthusiasm and a spring in their step and others muttering in discontent.

'I think you will have to replace one or two of those,' suggested Georgio, watching the fat captain attempt to climb the small dune out of the cove.

'I'm going to split them into two cohorts of five hundred and give you one of them, so feel free to demote the ones that give you trouble. We have often found that some serjeants are more effective, and the men tend to listen to them.'

Two of the disgruntled captains made their way to Altasparta. He was still inwardly fuming at his removal from control, but the threat of missing out on Constantinople had brought him back into line. He listened to the woes of Fumagalli, one of the two captains, but to their surprise, he only shrugged.

'We can do nothing at the moment; we are in the Emperor's lands and must do as he requests, but that does not have to stop all of our activities. There are several large villages to the south of us; I suggest we visit them one evening this week.'

They grinned and went on their way; they had always done well from these nighttime raids.

Later that afternoon, Conn watched in disgust at the array of soldiers on the beach, many missing even basic kit. It also took a long time for some cohorts to line up. Conn noticed several captains standing and watching their often exasperated serjeants cajoling the men into position. Finally, they were in some semblance of order, and Conn began to appreciate their problems with keeping control. He had given Captain Orontes his orders to hold back, and now he waved the Emperor's troops down onto the beach. They descended the slope in perfect order, four abreast, swords held high, all marching in step and perfectly turned out. The weapons shone, and their uniforms were brushed clean. The Lombard soldiers watched in almost silence as the Emperor's troops moved to line up in perfect rows on the far side.

Conn was pleased to see that the stark difference in the troops had the desired effect on most captains. At the same time, several of the serjeants were shaking their heads in embarrassment. For some time, he addressed them clearly and concisely, congratulating Captain Orontes on the turnout and discipline of his men. He assured the rest that this was the standard he expected them to reach as soon as possible. He then issued new duty rotas, with each cohort in charge of camp security for five days. This was different and far better, as each captain and their serjeants were responsible for the competence and actions of their men, with more accountability. He then asked the serjeants to choose ten men from each cohort to start digging the new latrines away from the camp. He then rode Diablo to stand on the slightly raised dune before them.

'There will be two-hour training sessions on the beach every morning; you are expected to be here if you are not on duty. You will shortly cross the Bosphorus and enter Anatolia and Syria, where you will find yourself in some of the most inhospitable territory you have ever encountered. Droves of enemy bowmen will be waiting for you, mounted on swift horses to sweep in, attack, and sweep out again, leaving many dead. You will need your skills in warfare to be honed to their best if you are to survive this journey. The Lombard troops used to be a force to be reckoned with and could be again. Over half of you will not reach Jerusalem; disease, heat exhaustion, thirst and attacks will decimate your ranks, and they will also slaughter or take as slaves, the women and children you are here to protect, some of whom may be your own. My men and I will do our best to prepare you for what lies ahead, but you must be ready to listen and learn.'

With that, he dismissed them, feeling pleased with the pale, shocked faces that had stared up at him. A movement on his left caught his eye; he realised it was Otto Altasparta turning away. The Lombard noble had watched and listened in annoyance as he knew Malvais was right. The man was a natural leader, which only highlighted his own inadequacies and failures with the troops. He glanced back again at Conn with loathing and strode away, determined to undermine him at every opportunity.

Chapter Eight

December 1100 – Rodosto
Fortunately, Conn's words resonated with many of the Lombard troops, and he was pleased to see so many of them turn up for the training session on the beach each morning. The poor quality of the swordsmanship soon became apparent as his Horse Warriors, and Georgio, repeatedly disarmed them. Nearly all the captains attended, and Conn set them to teach their men how to group quickly, using their shields to protect themselves from the Seljuk bowman. About halfway through the session, the fat, sweating captain arrived with another tall, thin, dark man with narrow-set eyes and what seemed to be a constant sneer on his face. They stood watching from a rocky outcrop.

Conn called Darius over; the young man had enthusiastically thrown himself into the sword and spear training, determined to become a Horse Warrior.

'Do we know the names of those two?'

'The fat one, no, but I can find out. The other one, who looks like a rat looking through the reeds, is Captain Fumagalli, Altasparta's right-hand man; he is also from Milan. I imagine that isn't his real name, for Fumagalli means 'chicken thief'. He is probably from the city's slums and has done well to rise so high; it certainly won't be through merit,' answered Darius.

Conn fixed his gaze on the two men for so long that they moved away. He put a hand on the young man's shoulder.

'Men like him, who operate in the shadows, tend to rise on the misfortune of others, often by theft, blackmail or threats. Try to keep an eye on them, Darius; use some of the young informers from the camp you are cultivating.' He smiled, waving an arm to indicate a dozen boys who seemed to know Darius and were watching the training wide-eyed. Darius shook his head but smiled as he turned away; Malvais had his eyes on everything.

The following day and the one after that, even more of the Lombard troops turned up, and Conn found some of the captains coming to him to share their concerns, and requests for new uniforms and equipment. Darius was sent into the camp and returned with laundry women and seamstresses among the crowd, and before long, new or mended clean uniforms appeared. Meanwhile, Georgio brought in leatherworkers and blacksmiths to repair leather doublets and replace or sharpen weapons. John Doukas had given him generous funds, and he happily spent it encouraging the Lombard troops to regain their pride in their appearance and hone their skills. They would certainly need them as they ventured south into the dangerous territories between Constantinople and Jerusalem.

The new duty rota also seemed to work well; Conn and Georgio rode through, and around, the large camp every evening for an hour before dusk. There were still resentful and sullen glances from some groups, but on the whole, most people appreciated how he had reorganised the camp. They now had equally distributed provisions, and teams of men delivered wood from the hills for their fires. He now appeared to have Count Albert and Guibert's reluctant respect, as they could see firsthand what he had achieved. Yuletide was now beginning, and the camp had a more festive feel. Conn had arranged for several herds of goats to be purchased, and brought down from the hills, to provide milk and cheese, and now a dozen older ones were to be killed and would be roasted on the beach along with several oxen. There would be music and singing, and the children were excited.

The leaders of the Lombards were leaving in three days for Constantinople, and he was escorting them there while reporting to John Doukas. They hoped to be able to persuade Alexios to allow them to move the camp closer to the city in the new year. Conn felt pleasantly tired as he unlaced his doublet and peeled off his clothes that evening. It had been a long day with many strenuous exercises, as he had made his men mount up and put the Horse Warriors through charge after charge against each other. The men and captains had watched in awe as the powerful horses had charged at each other, engaging in mock sword fights that looked frighteningly real as the clash of blades echoed across the water. More than one Horse Warrior ended up on the sand, to their embarrassment, usually when they fought Conn or Georgio.

'I'm astounded you did not kill each other,' Captain Orontes had murmured to Conn at the end, but the Breton Horse Warrior had just laughed before whispering, 'Almost every blow and strike is practised repeatedly; they know how, where and when to deflect. The biggest danger, Orontes, is with the horses; they fight for real, and it often takes a lot to restrain them.'

Conn lay down on his wooden cot and, putting his hands

behind his head, closed his eyes. Georgio was deeply asleep on the other side of the pavilion; it was at moments like this, just before sleep, that the trauma and flashbacks of the last summer, which he kept locked away, rose unbidden, no matter how he fought against it. He could see Marietta's grey eyes smiling up into his, the scattering of freckles across her nose and cheeks as he bent to kiss her, but then he would remember the feel of her limp body in his arms growing stiller and colder. The grey eyes had clouded, her hand clasped tightly in his had loosened, and he thought he would never forget the sound of her last breath as she whispered his name. The pain he felt at these times was unbearable; the guilt he felt at not getting to her sooner to prevent her death, or not charging into the hall to prevent the Sheikh's guard from stabbing her.

He gave a sharp intake of breath, and sitting up, he shook his head to clear it whilst swinging his legs back to the ground. He needed air, so he pulled his tunic over his head and boots back on. Untying the pavilion door, he went out into the night air and walked to the high bluff at the far end of the beach. It was a clear, bright night, with a three-quarter moon that shone onto the dark, deep waters of the Sea of Marmara.

It was here that Darius found him. Conn had been so preoccupied with his thoughts and emotions that he had not even noticed the young man's empty pallet bed. He had a dark-bearded young man with him.

'Sire, this is Matteo; he is one of Captain Fumagalli's serjeants; as you know, they took over the five-day duty rota yesterday; he has something to tell you,' he said in a low voice, glancing over his shoulder at the same time to check they had not been followed.

Conn nodded and stared at the dark Italian; he remembered

him for his frustration on the beach. He had a pleasant open face, but it was badly bruised on one side, and his chin was grazed; he had clearly sustained a blow or even several.

'Sire, I respect what you are doing with the camp, but many in my cohort do not, as they are under the sway of Captain Fumagalli, while others are very afraid of Sir Altasparta. They know what he is capable of doing.'

Conn was suddenly alert as if he knew what was coming; he raised a hand and ran a thumb over the young man's cheek to recognise the blow he had received for defying them.

'What are they planning?'

'There is a little fishing village to the south, almost a league away, called Panados. The young lord had lusted over the carpenter's wife there for some time, but the villagers gathered round to protect her; he was furious and threatened them with retribution. He swore he would burn their village to the ground, but then he was clever and bided his time with your arrival. Having heard of his reputation, the villagers set up nightly patrols, which went on for a few weeks, but they also became complacent, knowing the Emperor's men had taken over the camp. Altasparta is taking a large group of our cohort tonight; they will raid and loot the village in revenge. I told them all it was madness, and there would be more than retribution for us, but Fumagalli knocked me to the ground several times and reassured the men by saying it was so far away that no one would notice.'

Conn said nothing for a few moments as he thought this news through.

'I have ridden to the village several times. We have bought fish, cheese and fruit from them; there is a large ancient Greek shrine to the Goddess Amphitrite, the goddess of the sea.'

Matteo nodded, 'That is the one, but they left over an hour ago, Sire; I admit I struggled over betraying my cohort, or I would have come sooner, but what they plan to do is wrong.'

Conn placed a hand on the young man's shoulder.

'You did the right thing, Matteo, and I will ensure you are rewarded for your loyalty. Darius, rouse the men; I want them mounted and ready to ride immediately.'

Conn's anger was building as he made his way to Captain Orontes' pavilion. He needed the captain to be there when they caught up with them as another witness for John Doukas, for Altasparta was defying the direct command of Emperor Alexios. The whole camp had been told that justice would be swift and brutal for anyone caught raiding and looting; he intended to ensure it was. In no time, they were galloping along the stony track that led along the coast southwest to the small fishing villages.

Panados lay in a pretty bay further down the coast; like the town, it was surrounded on three sides by hills and a sheltered spot. The industrious villagers had terraced the east and south-facing slopes and planted olive trees, fruit trees and vines, which supplemented their fishing. Otto smiled as he rode into the village. His men were mainly on foot, and they had orders to take anything of value, including women and young girls, as he would sell them in the slave markets of Constantinople. He intended to make this village pay for their treatment of him. One woman, in particular, he would be taking with him.

He remembered the first time he had seen her, picking fruit on the terraces with the other women, but she stood out with her shining, bright auburn hair and blue eyes, no doubt the daughter of a slave or one of the Rus bastards that littered the city. He had approached her, but she had turned and fled; he had returned to the village again a few times, but on the last humiliating occasion, her young husband and the villagers had stood, stones in their hands, ready to drive him off. Now, they would pay. He smiled as he watched the scum of the back streets of Milan enter the houses, as he knew the screams would begin. Drawing his sword, he shouted for three other mounted men to follow him, and he kicked his horse into a canter to the carpenter's house, which lay on a slight rise at the village's far end. He sent one of his men to smash and destroy the ancient shrine above them; he would show this village what it meant to defy a Lombard knight.

The door was not barred as he entered, but the noise of the attack on the village had woken the inhabitants inside, and her husband had lit an oil lamp, pulled on his braies and was fastening them as Otto slammed the door back. They saw the outline of the armed men, and the young man immediately reached for his wooden staff as his wife screamed and pulled the cover over her naked body. Otto leapt forward and slashed at the young carpenter's arm before he could grip his staff; he then used the hilt of his sword under the man's chin to bring him to his knees. He called his men over to hold the husband; while laughing, he grabbed the cover with both hands and pulled it off the bed.

As Conn and his men crested the hill, they saw the flames leaping high from the houses in the village.

'We are too late! They have fired the village; I did not believe they meant it; why would those men follow his orders and do that?' shouted Matteo, in dismay, the emotion clear on his face.

Conn pulled on his reins and raised his hand to slow his

men behind him while drawing his sword.

'Maybe, but we can still stop this and punish those we find,' he growled, cold anger building inside him.

Shortening his reins, he kicked his horse into a canter and headed down the steep track into the village.

'Kill any man found looting or raping; we give no quarter,' he yelled back at his men, while kicking Diablo forward into a gallop when he reached better ground.

The sound of swords being drawn filled the air behind Darius. This was the first time he had taken part in an attack with the Horse Warriors, and he felt excitement but apprehension as well. He knotted his reins, gripped them in his left hand, and drew his sword.

They swept into the village, an unexpected avenging storm of hooves and swords. Realising what was happening, the raiders who saw them coming ran for cover in the houses or down the alleyways to the beach. Orontes and Conn dismounted and began clearing house by house, dragging any raiders out and throwing them to be beaten and tied by their men outside, killing any others who resisted in the slightest.

'Where is Altasparta?' demanded Conn of Captain Fumagalli, who was on his knees, blood trickling from his nose and mouth. The man said nothing but indicated, with his head, the house that sat further up the slope, at the end of the village.

As they reached the door, a sobbing, naked woman was pushed roughly through it by a grinning Altasparta. His face fell when he saw who stood outside, just as Conn delivered a punishing punch that knocked him back into the house and left him unconscious on the floor. Meanwhile, Orontes faced and ran through the man behind, who had raised his weapon. The third man backed away, hands held up in supplication as

CHAPTER EIGHT

Conn and Orontes saw the dead carpenter on the floor by the bed; his throat had been cut.

'I did not do that; I swear on the holy cross that I did not kill him. It was Altasparta. He made him kneel and watch him swive his wife, and then he killed him!' he cried, his voice cracking with fear. Conn turned away in anger and disgust and called in two of his men.

'Bind his hands behind his back; he is a witness, and take him to the others. Do the same with him,' he said, pointing to Otto's prone body.

Before long, it was all over; the cries and wailing went on as the locals mourned their dead in the village. The men started a chain of buckets to douse the flames and stop them from spreading to the other houses; the Horse Warriors helped them. Several of the dead attackers lay scattered around the village, and the rest, hands bound behind them, were on their knees in the centre.

Georgio, looking for Darius, found him helping with the buckets of water; his face was now smudged with smoke and with several streaks of blood.

'Are you injured?' he asked, in concern.

'No, it is from the man I killed; I pulled him out of the back room,' he said, pointing to a body at the side of the house.

'Well done,' he said, slapping him on the back before he went back to stand beside Conn.

As Darius stood waiting for the next line of buckets, he brushed away a tear or two; he had witnessed several attacks or murders, during his time on the streets of the city, but had never seen such pointless and unnecessary slaughter of innocents before. He thought he would never forget the smell of blood in the houses he entered; the scenes here would take a long time to erase from his mind.

Conn facing a crowd of angry and sobbing people, found that although he had done his best, he had few reassuring words to placate the village leaders; their homes had been attacked, their men killed, their women raped, and their holy shrine had been destroyed. He stood there wondering what else he could say, although Captain Orontes stepped in and promised them that punishment would be swift, and remunerations would be paid for the damage. At that point, the carpenter's wife, now wrapped in a blanket but wild-eyed with shock and grief, stepped forward.

'What payment do I get for a murdered husband? How will any amount of money ever replace him,' she shrieked, spitting in the captain's face. Orontes wiped it away, and, stepping forward, he gently touched her arm.

'I know there is no price that can compensate for that, but I promise they will pay if I have to do it myself,' he said softly and compassionately. Seeing that he truly meant it, she quietened and turned away, sobbing into the arms of an older woman who still glared at them.

Chapter Nine

Conn left the village of Panados as dawn was breaking; he had sent his wounded men back to the camp with Georgio, to be treated. Captain Orontes and his men had ruthlessly killed any of the wounded among the attackers.

'Less trouble for us later if they are dead and fewer wounded to slow us down when we move the camp. Also, it is a sobering lesson to the others that we mean what we say,' he explained, seeing Conn's raised eyebrow.

They had even gone in amongst the bound prisoners and killed the badly wounded, causing cries of panic as they thought they were all to be put to the sword. Now Conn stared stern-faced at the twenty or so survivors of the raid who, hands bound behind them, were sitting in the dirt. Amongst them was the Count of Biandrate's nephew, Otto Altasparta, who pushed himself to his knees as the captain approached on his horse. Conn had broken the Lombard noble's nose, and his face and tunic were covered in blood.

'How dare you treat me like this, Orontes? You know who I am. My uncle will have your head for this!' he yelled.

Orontes looked down on him with barely concealed contempt and disgust.

'I know what you are, Altasparta, the instigator of the attack on, and slaughter of, the villagers. Malvais tells me that Emperor Alexios will feed you to his lions for this, a sight I would like to see. Your uncle is a minor count and has no influence in the court of the Emperor. You are here in this land only on the sufferance of Alexios, and you have attacked and killed his people without justification.'

Otto paled as the significance of those words sank in but then glared at Conn; this was all his doing. Even Orontes now thought he was at the top of the dung heap because of this man, this arrogant Horse Warrior. However, he could do nothing until they returned to the camp, where his uncles would have him released.

The prisoners were roped together and made to stumble along the track back to the camp. Although it was early, most of the occupants in the camp sat outside their makeshift tents to watch the men being marched in. With the arrival of Georgio and the wounded an hour earlier, the story of the raid, and the brutal reprisals carried out, had gone around the camp like wildfire. Some were relieved to see their menfolk were part of the stumbling column. Others set up a wail that their men were not there, as it was rumoured that over twenty raiders had been caught and killed at the village. Some were fearful of what they saw, and some were stoic, for the raiders had got what was coming to them. Others were angry, and threatening revenge for the deaths of fathers, brothers or friends.

The Lombard leaders stood outside their pavilion, their faces reflecting their disbelief at what had happened, anger at their nephew, and then horror at seeing his bruised and bloody face amongst the bound prisoners being taken into the fenced palisade, used as a gaol. Guibert of Parma marched

CHAPTER NINE

down to remonstrate with Malvais as the gates were closed, and barred, on the prisoners. His brother, Count Albert, was close behind.

'What do you think you are doing, Malvais? You cannot possibly put our nephew in there with them like a common criminal,' he shouted at Conn, who glared down at them before wearily dismounting and handing his horse to Darius.

It had been a long night, and he was in no mood for the histrionics and demands of the Lombard nobles, with no right or jurisdiction here.

'He is far more than a common criminal, my Lord Count. He has fomented treason against Emperor Alexios by instigating a raid on one of the peaceful villages. He has encouraged the murder of the village men, the rape of the women and ordered the destruction of a sacred shrine, over a thousand years old, and sanctified by the Emperor himself. He then broke into the house of a twenty-four-year-old carpenter, swived his wife in front of him and then cut his throat. So what do you suggest I do with him? What would you do with a murdering treasonous rapist in Milan, Count Guibert?' he asked, in an ice-cold voice.

The two Lombard counts stood there, shocked at the litany of their nephew's crimes. Their mouths were working as they fought for something to say, but could come up with no argument to answer these charges.

'Let me give you both a suggestion. If I were you, I would consider how you will explain his actions to the Emperor when you leave for Constantinople in a few days. That is if you are still allowed to visit, which is doubtful. The actions of your nephew may result in the whole Lombard Crusade being ejected from the Byzantine lands with no provisions and no help. I'm sending a message to the Megas Doux about the events. He will no doubt decide the fate of your nephew, but I warn you it is likely he will be executed along with several others who committed murder and other atrocities.'

With that, Conn left them and headed to peel off his doublet and clothes; he needed a swim to try and wash away the tiredness but also all that he had witnessed and heard.

Otto had watched the conversation through the slight gaps in the palisade, although he could not hear what was said. Expecting his imminent release, he watched with astonishment as his two uncles, their faces pale, turned and followed by their guards made their way back up to the small plateau, where their pavilions were sited. He sank to his knees in the only small strip of shade behind the fence. It may be December, but the sun still beat down on them inside the high-fenced palisade from a cloudless sky.

The answer came back by bird from John Doukas the next day and was as expected. He wanted any man who committed murder or rape to be executed; he would expect Captain Orontes, as the Emperor's captain, to carry these orders out. Alexios was furious at the report of the attack and was still deciding the fate of Otto Altasparta; the message would arrive by messenger in a day or so. As far as the Lombard counts were concerned, he would still allow them to come to Constantinople, but they would now come as supplicants to explain, and pay reparations, for the behaviour of their men and nephew. They would no longer be guests.

Orontes was pleased, 'I will assess each prisoner in turn and use the villagers as witnesses to record their crimes; I'm furious that a few of my men had joined this raid, and I will make sure they suffer. I suggest that we carry out the executions as soon as possible; tomorrow afternoon will do, and give me time to organise everything we need.'

Conn agreed; he did not want discontent to build in the camp and promised the villagers swift justice. He relayed the information to the Lombard leaders. Count Albert silenced his brother's outburst of anger with a raised hand.

'You will achieve nothing with anger, Guibert. Malvais is right in what he says; this needs careful thought and diplomacy. I will draft a missive to the Emperor begging his forgiveness for the actions of a headstrong youth, who is simply impatient to reach Jerusalem. I will ask for mercy for Otto. I will also petition the Archbishop of Milan to intervene and, if possible, call for lenience. Can you see that these messengers are sent out, Malvais?' he asked.

Conn nodded, but was astounded at the idea of describing their thirty-five-year-old murdering nephew, who had a wife and four children in Milan, as a headstrong youth. However, Guibert had listened to his brother in growing disbelief.

'I cannot possibly face our sister, or his wife, if Otto is executed while we stood around and did nothing. We have nearly a thousand troops. Can we not take control here, Brother? Break our nephew out?' he demanded of his older sibling.

Conn gave a snort of astonishment and shook his head at their ignorance.

'That would not be a wise move; the Emperor has over forty thousand warriors within a few days marching distance. You would be annihilated, and your heads would be on spikes outside the city for all to see.'

Count Albert blustered immediately.

'I apologise for my brother, Malvais; he is understandably

shocked and upset. He is very close to Otto and spoke wildly, full of emotion without thinking.'

Conn turned and bowed, leaving them to go and warn Captain Orontes to be wary of any orders from Count Guibert to his men. He also ordered the guards on the prisoners to be doubled for their safety, as he knew the leaders of the village were coming to witness the executions this afternoon. Conn had to admire Captain Orontes for the way he carried out his investigation so quickly, bringing witnesses from the village to identify the murderers. Then, of course, the prisoners turned on each other, most of them blaming Altasparta for ordering them to attack and kill the men. By the end of the morning, Orontes had a clear picture of who had done what, and he divided the men into groups for punishment.

Otto sat on his own, his stomach tightly knotted as the men had turned on him, pointing, gesturing and shouting that he had forced them to take part. He tried to make himself as small as possible, his knees drawn up and his arms around them; for now, he realised he would have to pay for his actions. He had never considered himself a coward in any way, but the fingers of fear were beginning to clutch at his entrails.

The other groups sat as far from him as possible, as if the association would stain, but he listened to their comments, and they fed his fear.

'Vicious they are, over here in the east; their executions are never simple. Seen it several times in the last crusade, they drag them out for the crowds, taking a hand or a foot first, then their eyes,' announced an older man, while the younger ones shivered wide-eyed with horror at what they might have to endure.

'Rapists, now they always castrate them first, and then hand

CHAPTER NINE

them over to the relatives to tear limb from limb. I see the villagers are already arriving,' he said, pointing to a group walking past on the hillside above the palisade.

Otto could not help himself, and he turned to look up, meeting the eyes of a woman who had just lowered her hood. She stood still, glaring at the palisade with hatred. Otto went cold as he realised it was the carpenter's wife, although, with red and swollen eyes and hair torn and matted with grief, she was almost unrecognisable. For the first time, Otto realised the enormity of what he had done, not through guilt or remorse but because he may now have to suffer the consequences. Also, it was the stark realisation that his noble birth and powerful friends, who had always protected him, would not be useful to him here.

The punishments were to be carried out on the beach, and most of the camp were stood or sat around the bay on the sloping sand, dunes or the high bluffs behind. Not only had the villagers of Panados come to see vengeance and retribution delivered, but many of the wronged townsfolk of Rodosto had also come. There were three large T posts already embedded deep in the sand, which had been used for pell training, but now Captain Orontes had brought a large old barn door down to the beach, and his men had laid it deep into the sand, so it would not move but provide a platform.

The men from the palisade were taken out one group at a time. The first twelve men roped together were led to the beach, and the crowd parted like a wave before them. Some spat at them, some attacked them and had to be dragged off, and a few women sobbed and clung to their menfolk. Most of the men were terrified, although several were stoic and hoped the punishment would be swift and not leave them crippled or blinded for life. The men were pushed down to kneel in the sand and unroped from each other. Only two of these were the men from the cohort of Captain Orontes, and he shook his head sadly as he looked at them; no doubt they were offered silver from Altasparta. The remaining ten were from the gutters of Milan. Conn now stood, and in a loud, clear voice that carried over the crowd, he outlined the crimes of these men and announced the Emperor's decree that they should be executed.

Fortunately, Captain Orontes did not like to see men suffer; despite the local populace's wishes, who had cried out for several gruesome punishments, he had decided on swift justice. He had the men blindfolded, and in twos, they were brought to kneel on the wooden barn door, where a priest forgave their sins and sent them on their way to God with a blessing. Then, they were swiftly beheaded with a sharp sword by two of the serjeants. A huge cheer went up from the locals as the heads dropped onto the door; it was echoed by the fickle crowd, who had quickly forgotten that these men were once some of their own. Several of the waiting blindfolded men shook with fear, or emptied their bladders, as they were led forward to be next.

Otto sat white-faced as the older man of the remaining group in the palisade was pushed, with difficulty, onto the shoulders of another to see what was happening on the beach.

'Well, at least it will be quick; they are beheading them now,' he said in an eerily optimistic tone.

'We are just the looters; I reckon we'll lose a hand, the usual punishment for theft. It's not too bad unless it gets infected, then the rot starts, and they can take your arm off at the shoulder in a week. Happened to a friend of mine.'

CHAPTER NINE

'Did he live?' asked a young captive, his voice shuddering with the fear of what might happen to him.

'Nah, once it's in your blood, you're a goner!'

The cheers erupted again from the beach. Then, it went silent for some time.

'They're coming for us now!' he announced, which was too much for Otto, whose stomach was clenched in fear.

'God's blood, will you shut up, you gutterspawn!' he yelled, pushing himself to his feet with difficulty.

The others stared at him with hatred. From being the leader who had brought them all sorts of loot in the past, he was suddenly the bane and scourge of their lives, who had brought about their downfall with this reckless raid, and as one, they turned on him.

Although roped together and with hands tied behind their backs, they still managed to corner him, kicking and stamping on any part they could reach. They had managed to loop a rope around his neck and were starting to throttle him when the gate opened, and the guards pulled them off, leaving a gasping, bleeding Otto on the ground.

The crowd were becoming bolder now, physically attacking the prisoners as they were marched through. The guards only grinned and roughly pushed them forward. Conn and Captain Orontes were waiting with a full platoon of guards on the beach; they watched the progress of the bedraggled group of eight men coming through the hundreds gathered on that slope.

'I think we may need more guards to escort Altasparta down, or they will tear him apart before he arrives. Have you decided what to do with him? Surely you cannot let him live,' asked Captain Orontes.

Conn shrugged. 'I'm still waiting for a message from John Doukas. I can do nothing without that decision, but we can frighten the life out of him today.'

The next punishments were not as swift, as these men were stripped, and each led in turn to the T posts to receive twenty lashes and to be branded with the upturned V shape, for Lambda, to signify a looter. Again, the crowd roared its approval as men from the town and villages were allowed to deliver the punishment, and they laid it on with zeal.

Otto, now alone inside the palisade, was physically shaking as the sound of the ox whip carried over the heads of the crowd. During the final man's punishment, Darius pushed through to the beach; the imperial messenger Conn had been waiting for was following him. He had ridden hard from the city and was carrying a leather tube, which he presented, and Conn withdrew the rolled sheet of vellum and slowly opened it, as he knew that this would seal the fate of Otto Altasparta. He read the message before passing it to Captain Orontes, who gave a low whistle, but indicated the Lombard counts and their guards who were watching them intently, having recognised the insignia of the imperial messenger. Readying himself for the confrontation, Conn walked to where they were standing with their entourage and formally bowed, holding the open scroll before him.

'The Emperor has delivered his judgment. The crimes of your nephew are so heinous that he cannot go unpunished, despite his noble blood. The local people cannot see foreigners entering the land and breaking the laws with impunity. Usually, it would be a tooth for a tooth, and he would be handed to the family to tear apart. The Emperor has graciously listened to your pleas for leniency and is giving him a lesser punishment. It should have been a death sentence, but fortunately, the Archbishop of Milan interceded for him.'

The two counts looked relieved, and Albert smiled, which disappeared as he read the judgment from the scroll and silently handed it to his brother, who spluttered with rage.

'Impossible, this cannot be allowed to happen; you cannot flog and brand a noble of the House of Biandrate like a common criminal or slave.'

Conn could hear the crowd growing restless, and he knew they had to carry this punishment out immediately.

'If you try to stop it, the crowd will turn on you; look at their faces, their discontent at already waiting this long for his punishment,' he said, sweeping an arm in that direction.

Also, it seemed as if every member of the carpenter's family had moved down into a large group on the beach, waiting for Altasparta to be brought down. Conn doubted at that point if the young noble would survive.

'I suggest you use your private guards and our troops to bring him down. I will not read the Emperor's judgment until he is on the beach, and I warn you many of the crowd may see this as far too lenient, so Orontes will have his troops ready.'

Count Albert wearily nodded and sent twenty of his guards in the Briandata livery with the Emperor's men. Otto was not reassured by the sight of so many guards as he knew many of the crowd were baying for his blood. He had heard the shouts and cries for his head. However, even though blows still fell on him and his legs gave way several times, they managed to get him to the beach, where he was stripped and tied to the middle pell post. Like the others, he was branded between the shoulders with the upturned Greek Lambda letter, but below it, the blacksmith also put a large Greek letter P, which represented Rho or R for rapist. Otto could not believe this was happening to him, and he gritted his teeth, determined not to cry out. However, he could smell his burning flesh on the second one, and the pain was intense, so he could not hold back a strangled cry, and the crowd cheered.

Malvais came and stood in front of him, and unrolling the scroll, he read out the Emperor's judgement.

'Sir Otto Altasparta has been branded as a common felon. After various interventions and pleas for leniency, his execution has been commuted to twenty-five lashes. This is no easy punishment; many men will not survive twenty. His family have been ordered to pay the injured family a large sum of bloodwit or restitution. I will set this at fifty pieces of silver to be paid today.'

There was a grumble which became a roar of discontent from the local population, but Captain Orontes sent his men to encircle the punishment area, swords drawn. Otto could not believe what he was hearing; he had been bloodied, beaten, imprisoned, branded, and now they intended to flog him. He roared angrily and called for his uncles, trying to ignore the family of the young carpenter only twenty strides away. He could see the fury on their faces at the leniency of the sentence and expected them to break through and attack him.

At that moment, Orontes appeared before him; he held a thick piece of leather to his face, 'Something to bite on.'

Otto glared at him and shook his head.

'Don't be a fool, Altasparta. Now isn't the time for pride or false bravado; I have seen a man bite through his tongue at only ten lashes. It also stops you screaming as much.' Otto reluctantly opened his mouth and clamped his teeth on the hard, dry leather.

CHAPTER NINE

Conn had seen over a dozen men flogged; it was a common punishment for army soldiers. It was also a public event which humiliated a man. He loathed Otto Altasparta intensely, as he was the worst type of arrogant, vindictive, petty nobleman who thought he was above the law. So, Conn had to admit he felt some satisfaction knowing he was to be punished for his heinous crimes. However, after twenty lashes, the man was hanging on the pell post, his back raw and bloodied by the ox whip. The problem was that he dared not stop the punishment because the carpenter's grief-stricken wife was loudly counting each stroke of the whip. She screamed with rage as his uncles ordered him untied at the end.

'It should have been fifty or a hundred for what he did,' she yelled at them.

Conn stood a few feet away; he could see how beautiful she must have been before grief destroyed her, and stepping forward, he nodded in agreement.

'He will likely die. The wounds are deep, his blood is scattered all over the sand, and very few men can survive that punishment.'

Her eyes dulled with loss and pain. She turned away but then turned back.

'The worst part is that I am likely diseased from such a lecherous man like him, or worse; I could be carrying his child. If I find I am, I swear if he lives, I will come for him in the night and I will kill him, and then myself.'

Conn's stomach knotted as he watched her go. He had no answer for her or her heartbroken family, but he would ensure the bloodwit was paid today.

Altasparta's life hung in the balance for four or five days, he had lost so much blood. His uncles brought in the top physicians who worked on him night and day until his tenuous grasp on life improved. When Conn escorted the Lombard nobles to Constantinople several days later, Otto was expected to recover slowly, although he would be scarred for life in more ways than one.

As the party entered the gates of Constantinople two days later, Altasparta, drugged with theriac, floated in and out of consciousness, still in agony, as he lay on his stomach on his wooden cot. One thing that occupied his more lucid moments was his thirst for revenge against Alexios, John Doukas and Conn Fitz Malvais.

Chapter Ten

January 1101 – Westminster

Following his marriage and the coronation of his queen, King Henry felt a sense of relief for a few weeks as if his goal had been reached and his seizure of the crown had more legitimacy. This feeling did not last, as it became apparent he had too few supporters compared to his brother, Robert. He strode back and forth in the King's richly furnished chamber at Westminster Palace with Anselm, the Archbishop of Canterbury, and Queen Matilda. She tried to placate him.

'Yes, some will call you an oath-breaker, and they will openly support your brother's claim to the throne, but here we also have an opportunity, Henry, as we can see a lot of fence sitters, men who are unsure which way to jump. They are watching what you do and waiting to see if you keep your word with your Charter of Liberties, the promises you made to them.'

The Archbishop nodded in agreement, 'I will work on those who are undecided, Sire; I like to think that I have a reasonable amount of influence here in England.'

Matilda smiled at this understatement from the Archbishop of Canterbury, one of the most powerful church prelates in Europe, with the ear of the Pope.

'Also, do not forget that you have the powerful Beaumont

brothers firmly on your side, the Earls of Warwick and Leicester,' she added, placing a hand on his arm to stop him pacing.

Henry seemed to listen and be appeased, but his mind was still churning as he dismissed them. Several of the wealthiest and most powerful nobles have left his court at Westminster, ostensibly returning to their estates to celebrate Yuletide, but he knew better. His informers told him that some had even risked the dangerous winter sea journey, to return to Normandy, to be at Duke Robert's side. He knew that Robert had returned with his new wife to Rouen and was reportedly furious that Henry had deceived him, broken his oath of loyalty and stolen his crown. He did not doubt that his brother would be planning to invade, hence the disappearance of so many from his first Yuletide court.

That was not all, Henry was more alert to the atmosphere in his court, and he noticed the whispers and laughter that followed him from amongst the courtiers, and he marked those that seemed openly hostile. He knew he was at a disadvantage because they hardly knew him; he was eighteen years younger than Duke Robert and his powerful compatriots in arms. A younger child brought up in his mother, Matilda's, court in Caen. He was also different; he had no reputation as a warrior like Robert, the hero of Jerusalem, the man who had taken on his father and won. He had always been more intelligent and scholarly than his brothers, hence the nickname Henry Beauclerc, which had stuck. Some courtiers and nobles dared to deride and laugh at him behind his back, as they were not expecting him to hold the crown for long.

However, the one thing that Piers De Chatillon had taught him was that knowledge and information were everything.

CHAPTER TEN

The Papal Envoy had the biggest network of informers across Europe and the largest and swiftest communication system. As a very young man, when Secretary to Pope Gregory, Chatillon had set up a messenger pigeon system that was second to none. Henry had learnt from this and was building a network of paid informers, not only in his own court but in Robert's court in Rouen, and several other European cities. Henry was finding out exactly who was hostile behind his back and who could be bought. He also began to gather useful information about their debts and their families so that, as Flambard had done for William Rufus, he could exert pressure.

His two biggest problems were his cousin William, Count of Mortain, and Earl of Cornwall and Robert De Belleme, the Earl of Shrewsbury. Both were the largest and wealthiest landowners in England and Normandy and had considerable influence. Both disliked him, and derided him behind his back, or sometimes even openly in the court, making him the butt of their jokes. William also held the strategic Pevensey Castle and constantly harangued Henry to award him the Earldom of Kent as well. Matilda could see the arrogance and danger of these two powerful Anglo-Norman nobles, and she advised Henry to try and placate them without giving in to Mortain's demands.

'You cannot give him Kent; he is one of Duke Robert's supporters, and that will give him a long protected coastline in the southeast, to land their forces, if Robert decided to invade. I have an idea: why do we not offer him the hand of my sister, Princess Mary of Scotland? Let us try and tie Count William of Mortain to us by marriage, and with the attraction of the royal blood of both England and Scotland for his wife and heirs.'

Henry suddenly picked Matilda up and swung her around so that she laughed and demanded that he have more decorum as the King of England, while secretly enjoying every minute. What had been an arranged marriage had turned into a love match for her, and to have that love returned, she turned a blind eye to his many mistresses, tolerating his affairs and several bastard children at court.

Unfortunately, William, Count of Mortain, turned the marriage proposal down flat; there was no way he wanted to be tied to a cousin he had always disliked intensely, moreover, one who had stolen the crown of England from its rightful heir. Matilda was hurt, while Henry was angry and affronted by his refusal and swore he would see his day with Mortain.

'It is time to bring Ranulf Flambard to justice; he has been in the Tower of London for six months,' demanded the Archbishop, who had always despised the new Prince Bishop of Durham.

'You said in your Charter of Liberties that you would reverse the damage done by William Rufus and Flambard, and that he would be punished. However, he feasts and entertains in the Tower. Bring him to trial and execute him! That will show those undecided nobles that you meant those words and that no one is above the laws of the land. He is nothing but a low-born, self-important upstart, and he is widely detested; his death will be popular, Sire.'

Henry raised an eyebrow. 'What? Behead a Prince Bishop. I would not have thought you would want that set as a precedent in England, Archbishop!' he exclaimed.

Anselm gave a thin smile in recognition of the King's wit.

'Perhaps not, but you know that I'm right. It must be done, and soon.'

CHAPTER TEN

Henry nodded; he knew they were right. He would gather witnesses, and he would use the ceremony of the Easter Court at Winchester to put him on trial. It would be an appropriate venue, the treasury, for a man accused of misappropriating funds.

The news of Flambard's fate filtered through to the prisoner himself, in the great White Keep of the Tower of London, a week or so later. Flambard, still living in some state and using his charm and silver tongue to great effect, had won over his gaolers with presents and hospitality. This applied particularly to William de Mandeville, the Constable of the Tower of London. He was easily taken in by Flambard's flattery and friendship and began to believe that they had indeed wronged the King's advisor, who had, in reality, been working purely for the good of the country. It was Mandeville who brought him the news of Henry's decision. Flambard had thanked him and looked thoughtful as he poured Mandeville a goblet of wine.

'There is no doubt that this is Archbishop Anselm's doing; he has always hated me since his imposed exile in France, which he brought on himself,' he said, as he stretched out his legs to the roaring fire.

'I have heard as much, but the trial has been set for Easter, and unfortunately, I believe they will demand your head. You have made too many enemies among the nobles, my Lord Bishop.' Flambard nodded in exasperation and sighed.

'Purely by forcing them to pay what they owed, but I will outwit them yet, Mandeville, for I have a plan.'

The Constable pushed him for details, but Flambard refused to say anymore, stating the less he knew, the better, so no blame could be attached to him. Since the beginning of his incarceration, Flambard's servants had been given free rein to go in and out of the Tower, bringing him food delicacies, writing materials, manuscripts and visitors. The guards had nominally checked what was brought in, but several bribes had changed hands, and on this particular February night, they were given two large sacks of good quality wine, which brought smiles to their faces as it was a cold night outside and the fire in the guard room was beckoning.

Unbeknownst to them, a long rope was hidden in one of the other sacks of wine that made its way to Flambard's room. Lord Mandeville had agreed to stay in his quarters that evening. Pacing his room back and forth, Flambard waited impatiently until the guards were sufficiently drunk, then he took his chance to put his plan into action to escape, with his loyal servant's help.

'I will tie the rope tightly to the stone mullion of the window, Sire; it is strong and will hold your weight as you descend. I will go first and prepare the way, and your Chamberlain, Joffrey, will follow behind you.' Flambard was no coward, but his heart was in his mouth as he watched his young servant climb through the window and grasp the rope.

'You place your feet thus, Sire, flat on either side of the wall and gently lower yourself hand over hand. Do not go too fast, or you will tumble and lose your grip.'

'I'm more concerned with this thin stone mullion holding our weight!' exclaimed Flambard, fingering the carved stone. Standing behind him, Joffrey reassured him.

'It is solid stone, Sire, anchored into the stonework above and below; it will not move as long as we do not bounce or jerk on the rope too strongly.'

'I do not intend to hang myself with it!' he exclaimed, not

completely convinced by Joffrey's reassurances, but as he had no choice, he went next.

'Has it really come to this? A man of my position and power climbing out of windows in the middle of the night, possibly to plummet to my death,' he muttered, in disbelief, as he clambered out. For a moment, he sat on the sill, one leg in the room, one dangling against the stone wall, and he felt a moment of terror and froze as he looked down into the dark courtyard several floors below. Then he steadied his breathing and told himself that an executioner's axe was far more terrifying than climbing down a rope. He then surprised himself at how lithely he managed to descend, and soon, he was on the ground watching Joffrey descend above him.

'I have been assured that there will be no guard on the postern gate, Sire; we simply need to unbolt it, and pull it closed behind us,' whispered Joffrey, as he landed safely beside his master.

Flambard hurried after them, and before long, they were through the gate and racing along the dark, wet, London streets to where horses awaited them to take them to freedom.

The first prisoner in the Tower of London, Prince Bishop of Durham, Ranulph Flambard, thus became the first prisoner to escape from there, as they galloped out of London heading for the coast, where a ship awaited to take them to Normandy. Flambard had decided to throw himself on the mercy of Duke Robert. His Chamberlain, Joffrey, thought this could either be a clever move or a disastrous one, as they both knew Duke Robert had no great love for the cunning and devious Flambard.

The next morning, William de Mandeville had the unpleasant task of notifying the King that his prisoner had somehow escaped using a rope. He was immediately summoned in person and lambasted at great length by both the King and Archbishop Anselm.

'I cannot decide whether you purposefully assisted his escape or were just a careless gaoler. If it was the former, and I find evidence of that, I promise you will take his place in his cell and on the block. Your incompetence has allowed the most significant prisoner in England to escape, Mandeville, and you will pay for that. Prepare to bid farewell to your estates in Essex!' A pale and shaking Mandeville was escorted out.

Henry's men searched the countryside and ports for a week, but Flambard was long gone; a ship had been waiting at Pevensey with a chest full of treasure from Durham with his elderly mother. They cast off as soon as the Prince Bishop arrived. It was a perilous journey. The sea was rough, and the worried crew bailed out constantly while the captain prayed the large sail would hold, while he regretted the large amount of silver he had taken to risk it, at this time of year.

More unsettling was Flambard's mother, who the crew thought was moon-touched. Instead of cowering with Flambard in the covered cabin, she clung to the mast and howled into the storm. Some of the crew thought this was a bad omen, and they gathered on the deck, wanting to throw her overboard, but Flambard managed to convince them that she was summoning the old gods to protect them. It was with great relief from everyone concerned when they finally limped into the mouth of the River Seine, with a damaged sail and a pale-faced, exhausted crew eager to make their way to the wharves at Rouen.

CHAPTER TEN

January 1101 – The chateau at Chatillon Sous Bagneux

Piers De Chatillon, Papal Envoy, sat deep in thought at his desk. His friend, confidant and vavasseur, Edvard, sat opposite in silence, watching him for some time until he decided that he could take no more.

'This will not do, Piers; the situation is becoming untenable. It is now up to you to decide as Pope Paschal is leading us down a path that will not end well.'

Piers ran his hands through his hair; Edvard was right; this could not continue. Having been the Papal Envoy from a young age for five different popes, he had always given them the impression that he was acting on their wishes or in their interests. Or, he had guided them, sometimes gently, sometimes not, in the right direction. However, on the rare occasions when a pope's actions or orders could only lead to disaster, Chatillon would take control, and in one instance, he ensured that Cardinal Dauferio, who became a mad and dangerous pope, had a timely death to prevent him from doing harm.

The problem they faced now was complicated; for decades, the popes and Holy See, following Chatillon's advice, had actively supported and enhanced the career of Robert Curthose, the eldest son of William I. They had even secretly financed his campaign to defeat his father at Gerberoi. In return, Robert, now Duke of Normandy, had become a staunch advocate of the Holy See and one of the great military leaders of the First Crusade for Pope Urban.

However, for a brief time while Robert was attacking Jerusalem, the Holy See had agreed to back another horse, Henry Beauclerc, the youngest son of William I. This was because it suited the Holy See to have William Rufus, a most uncooperative king, removed from the throne, and Chatillon was permitted to facilitate the assassination. At that time, no one believed that Henry would have the ability, or support, to snatch the throne of England from his brother; they expected him to hold it as a regency for the return of Duke Robert, to whom Henry was oath-sworn. However, Henry had outwitted them all, and within a few days of his brother's death, he had ensured with almost impossible haste that he was crowned king.

The fly in the ointment, now, would be if Robert somehow learnt of the Holy See's actions in supporting Henry, in the assassination, and in not preventing him from seizing the crown that was rightfully his. Pope Paschal had ordered Chatillon to bide his time before going to Robert's side, and for once, Chatillon had found himself torn. But now, a message lay on the table before him, which meant he had to act immediately. It was from the unlikeliest of people, Robert De Belleme, the powerful Earl of Shrewsbury, and it contained only two sentences, but they were both of great significance.

It is time for Pope Paschal to get off the fence, Chatillon. Otherwise, I may have to relate to Duke Robert what happened in the forest when Rufus died and your involvement in letting him be crowned.

Also, Ranulph Flambard, who also has his suspicions about the sudden and unexpected death of the King, has escaped from the Tower of London and has suddenly arrived in Rouen to plead for sanctuary with Robert.

'I hate to say it, Piers, but Belleme has the right of it. I can see that loathsome snake, Flambard, whispering in Duke Robert's ear that you were in the forest beside the King when he died. You must deal with Flambard; no one will mourn if he breathes his last. I will even go and do it for you,' he offered, sitting forward in the chair with an earnest expression.

This brought a much-needed smile to Chatillon's face.

'We can no longer leave the situation as it is so we leave for Rouen this week, Edvard. Please arrange everything as usual. Daniel will be in charge of security at the chateau; I will tell him to give Gironde a more significant role as well. My son is growing up fast and is now old enough to take more responsibility for guarding our families here.'

'What of Gabriel?'

Chatillon stared out of the window over the garden briefly, as he considered his other twin son, younger than Gironde by an hour.

'It has taken Gabriel a long time to recover from the events at the villa in Aggio. The threat, yet again, to the lives of him and his mother, the death of Finian and the murder of Marietta in front of his eyes, has left its mark on him. He still has nightmares but with Ahmed's help they are becoming fewer.'

'He was very close to Marietta during the years when his mother was abducted; despite being young, she took Isabella's place, and he loved her dearly, as did we all. However, although sensitive, Gabriel is also resilient and he has his mother back at home. I would give him some role, no matter how small. As for Ahmed, he has a new lease of life now that Isabella has returned home. He has always thought of her as a daughter,' murmured Edvard.

For a while, they were lost in their thoughts, and there was no sound but the wind outside, which was rising and beginning to rattle the shutters.

'It was another fortunate day when I found Ahmed, the physician and apothecary, in the King's palace in Paris; like you, he has rarely been out of my life since. However, it is time I brought Conn back. I have no doubt now that there will be war, and I need Conn in England with access to the King's ear. Henry liked him; they spent a great deal of time together last spring and summer, which could prove very useful to us. Henry has few real male friends about him whom he can trust. Also, Conn was with Henry in the forest when the King was murdered; he helped with the plan, and I know he trusts him. I will send a message to Georgio.'

Edvard's eyebrows rose in surprise.

'Do you know where they are?' he asked, having not heard Chatillon mention the young Horse Warriors for months.

Chatillon rolled his eyes in mock horror at his friend.

'I cannot believe you just asked that of me as if I would not know where they were,' he laughed, and Edvard joined in.

'True, I spoke without thinking, and as you have not mentioned them, I suspect you have your reasons for not doing so.'

'They are in Byzantium, currently outside Constantinople, having been recruited into the Emperor's forces under the leadership of my old friend and sometime adversary, John Doukas, the Megas Doux. But I now need them back here.'

'Will Conn listen to you? Will he be ready to return? Marietta's death hit him very hard, Piers.'

'As it did to all of us, Edvard. We adopted and raised her; she was my ward and was beginning her new life with her mother's inheritance in Genoa. However, time moves on, and Conn Fitz Malvais owes me a great debt, one I have never called in, and he knows that. So yes, he'll struggle with the decision, but I hope to have them back here by the summer when Robert will no doubt invade England.'

Chapter Eleven

January 1101 – Constantinople
Albert of Biandrate and Guibert of Parma returned from their weeks in Constantinople much subdued and somewhat in awe of Emperor Alexios and his magnificent court. The Emperor had thoroughly chastised them for being unable to control their men and their nephew, a Lombard knight. They had dropped to their knees and apologised profusely, lamenting the actions of a frustrated young man's moment of madness. They swore that such an incident would never happen again. Their first week there was both humiliating and uncomfortable because they were there not as guests but as supplicants, and they read the contempt on the face of the famous Megas Doux, John Doukas, when he looked them up and down.

However, relations gradually thawed, and they were pleased to see the arrival of the Archbishop of Milan, who received a very different welcome from the Emperor. However, the short private meeting with him not long after his arrival, left them both shaken.

'How could you let this happen? Have you no authority or control over your family and your crusaders? You were given this group, a difficult one, I admit, because of your previous

CHAPTER ELEVEN

records as experienced knights at arms and your ability to control armed men. I arranged for you to have a thousand troops who you, surprisingly, put under the control of your wild and unpredictable nephew. Like a fox leading a flock of sheep, he could get away with anything unchallenged by you two. Words escaped me when John Doukas told me that; I could think of nothing to say to justify your foolish actions. You seem to have failed abysmally and done us untold damage with the Emperor and John Doukas, who is the real power behind the throne, and has the Emperor's ear.' He paced up and down the room for some time before turning on them again.

'What a mess you have given me, but of one thing I am certain, your nephew, if he survives, which is doubtful, is to be sent back to Milan, back to Lombardy, in disgrace, and I promise that the Pope will hear of this. He goes as soon as we are ready to cross the Bosphorus.'

The counts, who had sat heads bowed while the tirade broke over their heads, now reacted in alarm.

'We beg your grace to reconsider. Yes, they were rash and foolish actions in the heat of the moment, but he has paid dearly for them, and we promise he will not cause any more problems,' pleaded Albert.

'To join us, he would have had to be sent ahead by ship, for the Emperor refuses to have him enter his territory in Anatolia. I cannot take the risk of having that barbarous young man anywhere ahead of us creating mayhem, or near the rest of this crusade. I dread to think what the leaders of the French and German contingents will say when they arrive and hear what the Milanese have done. He has tainted our good reputation. When I heard the list of his crimes I wondered what I was thinking in asking for leniency for him. It would have been better for us all if he had been executed with the other murderers and rapists.'

Again, although thoroughly shocked at the Archbishop's words, they still pleaded for their nephew to be allowed to stay with them, but to no avail. As they were dismissed, Albert met Guibert's eyes as they left the Archbishop to his prayers.

'I do not know how we'll tell him when we return to the camp.'

Guibert shook his head in frustration.

'He will not take it well. You know as well as I that he gets this wildness and unpredictability from his father, who was uncontrollable at times and eventually died in a senseless brawl because of it.'

'I also fear our sister's wrath when she hears what has happened, but he has brought this on his head by his disgraceful actions,' murmured Albert.

'I think he has paid for that, Brother; he will bear the scars of his punishment for the rest of his life, if he survives it,' he said, grimly.

The counts remained in the court for the next two weeks, ensuring they were fulsome in their praise of Emperor Alexios and everything around them. In truth, they were overwhelmed by Constantinople; they had never experienced a city like it, the sights, the immense buildings and churches, the riches, silks, spices, and smells of the East laid out in shops and stalls. It certainly reflected the wealth and power of Alexios, sitting as it did in the heart of Byzantium.

Conn had returned two weeks before them, and the camp they returned to was a different place; the attack on the village and the subsequent swift and brutal punishments had

CHAPTER ELEVEN

subdued the rougher elements in the camp; some had even left. Fumagalli, the weasel-faced captain, had managed to escape, but had been caught, brought back and flogged. He had been demoted to the ranks and replaced by Serjeant Matteo, who had rapidly appointed new serjeants and restored discipline in the cohort. The camp, now set out in military lines, was an orderly place, with duties allocated and constant patrols. It had taken several months to achieve, but Conn was pleased with the orderly result.

He was with Georgio and two of his men when the Lombard counts returned; they pulled up their horses and addressed him.

'Commander, we have been granted permission by the Emperor to move closer to the city. He insists that we be at least half a league from the walls, but it means we can obtain better provisions and allow controlled groups to enter Constantinople and see the wonders therein. One of our escorts is a messenger, and he carries your orders to facilitate the move.'

Conn was surprised at this news after recent events, and Georgio gave a low whistle of surprise. However, Conn bowed his head in acceptance and waited for Captain Orontes, who had reluctantly agreed to travel to the city and escort them back. He dismounted, clasped arms with Conn and Georgio and then removed a leather tube tied behind his saddle.

'Orders from the great man himself, I don't envy you the task of planning this move. I have other news, but I will wait until we do not have so many interested ears around us,' he said, narrowing his eyes at the portly captain, who had only escaped punishment because he had slept through Altasparta's raid, when he should've been with them.

'Come to my tent later, Orontes. You can assist with the planning; you are not getting off that lightly,' he laughed.

There was the first hint of a warm breeze coming from the south, and Conn sat on his own on the rocky bluff at the end of the cove. Here, he unrolled and read the message from John Doukas.

Malvais,

By flattery and, I am sure, bribery, the Lombards have persuaded Alexios to allow them to set up camp closer to the city. This was against my initial advice, but the Emperor seems to be very impressed with the way you put down the recent raids, and therefore, he believes you and your men can control the camp wherever it may be. Having heard from Orontes how volatile large numbers of this group still are, I imagine it would be like holding down a lid on a bubbling volcano. We can only hope to move them all over the Bosphorus very soon.

I have no great hope of persuading the Emperor to change his mind. I'm therefore moving you to our small military base outside Hebdoman, where there is a large freshwater cistern, and I will provide more troops from the barracks there. You will need the extra men as I have heard that the other two Lombard groups will join you there in a few weeks. Hebdoman is over a league and a half from the city on the Via Egnatia and will give us a better distance to monitor and control any entries into the city. I have every faith in your ability to set up a similar structured and regulated military camp to the east of the town of Hebdoman. Let me know when you are settled, as I may ride out to visit you there.

John Doukas

CHAPTER ELEVEN

Conn rolled up the letter and replaced it in the leather tube; he stared across the Sea of Marmara, thinking the content of the message through. There was no doubt that this would be a momentous task; he called Darius over, whom he saw was hovering close by.

'Bring Orontes and Georgio to me now,' he ordered, before returning to his headquarters.

On the table in the pavilion were several maps given to him by John Doukas. Now, he unrolled and weighted down the one that showed the Via Egnatia, which ran along the coastline and entered Constantinople by the Golden Gate, in the far southern point of the city. He tracked back from there to Hebdoman and noticed that the large Roman cistern, or reservoir, was marked on the map. The others joined him, and Darius served wine and honeyed biscuits while Conn remained engrossed in the map until he waved the other two over to join him.

'Hebdoman is on the Sea of Marmara as well, so it is similar to here in that we have rising hills in the north and a sea barrier to the south. However, the camp needs to be far enough away from the town as I hear there are several smaller royal palaces, which might prove too much of a temptation to our guttersnipes from Milan.'

Orontes pointed to an area east of the great cistern. 'Knowing of these plans from John Doukas, I took the liberty of galloping up there to survey the area. There is an area called the Field of Mars, no doubt of Roman origin, which would be perfect for training. There are also more trees and sheltered areas on the slopes and several streams. It is an ideal spot to move the camp to, especially with double the number arriving,' he explained.

Conn drained his goblet and slapped Orontes on the shoulder.

'You have given yourself a task, Orontes. Take two dozen of your men and two dozen of the Milanese today. I want you to go and lay out the area of the camp and get the men digging the new latrines. It may be a temporary camp, but it will be a military camp, and we'll move them out quickly and quietly in groups with minimal discontent.'

Georgio gave a snort of amusement and disbelief.

'Is that even possible given the numbers that will be arriving, as it will mean splitting our forces in two, which will weaken us?'

'We will do it a quadrant at a time, each with an armed escort. The Lombard nobility and their large entourage and guards can go first. No doubt they will take the prime clearings and shaded slopes. Now, Orontes, what is this news you wished to share?' he asked the Byzantine captain, who was fast becoming a comrade and friend.

'The Emperor and Archbishop have decided that Otto Altasparta is not allowed to travel south through the Byzantine lands. When the Crusaders cross and go south to Jerusalem, he will be escorted north, under armed guard, to return to Lombardy.'

Conn raised an eyebrow; the Emperor had obviously neither forgotten nor forgiven Altasparta despite the punishments. 'Do his uncles know of this?'

'Yes, but they have chosen not to tell him until the time comes to move south. I think perhaps they are a little afraid of their volatile nephew, Malvais. John Doukas mentioned that once the other two large groups arrived from the north, within a month, the Emperor wanted them loaded onto ships and over the Bosphorus on their way to Nicomedia.'

Georgio shook his head, 'We are talking twenty to thirty thousand to contain here in the camp at first and then shepherd across Anatolia. Two-thirds of which are slow-moving civilians; we will definitely need more men, Conn,' he suggested, seeing the frown on his friend's face.

Conn did not reply, but dropping into a camp chair, he took a long draught of wine. If he had learnt anything from his real father, Morvan De Malvais, it was to break a large and complicated task down into smaller parts. His father had organised an army for Robert Curthose to defeat King Malcolm of Scotland, and the stories about that came back to him now. He sat forward and waved the other two to sit while Darius stood wide-eyed in the background, hanging on every word.

'The system we have established of dividing the soldiers into cohorts is working, so now each quadrant of the camp will have the cohort that will stay with it, establishing rotas and patrols of their own area. We will move this camp as quickly as possible before the end of the week. By the time the other two groups arrive in a week or so, we'll do the same with them, as we are getting another four hundred men from the barracks at Hebdoman.

Orontes nodded, seeing how this would work.

'This means that the captains and their serjeants have responsibility for one area; they are accountable and will answer directly to us. I suggest we promote more men to serjeants as we need them; I have several men in mind.'

Conn agreed, 'Paying them is no object as we've been given ample funds, so let us make a move and set this in motion immediately,' he said, standing and heading for the door.

Darius followed Georgio out at a trot while whispering, 'Is he always like this? So driven?'

Georgio laughed, 'You have no idea, Darius; this is nothing,' he answered, looking at their newly acquired would-be squire.

Good food and constant training had changed the gangling, thin youth he had met several months before into a different young man. He had filled out, put on muscle with weapon practice, and worked on his aim to be good enough to become a Horse Warrior.

Georgio had seen him taking the horses onto the beach with the grooms after dawn to exercise them. His skills in the saddle had come on apace, as had his sword skills. He now spent far less time on his back in the sand, as Georgio had taught him how to duck and dive to avoid the blows that would numb his shoulder and arm. Conn had also discovered that Darius was astoundingly good with a bow, so he occasionally included him in some of the more difficult training sessions on the beach when they set up targets. However, Georgio discovered that Darius could knot his reins and, hanging low on one side of the horse, fire his bow at a target, hitting it four times out of five. Conn had witnessed one of these runs and stopped dead, watching Darius release arrow after arrow at speed.

'Where did you say you found him, Georgio?' smiled Conn, standing beside his friend as a red-faced Darius came trotting up.

'You have just increased your already heavy workload, Darius; I will send you seven of the Horse Warriors, and you will teach them how to do that every morning before we leave this camp.'

Darius grinned, for he would happily lose sleep for such an opportunity.

CHAPTER ELEVEN

Conn meanwhile washed and then dressed, in his full regalia, to go and inform the Lombard nobles of the plans to move. When he entered the pavilion, the first person he saw was Otto Altasparta. The Lombard knight had spent his time recuperating and healing while his uncles were away, but he had stayed completely out of Conn's way, so they had not seen each other since that time on the beach.

Conn now completely ignored him, instead addressing Albert and Guibert using the diplomacy he had learnt in the courts of Spain. He used the language and flattery necessary to ensure that they followed his orders to the letter.

'On the orders of the Megas Doux, you have your wish to move closer to Constantinople. Captain Orontes and his men have already left to lay out the new camp. I want you to notify your servants and men and begin packing to leave here in two days.'

'Impossible. It will take at least five days to dismantle and pack the furniture, pavilions, our weapons and clothes. You overstep your orders, Horse Warrior,' shouted Altasparta, glaring at Malvais, as he hated him with every inch of his being. To his fury, Conn took no account of him, or his words, and did not even glance in his direction. Instead, he continued addressing Count Albert.

'I am giving you this chance to get there early and choose the best-shaded spots on the hillside for your pavilions. As you know, the other two groups will be with us shortly, and they may get there ahead of you if you delay, which will leave you little option but the flat sandy plain or the beach, where the wind will whip the sand around you. It will be exceptionally crowded once the whole Lombard contingent is together. I took the liberty of ordering your carts to be brought, so your servants can begin almost immediately.'

Count Albert nodded in agreement, but Otto looked on in fury and astonishment.

'Did you not hear what I said, Horse Warrior? We will not possibly be ready to leave in two days.'

For the first time, Conn turned and narrowed his eyes at him.

'Your opinion is of no interest or importance to me, Altasparta. Your uncle is the only one who makes decisions here.'

With that, Conn turned to go, but Altasparta, his hand on his sword hilt, stepped forward. His uncle's face showed alarm.

'Otto! Have you not already done enough damage to our reputation?' he shouted, red-faced with anger.

Conn smiling, shook his head at the nephew, gave a short laugh and as an ultimate insult, turned his back. When he reached the door, he bowed to the two nobles and left.

'Are you mad? Do you not think we have suffered enough at the Emperor's hands because of you?' he growled at him.

'I do not care, but I swear I will gut that arrogant Breton before we leave Constantinople!' he yelled before storming out of their tent.

Count Albert dropped into a chair, his hand over his eyes.

'We need to tell him and send him back as soon as possible, for by the Holy Face of Lucca, I swear I cannot take much more of this, Guibert.'

His brother, almost as angry as his nephew at the orders of the Commander, said nothing, and he hoped Altasparta carried out his threat.

Chapter Twelve

February 1101 – Hebdomon

To the surprise of everyone, the move to the new camp went smoothly, moving in orderly groups to the allocated areas. They had to spend one night on the road, and there were the usual thefts from each other, with goats and even full baskets of chickens disappearing. Fights broke out regularly, but the serjeants and their men quickly stamped them out and cracked heads together. When they reached Hebdomon, there was a buzz of excitement as it was a pleasant site, and they realised how close they were to the great city of Constantinople itself. Several of the guttersnipes from Milan left the camp on the first night, never to return, as they disappeared into the crowded streets of the city, disillusioned with their experience of the crusade so far. They certainly would not be missed, and word filtered back that several met with harsh and instant justice when caught stealing by the Emperor's patrols.

Conn rode in with the first quadrant, and was conscious of Altasparta's eyes burning a hole in his back. He was surprised that Altasparta could manage to ride, but Darius told him he had seen him walking up and down the beach, often doubled in pain with a few guards at his side, but he kept it up every evening, just before sunset.

'I see that he has gathered the surviving members of his raiding compatriots around him again, including Fumagalli; he will need watching,' stated Orontes, greeting Conn as they entered the new camp.

Conn gave a quick glance back, 'Like often attracts like; put a watch on him, Orontes.'

The captain saluted with a clenched fist and went back to chase up any stragglers to catch up, as they had the rest of the camp to move.

A week later, just as things began to settle in the new camp, the first group from the north arrived. Conn could see at once that they would have little trouble; the rich clothes, the quality horse flesh, and wagons piled high with personal items, furniture, wine and food showed that most of these were lesser knights, or well-to-do traders and merchants, who had separated from the Milanese slum dwellers at the earliest opportunity. Conn met with the leaders and laid out the ground rules of the camp, which were accepted without a murmur. However, he found a grinning Georgio and Darius sitting on their horses, watching this group leave a wide gap between themselves and the rabble from Rodosto. The Lombard knights were delighted to have additional company and entertained lavishly for several nights, sending into the city for choice food and wines.

Three days later, the final group arrived. Darius named them the Church group, but they were a mix of people. Yes, there were bishops, priests, clerics and academics, but there was a group of several thousand dedicated religious pilgrims who truly wanted to reach Jerusalem and pray in the Holy Sepulchre. They held mass on the beach twice a day.

Keeping the thousands in the camp supplied with food

CHAPTER TWELVE

and water became a gargantuan task that filled almost every waking hour for Conn and Captain Orontes, leaving them with little time to be concerned about Altasparta and his cronies. At Conn's request, John Doukas sent more men and even rode out himself to view the camp. They rode to a hill that overlooked the area and dismounted to stand and stare down at the enormous sprawling camp.

'The Emperor expects the stay of this Lombard group here at Hebdomon to be a short one, a month at the most, and then they will be sent on their way. If a tenth of them survive, it will be a miracle; there are more there than I imagined would make it this far,' he said, shaking his head. He felt some frustration, looking down across the tens of thousands of civilians, women, and children playing on the beach with little knowledge of the inhospitable conditions and dangers they would face ahead, with few weapons to defend themselves.

'The Emperor has also received news that two further groups are on the road from Europe, one from France under the leadership of Stephen de Blois and the French king's brother, Henry. The other is from Germany, led by Duke Welf of Bavaria and the nobles from the court of the Holy Roman Emperor. We must have this group over the Bosphorus, outside our military base in Nicomedia, before these other two groups arrive. Keep this information quiet, Malvais. I do not want the Lombard nobles to get a whisper of these other groups yet, for they may decide to wait for them, a situation we could not cope with logistically without drawing our resources from other areas, and *that,* I'm not prepared to do.'

So saying, he waved his servant forward, who handed Conn a leather pouch.

'More orders, Sire?' asked Conn.

'No, I was told to put this into your hands, and your hands only, by someone for whom I have a great deal of respect.'

Georgio, standing just behind Conn, knew exactly what this would be. He tried to steel his expression so no trace of guilt showed, as he knew he would never forgive him if he thought he had gone behind his back.

Conn lifted the leather flap and took out the folded square of vellum. As soon as he opened it, he recognised the distinctive writing and the dark violet ink of the Papal Envoy. John Doukas had now moved away, and mounting his horse, said,

'I will leave you to read that in peace, but send me regular reports on the mood in the camp and of any problems that may be brewing,' he said to Georgio.

With a wave of his hand, John Doukas was gone. Leaving Conn holding the letter from his mentor and friend, Piers De Chatillon. It was with great reluctance that Conn forced himself to face the words in front of him. He had left that life behind, and in his darkest pain-wrenching hours, he knew he was running from the heart-rending trauma of what had happened.

Suddenly, he could not bring himself to read it, and he refolded the letter. Without a word or glance at Georgio, he mounted Diablo, tucked the letter inside his doublet and rode out of the camp as if the devil was on his heels. Conn pushed the big horse into a fast gallop, leaning low over its neck, urging it on until he finally came to the forested slopes of a far hill. Diablo's sides were heaving as he leapt from the saddle. Dropping the reins, he lent his head against the big warhorse's neck and stroked it in thanks. There was an outcrop of rock ahead, and climbing nimbly up, he perched

CHAPTER TWELVE

on the highest point. With the backs of his hands, he brushed away the tears on his face, telling himself it was the harsh wind in his eyes as he galloped. He took several deep breaths and then, removing the letter from his doublet, he opened it. There was no greeting....

I know you will not want to hear this at the moment, for, like me, I know you are grieving. I imagine you are also racked with guilt that we were unable to get there sooner and act quicker to prevent the deaths of Marietta and Finian. However, we must put this aside, for I need you back here, Conn. The situation in Normandy is on a knife edge, and there is a chance that knowledge of how you and I facilitated a certain assassination may come to light. I will work to ensure that does not happen, but I urgently need your help.

I never expected to be in a position where I would use these words to you, as you have risked your life for me recently in our attacks against Sheikh Ishmael, but I am afraid I have to use them now.

You owe me a great debt, Conn Fitz Malvais, and we both know only a fraction of it has been paid. I need your help back in England as soon as possible. I am relying on you.

Please burn this letter immediately. You know and understand my dislike of the written word and it should be a practice that you always follow.
Piers De Chatillon

Conn read the letter a second time and then a third before walking to his horse, opening a flap in his saddle bag, and taking out his small wooden tinderbox and flint. He crouched down, and within minutes, he had a decent flame, and he held the letter to it until it was reduced to ashes.

He then stood, clenched his fists and gave a roar of utmost rage to the sky, that disturbed the roosting guinea fowl in the nearby trees, but it released some of the anger and emotion he was feeling. He knew the letter from Chatillon meant he had to return, but he would ignore it for now.

It was late when he returned to the camp; in the pavilion, both Darius and Georgio were wrapped in their blankets, both asleep. He lay down fully clothed, not even removing his leather doublet. He was weary, bone weary, as it had been a hard week moving the camp, long days and nights. He was asleep very quickly but he woke with Georgio shaking him and found he was drenched in sweat, his hair stuck to his forehead.

'You were shouting Marietta's name, over and over,' his friend said, handing him a cool, damp cloth.

Conn sat up and muttered a quick word of thanks. It had been several months since the nightmares and night sweats had happened. It was as if he had to relive the events in the villa at Aggio over and over again. As Georgio returned to his camp cot, Conn unlaced his doublet and wiped his face and neck with the cloth.

He thought of the letter, which no doubt had triggered this flashback. He sighed and decided he would go back, but he was not sure when, as he was certainly nowhere near ready. Piers De Chatillon would have to wait.

Chapter Thirteen

February 1100 – Hebdomon
'Unfortunately, as is the way, information seems to find its way out, no matter how we try to keep it quiet,' muttered Georgio, to a silent and brooding Conn, who had hardly spoken a word to him, or anyone else, that was not an order, since the letter arrived. Now, he just shrugged, intent on cleaning his bridle until the leather shone.

In a matter of days, the whole camp seemed to know of the other groups making their way across Europe towards them, and Altasparta had somehow learnt that he was being sent back to Lombardy; the volcano that John Doukas had described was bubbling again.

Otto Altasparta was now beyond violent emotion; he had reached a point of ice-cold anger and hatred. He had been humiliated, treated and punished like a common criminal instead of being given the right of trial by combat as a knight should. Now, overhearing his uncle's conversation one night, he found he was being sent back to Milan in disgrace and prevented from travelling to Jerusalem. These thoughts went around in his head, and he came to one conclusion: all of this was the fault of the Horse Warrior. He now did not doubt that Malvais had suggested this banishment to John Doukas and Emperor Alexios. So now he was planning his revenge on them all. He knew, despite his preoccupation with his own fate, that there was discontent in the camp. It had spread like wildfire and the French and German contingents, each with a much larger military cohort, were on their way, and the Lombards were aware that they needed this extra military protection.

The Archbishop and Lombard nobles approached Conn and demanded a meeting with John Doukas, to insist they stay at Hebdomon until the other groups from Europe arrived. They refused to be forced into crossing the Bosphorus into enemy territory, where they would be vulnerable with such a high percentage of civilians. Conn was at the meeting, which took place in a small royal palace in Hebdomon, standing by the side of the Megas Doux as they aired their demands. He noticed that Altasparta had ridden in with his uncles but seemed to be keeping a low profile, standing behind them, listening to all that was said. However, Conn was on alert as he saw Count Albert glancing nervously back at his nephew several times.

Otto was, in fact, slightly in awe of the famous Megas Doux. This was the first time he had seen him, although everyone knew the reputation of this great warrior. With his dark patrician good looks, John Doukas was younger than he expected, but there was no doubt that his tall broad shouldered presence filled a room, and his dark, piercing eyes seemed to take in everything. He listened to their requests and then patiently explained why this was impossible. Finding enough provisions for the size of the camp at present was a problem, with thirty thousand. It would be impossible with sixty to seventy thousand; rationing would have to be put into place or some would starve. It was essential that the Lombard group

CHAPTER THIRTEEN

moved east to Nicomedia, where there were plentiful orchards and harvests to help feed them.

Count Guibert snorted with disdain.

'Are you trying to tell us that the wealthy and powerful Alexios could not have food brought from these regions to feed us all? I find that difficult to believe; I think he is just punishing the Lombard Crusade for the rash actions of my nephew.'

John Doukas looked at the Lombard count with disbelief and then annoyance in his face, and his next words were to the Archbishop of Milan.

'Excellence, you are aware that the Emperor is under no commitment to feed your crusaders, for you are not here to support him or help keep the Seljuk Turks from the walls of Constantinople. Instead, you are merely passing through to help your compatriots in Jerusalem. You could have hired ships to take you across the Mediterranean. Instead, you impose upon the Emperor, demand safe passage through his lands and expect him to provision the thousands you bring. He is doing this from Christian goodwill at the moment, but I warn you, do not try his patience. It has been arranged that you will cross the Bosphorus in three weeks. Again, he has arranged and paid for dozens of ships to help you cross the water, and his troops will guard you until you reach the large military base in the valley at Nicomedia. The French and German cohorts will join you there shortly afterwards.'

With that, he nodded to the Archbishop and the nobles and dismissed them.

'The Emperor will not tolerate dissent, Malvais. Such ingratitude from these people turns my stomach, and I will report this conversation to him. I trust you to get the camp ready to move; they will need to jettison their non-essential belongings, as they cannot expect to take a league-long line of loaded carts through the rough terrain, mountains and deserts of Anatolia on their way to Antioch. Moving so slowly will make them even more of a target.'

'The thousands of women and children alone will make them that,' murmured Conn. 'I feel that this group are destined to be wiped out as was the People's Crusade led by the mad priest, Peter the Hermit. They were thirty thousand strong, mainly pilgrims, and only two thousand survived the attacks. They also believed that God and their faith would protect them.'

John Doukas shook his head in frustration and clasping arms with his young commander, he left to ride back to the city.

Conn remained in the cool, marble-floored palace and summoned Georgio and all ten of his captains to him.

'We have a difficult few weeks ahead to contain the Lombard crusaders who are now simmering with discontent. I need you and your serjeants to be vigilant, contact your informers amongst them and find out if anything untoward or suspicious is afoot. Our positive message to them is that Jerusalem is ahead, and the Emperor has generously agreed to send them troops to protect them in Anatolia.'

'I have set up the training sessions on the field for the civilian men who want to learn how to defend themselves; you would be surprised at how many priests and clerics are turning up amongst them,' said Orontes, as they mounted their horses to return to the camp.

'I can remember Finian Ui Neill telling me about Bishop Odo of Bayeux, who was a terrifying sight galloping into battle

CHAPTER THIRTEEN

with a massive club, and breaking heads around him. He always came out with barely a scratch,' said Conn, laughing for the first time in a week.

Back at the camp, Altasparta made the most of the situation by spreading disinformation and increasing the discontent. He purposefully gathered groups of thirty or so at a time, asking the question, why should we move into danger? His sidekicks, such as Fumagalli, did the same, and before long, the rumours were rife around the camp that they were to be herded like lambs to the slaughter with no protection, and few possessions, into Anatolia.

Panic and alarm began to spread amongst the women who demanded that the men take a stand, for they were frightened. They had heard the stories and tales of what had happened to the other crusades. It was always the women and children who were vulnerable and were either killed or taken. This included the families of many of the Lombard troops, and word soon came that these troops were suddenly becoming resentful and not turning up for duty. By the end of the second week, groups were openly protesting and shouting that they would not move from Hebdomon. Count Guibert took the lead and openly encouraged them.

On Saturday evening, Darius came hotfoot to find Conn; he had run most of the way, and catching his breath, he said that Georgio needed him immediately on the Field of Mars. This was a huge space, but when Conn arrived, there must have been ten thousand, mainly men, shouting their protest and refusing to leave the field until they had reassurances that they, and their families, would be allowed to stay.

'Georgio, ride for the city and tell John Doukas what is happening here; ask him how he wants me to deal with this.

Darius get the Horse Warriors mounted and get Orontes to bring his men, as many as he can muster - fully armed. This could easily get out of hand and turn violent.'

The sight of the mounted and armed troops around the field subdued the crowd somewhat, but Conn was suspicious at the speed with which they calmed and dispersed as if it was all orchestrated, and Darius confirmed his fears.

'I slipped into the crowd; there were runners who appeared and ordered them to disperse now that the protest had been heard. At that point, they began to drift away with only a hardened few still protesting.'

Several hours later, Georgio returned from the city with a message from John Doukas that Conn did not expect and one that worried him, as this would escalate the protests and discontent.

Malvais

The Emperor has ordered all provisioning of the camp to cease. They may have access to water and nothing more. If they want provisions, they can now buy them with their own coin from the city. I am aware that this may cause you problems with further looting and raids, but I suggest you explain to the Lombard leaders that the Emperor's patience is now at an end. The provisioning will begin again when they are on the other side of the Bosphorus, where they have been ordered to proceed.

As expected, when the message was shared, this did not go well with the nobility and knights, who now had to not only provision and feed their own large retinues, but also the tens of thousands of pilgrims, who had little or no money. These were now the responsibility of the Church, and the Archbishop was furious. They protested, blustered and shouted at this outrage, but Conn only shrugged.

'You have brought this on yourselves by throwing the Emperor's generosity back in his face. What did you expect with the protests you have organised? The Emperor expects you to move to the ships next week, or you can stay here in Hebdomon, waiting many months for the others to arrive, while emptying your own coffers and watching your pilgrims starve,' he said, and turned to leave. He caught a smile of pure satisfaction on Altasparta's face that worried him; he again stood quietly at the back, and it had quickly changed into a sneer, but Conn was convinced that he and his Uncle Guibert had been behind the protests. Now, he wondered if they were, in fact, playing right into Altasparta's hands by enforcing the harder measures, and building resentment, that could bubble over into violence.

The following day, Otto Altasparta left the camp with ten men and half a dozen carts, ostensibly to buy flour and provisions in the markets. Once through the gates, Otto and Fumagalli left their men, turned left and headed north. Otto was determined to strike a blow against this Emperor and his minions, and he believed that he had worked out how to do it.

He intended to launch an attack on the Emperor's Blachernae Palace. Today was a reconnaissance trip to assess the weakest points of the palace walls. The Emperor had several palaces, but this smaller one in the cooler northwest of the city was his favourite. Otto was determined to bring hundreds of men into the city to buy supplies over several days, but most would stay inside the walls; only the two men driving the laden carts would return to the camp with the supplies.

Then at the crucial moment, Otto would have hundreds of his men ready to attack the palace without warning. He would make the Emperor Alexios and John Doukas pay for what they had done to him, and if things worked out the way he hoped, he would lay a trap to kill the Horse Warrior at the same time.

Chapter Fourteen

March 1101 – Rouen

Flambard had expected it to be difficult to gain any acceptance in Normandy at the court of Duke Robert, and he was right. He had exchanged one prison for another when he was placed under an armed guard, in one of the lesser rooms in the palace, for a month. During that time, few came near him; however, he received a very unpleasant visit from the Earl of Shrewsbury, Robert de Belleme, who mainly came to gloat.

'How the mighty are fallen, Flambard. Were you mad to think of coming here to claim sanctuary? Surely, any court in Europe would have done. You are seen as the enemy here, Flambard, having been the architect of several measures and attacks against the Duke, and now you seek his patronage! I believe he is thinking of having you publically executed; that is the only thing that he and his usurping brother, Henry, have in common at the moment - they both want you dead.'

Flambard gave him a weak smile. He had always hated the sneering, sarcastic Earl of Shrewsbury, but he knew the wealth and power that Belleme held, and he was one of Duke Robert's closest advisors.

'I have always found your cutting wit amusing, Sire, but if I could have a moment of the Duke's time, he would find out how useful I could be to him. You know my capabilities, my Lord Earl; surely you can put in a word for me,' he pleaded.

Belleme gave a bark of laughter, 'I know your underhand, devious methods and your crimes, Flambard; I would not trust you an inch, and why on earth would I become your advocate? You must be as moon-touched as your mad mother if you think I will say a good word about you; I have always despised you.'

'Where is my mother, Belleme? Is she safe?' he asked, in concern.

'Was that a quick glimpse of a heart under there, Flambard? Can you care for another human being other than yourself? Do not fear; the Duke placed her in the nearest convent, and she'll no doubt be cared for.'

With that, he stood and left, the usual sneer of amusement on his lips. Flambard did not see anyone apart from servants for another week. Finally, the door was unlocked, and he was escorted to see the Duke; he had hoped for a private audience, but he was shown into the crowded court. He was pushed forward to kneel before Duke Robert and his wife, Sibylla.

'Ranulf Flambard, your audacity astounds me. After everything you and my brother, William, tried to do to me, including sending in armies to invade and occupy the northern part of Normandy, you have the gall to come here and seek my help as a fugitive fleeing for his life. Give me one good reason to consider letting you stay in my country, never mind my court. People around me tell me I should execute you forthwith!' exclaimed Robert, looking at the man in front of him with contempt.

There had been much laughter, insults, spitting and derision aimed at Flambard as he was brought into the packed court, that he had feared it would soon come to blows, but now they all quietened as they waited for his answer. Despite his current predicament, Flambard had been a man of power, a man people feared, a man with significant influence who could make or break many people with his knowledge. Several people in that court still owed him large amounts of money or land, which they hoped would now be forgotten as he did not have the wherewithal to collect his debts.

'My Lord Duke, I must remind you that it was I who insisted that King William Rufus legally make you his heir, for I knew he would never marry. I drew up those documents in your favour and ensured the King and Henry Beauclerc took the oath. It was I who drew up the vifgage, the loan that allowed you to equip yourself and your immense armed entourage for the crusade, enabling you to become the hero you undoubtedly are. I also ensured that it was a personal, not a state loan, to William Rufus rather than the English treasury. So now, as I'm sure you are aware, the loan does not have to be repaid. But, more than that, Sire, I am outraged that the usurper, the oath-breaker, Henry Beauclerc, has stolen the crown which was rightfully yours. As the Earl of Shrewsbury pointed out, I could have gone to any court in Europe and been accepted, but I came here to offer my skills, knowledge, and information to help you take England back as soon as possible.'

Silence hung in the great hall of the castle at Rouen; not even the sound of a cough or a shuffling foot disturbed it, from the dozens of nobles and courtiers watching Duke Robert intently and waiting for his response.

Belleme watched as the Duchess Sibylla leant and whispered in her husband's ear. He had discovered that she was highly astute when it came to politics. Then he turned his gaze on

Flambard; he could see the beads of sweat on his brow as he waited. Belleme had given a consummate performance describing his skills, combined with flattery. Every sentence had been weighed and crafted for impact before it came out of his mouth. Finally, Robert stood and stared down at the man kneeling before him.

'Much of what you say is true, Flambard, but you also left much unsaid. I assure you that you will not easily be forgiven. I will discuss your offer with my council, and only then will I decide on your fate.'

With that, the crowd seemed to breathe again, and chatter broke out as the Duke waved the guards forward to take Flambard back to his small chamber. Belleme caught his eye and inclined his head slightly in cynical recognition of a good ploy, and for a moment, Flambard felt a glimmer of hope.

Meanwhile, Piers De Chatillon and his friend, Edvard, were cantering northwest towards Rouen. Chatillon felt an unusual twinge of guilt at disregarding Pope Paschal's directive, but there was too much at stake, and he needed to be at Duke Robert's side. After five hours in the saddle, they pulled into an inn not far from Rouen, where they were well known and, before long, were sitting in front of the fire partaking of a hearty venison stew. Staring into the dancing flames, Chatillon hoped that Conn Fitz Malvais had received his missive and that he was considering returning, as he had a crucial role for him to play at the court of King Henry. He turned to Edvard, who happily mopped up the last of the rich gravy with a piece of bread; it had been a cold ride in a biting wind.

'I received interesting news from Count Robert of Flanders shortly before we left. Henry has requested him to provide one thousand Flemish knights to be available as soon as possible, so it looks as though Henry is already preparing for the war he knows will come.'

'That sounds expensive, Piers; I know they are cousins, but will the Count provide them?'

'Henry has a well-filled treasury behind him, filled by the excessive taxes taken by Ranulph Flambard, and he has offered to pay Count Robert an annual retainer of five hundred pounds of silver pennies, not an insignificant sum. As to whether the Count will provide them, I think young Henry is forgetting that the Count of Flanders is also Duke Robert's cousin, and they fought side by side for years on the crusade, becoming firm friends. So the answer is no. The Count may accept the money, but the knights may never arrive. However, it shows Henry's state of mind that he is already thinking of buying foreign mercenaries.'

The next day, they clattered through the gates of Duke Robert's great castle at Rouen. Chatillon had spent so much time here over the years at Robert's side that it almost felt like a second home. Several serjeants and guards recognised them and saluted before sending for the Steward. As they dismounted, Edvard, glancing around the bustling courtyard and bailey, gave a low whistle at the dozens of men, banners, and pavilions.

'I would say that the allies of Duke Robert are certainly gathering here in Rouen.'

Chatillon glanced around at the significant banners planted in the bailey; almost all the great houses of England and Normandy appeared to be there.

'All uniting against an oath breaker. If Robert decides to invade England this time, I cannot see how Henry can possibly stop him with forces such as these arrayed against him,' he murmured.

The Steward appeared, gushing with his usual welcome as he knew the Papal Envoy well.

'Your Eminence, Duke Robert will be delighted to see you; he has been watching for your arrival daily.'

Chatillon smiled and inclined his head in recognition.

'Are my usual rooms available, Alain? You seem to be bursting at the seams.'

'Of course, Sire, the Papal Envoy takes precedence over most guests, and the Duke told me to keep your rooms available; he knew you would come. I will take you to him; he is with the Duchess in the solar.'

Chatillon, laughing at this diplomatic answer, waved him aside.

'Go and eject whoever is in my rooms, Alain; I will go to the Duke. I know my way.'

The Steward smiled; nothing could ever be hidden from Chatillon.

A buzz of conversation broke out as the Papal Envoy appeared in the Great Hall in his distinctive dark purple cloak with the gold papal insignia. He nodded to many well-known nobles as he walked up the stone staircase to the private apartments above. He was placing his foot on the first step as he noticed Robert De Belleme limping towards him.

'At long last, we have great need of you, Chatillon. We cannot have a repeat of the disastrous summer of 1088, when Robert had a full fleet ready to invade but never even got on the ship.'

'Do not fear, Belleme; the odds are stacked in his favour, and I will ensure it comes to fruition this time. The crown

CHAPTER FOURTEEN

should be his.'

Chatillon made to continue, but Belleme put a hand on his arm and lowered his voice to a soft hiss.

'Even though you helped put Henry on the throne.'

Edvard, ever watchful, stepped forward, his hand moving towards the hidden dagger in his belt, but Chatillon held up a hand to stop him.

'I still consider the Earl of Shrewsbury to be a friend, Edvard, for now. I'm not sure where you get your information, Belleme, but like you, I was a helpless bystander in the forest when William Rufus was killed. What happened afterwards were a few temporary measures, to ensure stability in England, as Robert was still God knows where en route to Normandy. I never doubted for a second that Robert would return and reclaim the throne.'

Belleme gave a snort of disdain, and his trademark sneer appeared as he removed his hand. 'Helpless bystander,' he muttered, and laughed as he turned away.

Chatillon continued up the stairs while nearly all the eyes in the hall were on him. They all knew the influence he had and the power he wielded. When he knocked and entered the solar, Duke Robert sprang to his feet and came to clasp arms with his old friend.

'I knew you would come, Chatillon, despite what some were saying. You have never let me down. You remember my wife, Sibylla,' he said, while waving his friend to a seat and calling for wine.

Chatillon bowed to the tall, elegant beauty he had last seen at their wedding a year before.

'Unfortunately, it was family matters that detained me, Sire; you no doubt heard of the trauma we endured in the summer.'

'Of course, I was deeply saddened to hear of the death of your ward, Marietta, and of Finian Ui Neill, a great warrior who fought alongside and served me on several occasions. However, you must be relieved to have your wife back at home finally.'

'Yes, indeed, but the last few years have taken their toll on both her and my sons, and I suddenly find that my family and their happiness has become my priority. Now, however, I am here to advise and support you in any way I can.'

'Information, Chatillon, that is always your stock in trade; you know and discover things in days that it takes others weeks or months to hear.'

Chatillon glanced significantly around the room and then let his gaze fall on Sibylla. Duke Robert took the hint and dismissed all of the servants, squire and ladies-in-waiting who had been sitting quietly embroidering near the window before turning back to Piers.

'I share everything with Sibylla; I trust her implicitly,' he announced.

Chatillon raised an eyebrow in surprise, but then told him the gist of what he knew, including the attempt to recruit mercenaries.

'My brother, Henry, is no soldier, Piers; he has always been an intellectual soul. This is why his move has shocked and surprised me.'

'You have been away for many years, Sire, and during that time, your brother has changed. He spent many months exiled in Leon and fought alongside his cousin, King Alphonse, in the Reconquista wars. Yes, he was studious, but he is bright and intelligent; he picks things up quickly. I was sent to London last summer and had several weeks to observe him. He isn't the young man we once knew; he is ruthless, ambitious and decisive. Fortunately, he does not have the support he needs to hold onto his crown as yet. However, we both know there are still some significant nobles who have yet to make up their minds on which way to jump. I will show them which side the Holy See is inclining; they will not be able to ignore that.'

While grateful for this information, which he did not have, Robert looked taken aback at that last sentence, and he frowned, but before he could reply, Sibylla jumped in.

'Inclining? Surely, the Holy See should be firmly on Duke Robert's side after he gave years of his life and wealth, risking everything to lead the crusade to the Holy Land. The Holy See owes Robert a debt, and now is the time to repay that debt!' she exclaimed, her face suffused with anger.

Chatillon knew that she had the right of it, and when he replied, he chose his words carefully so as not to sound patronising in any way.

'It is more complicated than that, my lady. King William Rufus worked against the Holy See for more than a decade, refusing all of the requests made by various popes. At the same time, he and his creature, Flambard, robbed the Church blind, taking all the revenue from the bishopric lands that they refused to fill. The Pope was relieved at the news of the King's death, and Henry was very clever, for working through the Archbishop of Canterbury, Anselm, he made promises to the Holy See that he would make everything right and that in England, once again, Church and State would come together in agreement and harmony. Due to these promises, the Archbishop recognised Henry's claim to the throne under the laws of porphyrogenita, that he was born in the purple, as is his new wife. So, things are not as clear-cut as I would like.

Duke Robert must make the same promises, and I will report to Pope Paschal the overwhelming support you have gathered here. You know I will always be truthful to you, my friend. Do not put any great hope in securing the papal banner for your cause just yet.'

Robert shook his head, 'My father, when he was Duke of Normandy, secured the papal banner for his invasion of England, and he had the same just cause as I. That we are taking the war to an oath breaker as my brother Henry, like King Harold before him, swore an oath with his hand resting on sacred and holy relics.'

Chatillon shrugged, and Robert realised that he had no choice but to accept the situation, as the Papal Envoy swore them to secrecy about what had been discussed.

'Now, tell me of Flambard,' he asked, which was met by a shout of laughter from Robert, who could still look almost boyish at times.

'I was never more astonished in my life, Piers, at the pure blatant effrontery of the man,' he replied. Chatillon smiled.

'He is a survivor, Robert, a rat leaving a sinking ship. Swimming to find another one. I know you will never underestimate him, for he is cunning and devious and an expert at delivering what people want to hear, but he may prove useful to us. Like me, he gathers information, but with him, it is to manipulate or threaten people and some of that we will be able to use. With your permission, I would speak with him and then tell you what I think.'

Robert nodded in agreement, and Chatillon saw the relief on his face; Robert was a brave warrior but had always been more of a soldier, acting and doing rather than politics and diplomacy.

'Mind you, Edvard here is itching to cut his throat for what they did to Finian back in 1088, and if I do not like what I hear from him, then I must admit, it could be a pleasant alternative.'

Robert sent a look at his friend, but then they all laughed. Sibylla, looking from one face to another, suddenly shivered, for she knew of Chatillon's reputation, and she could see this was not a throwaway remark, they meant it. With that meaningful glance at Chatillon, Robert had given tacit permission, and they would carry out the threat without a backward glance if they wished.

Chapter Fifteen

March 1100 - Constantinople
The only information Otto Altasparta had on the Blachernae Palace came from his uncles, who had gushed over the splendours they saw during their visit. His Uncle Guibert had told him it was built on the slopes of a hill, and he said that the silver and gold throne room was awe-inspiring. He was not sure what to expect, but he knew that Alexios Komnenos preferred it to his main residence because it was smaller, more compact and gave him more privacy than the Great Palace in the centre of Constantinople, which was more of a busy administrative centre. It was also more isolated in the top northwestern corner of the city. He had been told there was a cohort of the Varangian guards in residence, who had a fearsome reputation, but apparently, there were only about twenty of them. He did not doubt that when his hundreds of armed men attacked, they could overwhelm and kill them.

However, when he and Fumagalli had finally trudged up what seemed an endless hill, he was shocked by what met his eyes. It was not just one palace; this was an enormous palace complex laid out in front of him that stretched across the face of the hill. It had high walls with great towers and gatehouses, and on the eastern side, there was row after row of immense tall and wide stone-built terraces, thirty or forty feet high, planted with flowering bushes and fruit trees. There was no way anyone could access the palace complex from the east, not without long scaling ladders. Behind the Blachernae Palace rose steep, high cliffs; it looked impregnable.

He shook his head at Fumagalli in frustration; he noticed a very large and prosperous inn at the bottom of the slope, obviously used by the many visitors to the Blachernae Palace. He dropped to sit on the edge of a stone trough in the spring sunshine.

'Impressive, isn't it,' commented the innkeeper, coming out to enquire if they wanted refreshments. They agreed, ordered drinks, and he waved them to a sturdy bench under the inn windows, which still gave them a good view up the hill on the western side of the palace.

'There are two large gates in that stretch of wall,' commented Fumagalli in a whisper as the portly innkeeper returned.

'Are they the main entrances to the Blachernae Palace?' asked Otto, innocently.

'Yes, the first you can see is the main gate, which remains closed most of the time; you can see the fierce Varangian guards standing outside. Further up the hill are the stables, trades entrance and the Varangian barracks. That entrance is always busy, with carts coming and going at all hours, keeping us awake rumbling over the cobbles.'

'I hear that on the far side, there are a few postern gates; rumour has it that the Emperor uses one to escape privately into the countryside, as the royal hunting grounds are nearby. Is that true?' asked Otto, but he could see from his face that the innkeeper was becoming suspicious, so he allayed his fears by telling a partial truth.

'My uncles, the Lombard counts, were here a few weeks ago. I was supposed to be with them, but I was brought down with a winter ague and was so disappointed. I heard such praise for the palace; I wanted to see it myself.' Somewhat mollified, the innkeeper left them while Fumagalli watched the constant stream of traffic and messengers.

'Carts are coming and going all the time through that top gate; the guards barely glance at them. Give me some coin, Sire. I intend to bribe my way onto a cart.'

Otto smiled, Fumagalli was such a useful man, an opportunist. A short time later, Otto spotted him sitting beside the driver of a wine cart trundling up the hill. He winked as he passed his master and was soon out of sight as they turned through the massive stone arch of the top entrance. Otto, who was still recovering from his punishment ordeal, fell asleep on the bench in the warmth of the spring sunshine. The next thing he knew, Fumagalli's narrow weasel face was leaning over him, telling him to wake up.

'It is well guarded as we expected. I saw at least ten axe-bearing Varangians around the gates and patrolling the top of walls and the towers. However, in that yard, there are several servant's entrances and one or two buxom girls who caught my eye. I threw a silver coin in the air to get the attention of one, and she smiled and nodded. The wine trader has gone to get the next load, so I'm going back in with him, and once I have helped him roll the casks down into the cellar, I will make her acquaintance. The only way an attack on this palace will be successful will be if we have someone on the inside. I may not come out again today, so I will meet you back at the inn in the early hours.'

Otto slapped him on the back and set off down the hill to

send the message for the next hundred men to enter the city tomorrow. If things went to plan, then they would attack, do the utmost damage, and he would escape through one of these postern gates to the east. If he were clever, no one would ever know he had been there. It was just a mob of frustrated pilgrims taking out their anger at the lack of food and supplies. He needed to make or buy a mask or helmet to cover his face so he would not be recognised. He also needed to bring down an imperial messenger as he needed that man's livery; he would send a message to the camp to summon Conn Fitz Malvais to the Blachernae Palace. When Malvais arrived, Fumagalli and his men would be waiting for him in the stables. Otto smiled at the thought.

The atmosphere in the camp was tense, although most were obeying his instructions to get rid of any non-essential possessions, and now hundreds of items were up for sale. News of this had spread, and tradesmen were coming out of the city and buying everything from spare saddles to furniture items. There was a constant stream of carts going back and forth along the Via Egnatia into Constantinople, and Conn, patrolling the camp and preventing looting in nearby Hebdomon, did not notice the large number of men leaving. However, Darius did, and he took his concerns to Georgio.

'There are hundreds of men and carts going into the city, but very few are coming back to the camp,' he commented to Georgio, who was cleaning his tack, piece by piece. He looked up at the worried tone of his young servants voice for Darius was astute and noticed things that other people missed, probably due to being on the streets of the city where he had to be constantly alert. However, this time, having weighed it up, he shrugged it off.

'They know they are going onto the ships in four or five days; they are no doubt taking the chance to see the wonders of the city, enjoy the charms of the local whores and buy items or foods they cannot get in Anatolia.'

Darius stood chewing the corner of his lip; he was not convinced.

'Have you seen Altasparta recently? I am sure I saw him riding into the city a few days ago,' he added.

'The further that man is from the camp, the happier I am, Darius. If he is in there enjoying the city, then he isn't here fomenting rebellion and discontent,' answered Georgio. However, by the expression on his servant's face, he knew Darius was not ready to let this go yet.

'Do you not notice that now he isn't here, the protests in the camp have stopped?'

'Of course, we knew it was him and his devious uncle, but let us be grateful for that. Soon, we will all be on the other side of the Bosphorus, and the pilgrims will have other things to consider in the bleak deserts and rocky hills, such as survival.'

Darius subsided for a while deep in thought and disappointed at Georgio's response, before asking, 'Can I have your permission to visit my mother tonight to bid farewell as I may not see her for some time.'

Georgio looked at the seemingly innocent face before him, convinced there was more to it, but he nodded as he had been about to suggest it before they boarded the ships.

CHAPTER FIFTEEN

'Of course, but be back here tomorrow morning, prompt, as we have many things to do.'

Darius grinned and raced away to saddle one of the riding horses. He knew the city like the back of his hand and had friends everywhere. He was not quite sure exactly what Altasparta was doing but if there were anything strange afoot, he would find out.

It was not yet dawn when Fumagalli shook Altasparta awake; the Lombard knight was not happy at being woken despite the man's grin.

'I'm happy to say that my new lady love who has a job in the kitchens, has wangled me a temporary job in the stables for a week, as one of the grooms was badly kicked and cannot walk. I told her I was good with horses, and she took me to the head groom, who said I could stand in for a while. I persuaded her to show me around while it was quiet; the place is like a warren, Sire, rooms into rooms, staircases everywhere. I was nearly caught twice looking for the way to your postern gate; I will try again tomorrow.'

Otto nodded and yawned, 'Any problems we might face?'

'Yes, the Varangians, it's the first time I have come up against them. I was led to believe they were Rus or Vikings, but most of them are large Anglo-Saxon warriors who fled with their fathers after their defeat by the Normans in England. Even the servants are frightened of them; they have short swords, but all carry a large single-bladed axe so sharp it could split a hair. It would take three or four men to take one down.'

Otto looked thoughtful, 'Only so many will be on duty at once; the others must be in a guardroom or barracks. Find out where that is and see if the door can be barred or locked.'

Fumagalli quickly nodded, 'I must go back as I have to take

the horses out for their dawn exercise. When are you thinking of launching the attack? I notice that many seem to have a rest period in the afternoon, and the place is deathly quiet; that would be the best time.'

Otto agreed, 'Have another look around later today, and we'll launch the attack tomorrow if everything is in place. My men captured an imperial messenger tonight, so we have the blue livery to send a message to summon Malvais to the palace later in the afternoon tomorrow; he always stables his horse himself, and you and your men will be waiting for him.'

Fumagalli spent the rest of the time that morning exploring the palace. He discovered the Varangians had two basement rooms off the cobbled yard. It was fortunate that those rooms came out onto a long, narrow, windowless corridor with several steps up to a great, heavy, wooden door. He was immediately challenged as he stood at the entrance, but he said he was new and lost and made a quick exit. However, the outside door had a lock, and the key was on a small board with two others inside the corridor. It was a thick oak door, and with the corridor being so narrow, fortunately, there was not enough room for them to batter it from the inside.

An hour later, he crept back, his heart in his mouth, while all was quiet, and he pocketed the key without being seen. He continued his exploration of the palace late that afternoon, carrying a large water jug so he looked as if he was on an errand. He made his way down a long, narrow spiral staircase at the northern side of the palace, and at the bottom, he found a landing with a door on either side.

He quickly opened the one on the left, expecting a storeroom, but was astounded to find a church under the main chambers above. It was empty, but dozens of candles had been lit, high windows had been built into the outer walls of the palace, which meant that light streamed in through the coloured glass. He noticed an open door and staircase on the far side of the church that led upwards; he presumed that this was the large private chapel of the family, and it led to their apartments, which might be useful to know. He crept back out and, closing the door behind him, he opened the door opposite, once again, expecting a storeroom in the bowels of the palace.

Again, he was surprised to find more steps leading down into a long stone corridor, torches burned at intervals to light the way. At the end was a sturdy door with two heavy metal bars; he noticed that these were well-oiled and slid them back whilst glancing back over his shoulder to ensure no one had followed him. He pulled the door open, and light streamed in; Fumagalli grinned; it looked as if he had found the Emperor's private postern gate on the eastern side.

There was a wide terrace outside full of early flowering spring bushes and a view across the countryside; on the left was a narrow stone staircase which led to the fields below. He saw immediately that there was another barred door, but again, the oiled bolts moved easily, and within moments, he was gazing out at the fields and forests beyond. Pleased with himself, he carefully and quietly returned, carrying his jug across the immense, empty, echoing audience chamber. He returned the jug to the pantry and headed for the servant's quarters; taking a laughing Maria by the hand, he pulled her back to her bed. Pleasure first, and then he would report to Altasparta for it seemed that it would be far easier to carry out tomorrow's raid than he expected.

Conn had ridden out the next morning when the imperial messenger arrived, so the man had left the summons with Georgio, who, at the sound of hooves, had hoped it was Darius returning. However, it was to be another hour before his laggardly squire arrived, heavy-eyed and weary.

'Make a night of it, did you? I thought you were visiting your mother.'

Darius dismounted and began to untack the horse before he answered while Georgio, hands on hips, waited impatiently.

'I spent the night, after having dinner with my mother, prowling the inns and streets on your business. I have had less than an hour's sleep. I found many men from the camp, and yes, they are of the worst type, but there are several hundred of them spread across the city.'

'What are they doing? Is there truly any reason for concern?' asked Georgio, slightly mollified.

'They are carousing, drinking, swiving the whores and getting into fights,' he replied.

'So, nothing more than we expected. I would imagine many might not return to cross into Anatolia; the city's attractions might keep them there. After all, Constantinople is ten times the size of Milan, with more opportunities for the guttersnipes. They are not our concern now, Darius. We aim to get the camp's inhabitants down to the ships in an orderly fashion, which will take days at least. Conn is down there now.'

'I tell you, Sire, there is something afoot in the city; it does not feel right. The fat captain was there with two of the men who were flogged, and they were not drunk. It was as if they were waiting for something, and I saw no sign of Fumagalli or Altasparta.'

Georgio stood and stared at Darius; the young man was not one to raise alarms unduly.

'Conn has been summoned to the Emperor Alexios this afternoon; a messenger has just been; no doubt John Doukas will be there, so I will share your concerns with him and he can raise them when he enters the city.'

Darius had to be content with that as he led his horse away to the meadow above. He had passed the imperial messenger on the road and raised a hand in greeting, but the man had looked away; there was something familiar about him with his black beard, but Darius just presumed he came to the camp regularly.

Darius did not see Conn before he left as he was employed packing their accoutrements, the spare tack, weapons, and chests of clothes onto the carts ready to move in two days. Then, one of the horses had sustained a small cut to its fetlock, so he took it down to the sea and walked it back and forth in the salt water to help it heal. Several women were there, washing clothes and beating them on the rocks; he had some enjoyable and bawdy banter with them. It was as he led the horse out he heard one shout to another.

'When is your man back, Leah?'

'I do not know, but he will get the edge of my tongue when he does, as he rode into the camp this morning in a smart uniform. I waved and shouted, but he looked through me as if I did not exist. I tell you, he better have money when he comes back after dragging us to this godforsaken land,' she spat, attacking the clothes with even more vigour.

Darius stopped in his tracks and stared at the woman. 'You say he was in uniform. Was it a blue livery?'

The woman was reluctant to answer at first, but Darius encouraged her.

'If it was blue, then he is a very lucky man and could have lots of money, for he has found employment with the Emperor's men,' he exclaimed with a grin. This pleased her.

'Yes, it was blue, with a silver badge on the breast,' she volunteered.

Darius smiled in thanks, but his face was grim as he set off up the sandy incline at a fast pace towards the pavilion. Leaving the horse outside, he burst in, but neither Conn nor Georgio were anywhere to be seen. *Had he gone with Conn, he wondered?* He grabbed a boy to return the horse to the lines and asked around. Georgio had gone with Orontes to sort out an argument with the counts about what belongings they could take with them.

When Darius arrived, the argument was becoming heated as Count Guibert was still refusing point blank to leave the camp while Albert was wringing his hands and looking nervous.

'You cannot take eight carts of furniture onto the ships; you would need a ship of your own. You must go through the carts and discard everything that isn't essential for your protection and survival while travelling across the desert,' explained Georgio in an exasperated voice. Darius ran to his side and put a hand on his arm.

'I must speak to you urgently,' he whispered, but Georgio shook him off.

'In a few moments, can you not see we are busy here?'

'No! I must speak to you now; I believe Malvais is in danger,' he exclaimed, in a much louder voice.

CHAPTER FIFTEEN

That got the attention of everyone, and Georgio caught a fleeting glimpse of a satisfied smile on Guibert's face.

'The messenger this morning was not from the Emperor; it was one of Fumagalli's men dressed in livery. I think Malvais is riding into a trap or attack,' he added.

In seconds, Georgio had drawn his sword and stepped forward; he held the tip of it at Guibert's throat. Count Albert shouted out in alarm as Guibert stood pale and shaking.

'You know about this; I saw your face at what Darius said,' he said in an ice cold voice and jabbed the sword forward. The Count toppled over backwards; the blade followed at his throat as he fell and Georgio stood astride him.

'Tell me what is happening, and I may let you live, you traitorous dog!'

Guibert blustered, holding up his hands while his brother stared at him in shock.

'I don't know the details, I swear. I know my nephew is planning a protest or attack on the Blachernae Palace to demand the Emperor restores the provisions and lets us stay here at Hebdomon until the French arrive.'

'Are they mad? The Emperor has thousands of troops in the city, and they will slaughter them all,' gasped Darius.

'I did tell him that this was unwise, but you have seen how hot headed he is, how difficult to control,' mumbled Guibert while his brother gaped in horror at what he had heard.

'I don't believe a word you say, and if I find you are behind this or encouraged him to attack Emperor Alexios, I promise I will march you to the square, I will even take your head myself. Darius, gather all the men; we ride for the city. Orontes, muster as many as you can without leaving the camp unguarded, as they may be planning a rising here as well.'

155

With that, they ran for the horses; Georgio prayed that Conn was safe. He was a few hours ahead of them and had ridden in on his own, refusing the usual escort.

'Where are they likely to attack Malvais, Darius? He was riding for the Blachernae Palace,' he shouted, knowing the knowledge that he had of the city.

'It sounds as if they are mad enough to gather at the palace itself; we should ride for there. They could jump and surround him anywhere in the narrow streets beside the western wall,' replied Darius in a frustrated voice.

As soon as we enter through the Golden Gate, pull one of the men out to send to John Doukas at the Grand Palace, tell him what is happening and that time is of the essence. There is no doubt that Altasparta is behind this; I swear I will also take his head from his shoulders if Conn is harmed!' he yelled as they headed for the camp gates and galloped towards the city.

Chapter Sixteen

March 1101 – Constantinople
Conn was surprised at the suddenness, the urgency of the summons to see the Emperor and his mind searched for any of his actions that might have caused it as he rode towards the city. He had been in the presence of the Emperor twice, both times at the side of John Doukas, who had always relayed any orders from Alexios. Perhaps John Doukas had been called elsewhere, and the Emperor needed reassurance that the camp was now compliant and ready to move.

He rode through the Golden Gate and turned left for the long climb up to the Blachernae Palace; the city was as busy as ever, the streets packed with people and traders. However, most of them moved at the sight of the armed Horse Warrior on an enormous snorting Destrier that showed the whites of its eyes and snapped its teeth at any obstacle or person.

In the palace compound, everything had gone according to plan. Half of the men, helped by the element of surprise, had stormed the top gate and, with difficulty at first but then with sheer numbers, had overpowered seven of the large Varangian guards. The big men took several of the attackers out, but with eight or nine men attacking them with daggers, they quickly dropped to their knees. One, however, took out eight men with his axe before the rest managed to subdue him. Fumagalli had helped by locking the remainder of the guard in the barracks; the sound of muffled thumping on the door could be heard for quite a while until they realised it was pointless. The wounded on both sides were cold-bloodedly dispatched on Altasparta's orders, and the dead bodies were pulled into a storeroom out of sight; water was sluiced over the blood-stained cobbles.

The servants were all cowering in the kitchens where Fumagalli and two of his men had herded them at sword point, telling them that if they put a foot out of the door, they would be cut down. Fumagalli laughed at the accusing glaring eyes of his lover, Marie, before saying he might return for her and take her with him. She let out a torrent of abuse and spat at him as he locked them all in the large, cold store, which had no windows.

Meanwhile, Altasparta led another hundred or so men across the fields and through the postern gate which had been opened by Fumagalli, this gave them unchallenged entry into the northeastern side of the palace. Otto had found a mask on the market, a thin, tin, Greek tragedy mask used in plays and festivals. It gave him almost a demonic look as he raced up the stairs and into the vast silver and gold audience hall, which ran almost the full length of the palace. There were huge statues of lions everywhere, and he realised his uncles were right; it was an awesome sight, as were the full wall mosaics of palm trees and wild animals.

So far, so good; they had been undetected, and none of the Emperor's guards had appeared from the massive doors to stop them. Fumagalli had told him the Emperor and his family retired to their suite of private rooms during the afternoon rest period, so he knew they were somewhere behind this huge chamber. Despite what the Emperor had ordered done to him, Otto did not want to kill or harm Alexios; he wanted to frighten and threaten him. To show him who he was dealing with, the Lombard nobles would not be treated as if they were of no account, but he also wanted him to reverse the decision that prevented him from going to Jerusalem.

He turned to his men, milling around the vast space and staring awestruck at the chamber's walls. There was more gold and silver on their decoration than they expected to see in many lifetimes, and several were using their daggers to try and prise some off. He smiled and waved them forward.

'You may loot as much as you wish from the palace, but Emperor Alexios and his family are not to be harmed,' he shouted, making towards the large carved double doors. However, as he reached them, one opened, and the Emperor's head Steward appeared attracted by the noise. He stopped in shock at the mob of armed men in front of him and quickly slammed the door in Otto's face, locking it and yelling in alarm as he slotted two large iron bars across the middle of the doors.

Fumagalli had never been through here before into this extensive set of rooms, so he did not know of the additional five Varangians who were always on duty in the richly decorated atrium leading to the Emperor's apartments. They surged forward, but the Steward, with his back to the doors, stopped them.

'There is a mob of hundreds out there; you cannot possibly take that many, your job is to guard the Emperor Alexios and his family and get them to safety. 'Go!' he yelled, they obeyed his orders immediately running through the heavily carved and decorated single door, leaving one guard with the Steward. The man wiped the sweat from his brow as he turned to the large blonde warrior beside him.

'We now have no way to escape, but the Emperor Alexios will know of our sacrifice so be glad we have done our duty, give me your sword,' he said. Indicating that they should stand either side of the great doors but out of the line of sight of any that broke through.

Meanwhile, outside, Conn had ridden through the large archway into the courtyard, which was strangely quiet. There were several Varangian guards on the gate, the largest of Altasparta's men who had pulled on the Varangian uniforms, and they nodded at him in recognition. Suddenly, Diablo became very skittish; he could smell the blood and he stalled, sidling away from it towards the stables, but Conn could see nothing to alarm him, so he dismounted and led the unhappy horse into the stable block.

As befits a royal palace, it was an exceptionally long building in pristine condition; the stalls were large with carved and decorated partitions and several large box stalls at the far end for injured or recovering horses. There were air vents high on the walls which let in light, and a sluice channel ran the full length; a few grooms were mucking out on the right-hand side. One began to approach him, but he waved him away, so the lad grinned and told him there were clean stalls at the far end; the dark-haired boy looked familiar, but Conn presumed he must have been here last time he was at the palace. He led Diablo down and into one of the last stalls, which had clean straw, hay in the rack and a full water bucket. He spotted a feed bag full of oats hanging on the end of the partition, and untacking Diablo, he carried it forward and bent down to hook it over his horse's nose.

He did not hear them coming until the last minute; they had been crouched in the dark shadows a few stalls away. Thinking it was the groom behind him, he turned and caught a glimpse of Fumagalli's grinning face as the heavy cudgel came down on his head, and he dropped like a stone. Diablo stamped and tried to rear, kicking out at the three men as they pulled Conn's prone body out and into the large box stall at the end. Fumagalli stripped Conn's harness and twin swords away before using his dagger to cut the ties at the sides of the heavy leather doublet.

'We want every kick to count, boys; he has made our lives a misery; now it is our turn,' he said as he launched several vicious kicks into Conn's body, and they joined in until Fumagalli called a halt.

'Tie his hands and feet tightly, close the stall door and stay with him; I will return when we know what Altasparta wants to do with him.'

Fumagalli entered the palace; he could hear the whoops of the men as they seized anything they could lay their hands on. He found Otto and his men in the audience room before the locked doors to the Emperor's chambers. They had lifted a large carved couch and were using it as a battering ram. However, the doors, locked and now barred from within was not giving much under the blows, although the small bottom panels were beginning to splinter.

Inside his chambers, Alexios was in a towering rage. He sent his wife, the Empress Irene and seven of the youngest children with their armed servants and two Varangian guards down the hidden back staircase to escape through another postern gate into the secret caves behind the cliffs. The Emperor's eldest son, John Komnenos, who was now fourteen, insisted on staying with his father. He was a renowned archer, so his father placed him at the side of the chamber with his bow, shielded by a pillar.

'Kill any enemy who comes through that door, arrow after arrow, my son, then flee after your mother down the stairway, locking all the doors behind you. It is your job to protect them and to stay alive. It would be best if you did not let them take you, for you are my heir, so once deep in the caves, you do not emerge until I or the Megas Doux sends for you,' he ordered.

Young John Komnenos was outwardly calm; he would never dare show fear in front of his father, but he could hear every shuddering crash against the doors out in the atrium, and he worked hard to keep the shudder of fear under control.

Finally, the small bottom panel on the right gave way and one of the men kicked it through, shouting in triumph. Kneeling and peering through, he saw nothing but an empty room ahead.

'They have gone,' he declared, putting his head through to check.

In seconds, the axe of the Varangian had descended and taken his head; the body fell back, blood pumping from the severed neck. Altasparta's lips drew back in distaste.

'We need the whole door down; move him out of the way, keep trying,' he declared, but Fumagalli whispered in his ear.

'We are running out of time, Sire. Messages will have been sent, and soon hundreds of imperial troops could be thundering towards us from the barracks, and we'll be trapped. I have the Horse Warrior in the stables; he has been beaten, but what do you want me to do with him? He is one of the Emperor's commanders; I do not think we can kill him.'

CHAPTER SIXTEEN

Altasparta pulled the tin mask back down over his face and gave a harsh laugh.

'We have already killed a dozen of the Emperor's Varangian guard, one more will not make a difference. Find a rope, Fumagalli, and hang him; I want him to know real fear before he dies but do not tarry. I'm taking a few men to find another way into the royal chambers, there must be one, so I can confront Alexios. I will meet you at the postern gate shortly, and then we'll escape across the fields.'

When Fumagalli returned, Conn was conscious and glaring at him.

'Have you lost your mind, Fumagalli, they will gut you on the public square for this?'

To his surprise, the demoted captain just shrugged.

'We will be long gone by then, Malvais, and only an enraged looting mob will be left. We have witnesses to say we were never here. We are upstairs with half a dozen whores and our friends at an inn on the other side of the city. The innkeeper will swear we were there all day and night.'

To his alarm, Conn saw that Fumagalli held a noose in his hands, which, stepping forward, he slipped over Conn's head and tightened behind his ear.

'Get him on his feet,' he said, throwing the other end of the rope over the beam above.

There was no box or stool in sight, but the blacksmith used a small, narrow bench, and they carried it to the box stall and pushed Conn onto it with difficulty; as Conn grimaced and cried out in pain, he was sure they had broken several ribs. Fumagalli pulled and tied off the rope so that Conn was only just balancing on the bench. The three other men had been drinking heavily from the wine sacks they carried; they now laughed at Conn's pale face and began laying bets on how long he would last when the bench was kicked away.

For the first time, Conn felt a real stab of fear; he expected the Emperor's troops to arrive any second, for surely the palace could not be attacked by such a rabble without the alarm being raised. With an awful finality, he realised they might not get here in time and he could feel his stomach knotting and the sweat began to stand out on his brow, as the drunken men launched an occasional kick at the bench which made it rock and his feet scrabbled for purchase. His hands clenched in fear as he suddenly realised that life was still precious to him. After last summer, he was so full of anger he was looking for a quick death in a fight or attack, a clean death with a sword, anything to take the pain away. Not however, a long struggling death kicking on the end of a rope while his bladder emptied in terror, for there was no long drop to break his neck, it would not be a good death. He had lost a lot of his faith after what happened in the villa in Aggio, but now he realised that he wanted to live and he began to pray.

Chapter Seventeen

March 1100 – Rouen
Duke Robert had ridden out early that morning; the castle at Rouen seemed to be bursting at the seams with his supporters and their retinues, which was reassuring in itself, but he felt that he rarely had a moment on his own. His cousin, William, Count of Mortain, was keeping him company, which Robert did not object to, for although he found the young man intense, he had a ready and sardonic wit. He found the tale of Henry and Matilda trying to marry William to a Scots princess and his refusal of the marriage highly amusing. As Duke of Cornwall, he was a powerful and outspoken ally to have.

'Have you decided what to do with that snake, Flambard, Sire?' he asked as they pulled the horses down to a walk.

'I have let him stew for a week, but Chatillon is going to visit him this morning, find his true purpose and, more importantly, find out what information he is prepared to offer us for what reward.'

'Reward!' spat William. 'He is lucky to have his limbs intact; I would have taken both hands off when he arrived.'

Robert raised an eyebrow at his bloodthirsty young cousin, 'Yes, you and my father both, Mortain, but first I want to know how useful he is to us, preferably with both hands still attached. Let us canter along the river and back to the castle; I'm beginning to feel hungry.'

The meadows were still covered in a light frost as they turned towards the castle, and suddenly Duke Robert swore long and loudly, as he saw a horsewoman approaching, and he knew immediately who it was. William laughed as he recognised her.

'She is nothing if not persistent, Sire; she must have been sitting out here in the chill breeze for an hour to see which way you would return to the castle.' Robert smiled at his jibe but frowned as she came close.

'Good morrow, my Lord Duke. May I have a moment of your time, preferably alone?' She stared pointedly at Count William, who stared back but did not move.

'We are returning for a meeting of the Council, so I can give you only a moment or two, and you can say what you will in front of my cousin. You know the Countess of Buckingham, I believe, William.' The Count nodded, straight-faced, and inclined his head in a slight bow.

William could see the flash of anger in her eyes at this reply, and he noticed her knuckles were white on her reins. He had heard about her outbursts of temper.

'How is it, my lord, that we had such an intense love affair for so long, and yet you now treat me unkindly? We share a son, my lord, and my love for you has never diminished.'

As she said this, she moved her palfrey forward, and reaching out, placed a hand on his, but to no avail as he gently withdrew his.

'Of course, I still care for you, Agness, but our affair finished when I left on the crusades. Since then, I have married, and

I find that not only do I love my wife, but I respect her and intend to remain faithful to her. I also came to the conclusion, as I cleansed my soul in the confessional before the crusade that we had cuckolded your husband for too long.'

Mortain watched as the woman's face contorted in rage, all pretence of any gentleness gone.

'You cannot cast me aside like this, Robert; you know I deserve more than that,' she protested.

'I have given you much over the years, Agness, not only my love, but you know I have provided for our son, I made him the Lord of Tortosa. Now I must leave you.'

With that, he kicked his horse into a canter and rode up towards the castle. William quickly caught up with him as he trotted through the gates into the crowded bailey.

'You need to keep a watch on her, Robert, a woman scorned and all that. Looking at her face, I could swear that she positively hates you, and I can imagine she could be very vindictive, particularly if you have shared past secrets with her that she could reveal.'

Robert dismounted but stood for a moment looking up into his young cousin's face.

'As I watched her anger, I remembered something Chatillon said to me when he came to our wedding in Italy. He warned me about her, and he does not do that lightly or without reason. Now we have more momentous matters to discuss, and I imagine she'll scuttle back across the channel to join her treacherous husband, Walter Gifford, who is advising my brother.'

William looked perplexed, 'Are you not afraid she will take everything she hears from here, to the English court?' he asked in a concerned voice.

Robert gave a shout of laughter, 'Henry will already have several informers in my court, William; he learnt that from watching Chatillon at my side. I do not care if he knows we are coming to take back my crown, but I will ensure that where we land, and when, will be known only to a select few.'

Chatillon settled in the chair opposite a wary Ranulph Flambard.

'For God's sake, do not use the phrase, how the mighty are fallen, Chatillon, as I assure you it has been much overused already.'

Piers smiled at his old adversary, 'I was going to say congratulations on a clever move in coming to Normandy. They are not quite sure what to do with you, Flambard, for you fall into that interesting category between fish and foul, neither one nor the other. Half of the court want to see you publically executed, a quarter want to see you maimed, and most of the rest are undecided but could be easily swayed either way. Only a handful can see that you may be of value. Tell me, Flambard, are these the odds you were hoping for?' he asked, noticing that Flambard's face had paled.

'I had little choice, as you know, Chatillon. Henry Beauclerc was the last person I wished to see on the throne of England, and I am ready to use all of my skills and information to help Robert regain the crown that is rightfully his.'

The Papal Envoy steepled his fingers and regarded him over the top of them for some time and Flambard became uncomfortable and shifted in his chair. He had always found Chatillon's penetrating dark eyes unsettling; they seemed to know so much and gaze into the very soul. He also knew that his fate hung in this man's hands; one word from him and his life would be extinguished.

'God's blood, Chatillon, you cannot let them kill me; think of the precedent it would set. I am the Prince Bishop of Durham; you cannot let them kill a cleric of my stature in cold blood,' he pleaded.

'Oh, it won't be in *cold* blood, Flambard; I have seen the list of your crimes and the names of your accusers; it fills two full sheets of vellum. I imagine they will prolong your death for some time.'

Flambard sat back in his chair. His shoulders slumped as he realised that Chatillon was not here to offer him hope; he was here as judge and jury. Seeing his expression, Piers smiled and decided to rekindle the hope, although he had to admit he was enjoying tormenting his old foe.

'So, tell me, Ranulph, on the off chance that I decide to put a case to Robert to keep you alive because you have so much to offer him, what are you hoping for in return?'

Flambard sat forward, his hands on his knees, his eyes wide in surprise.

'Very little, Chatillon, the chance to assist in putting Robert back on the throne. I do not want a position at court, I have had my fill of that. An amnesty for any past crimes and the chance to live a peaceful life; I have money, so I want for very little.'

To Flambard's dismay, Chatillon laughed out loud at this and pretended to wipe the tears of laughter from his eyes.

'This is me you are talking to, Flambard, not some naïve,

easily taken in courtier. I know you inside out; I have seen all of your tricks; you are cunning, manipulative, deceitful, and you lie repeatedly. However, I am of the mind that you could be useful, but you had better deliver the information we need. You will find that your finances are not what you thought as your mother handed over the chest full of silver and gold from Durham. But you will no doubt be relieved to hear that it has been put to good use as part of Duke Robert's war chest.'

Chatillon stood to leave, as Flambard put his head in his hands and groaned, for that had been the equivalent of over a thousand ducats of gold. He waited for several minutes after the door had been closed and locked behind Chatillon before he let out the roar of rage and frustration that had been building inside him.

Chapter Eighteen

March 1101 – Blachernae Place, Constantinople
Georgio and the Horse Warriors clattered at speed through the Golden Gate and towards the palace, shouting warnings for people to escape their path. They slowed as they approached the palace, and Georgio reined in outside the inn.

'We must leave the horses here and go on foot through those gates, as we have no idea what awaits us. Darius tells us that a few hundred men have hidden in the city over the last few days, ready to launch an attack, which may have happened or may still do so. I suspect they are already inside the main gates as they are locked and closed, which is unusual, and there is no sign of the Varangian guards who usually stand at the gates further up the hill. If the rebels are inside, they have dared to attack the Emperor, and the order is to give no quarter to any rebels we find. We know that Malvais was riding into a trap; he may be dead or a prisoner, but we hope to find and get him out alive. Darius, get help to tie up or stable the horses.'

The grim-faced twenty or so warriors raised their fists in salute as they followed Georgio at a run up the hill to the large arched gateway. As they approached, Georgio could hear laughter and chatter, and he flattened against the outside wall. He waved Gracchus and half a dozen of his men forward to attack, and he and the rest followed moments later. The half dozen men dressed in Varangian uniforms whirled in shock as the Horse Warriors attacked.

'I want one alive, Gracchus!' shouted Georgio as the big man lifted one of the rebels in the air and slammed him to the ground before putting his foot on his throat. Georgio scanned the courtyard; there was no sign of the several hundred rebels described by Darius. He grabbed the man by the hair, nodding at Gracchus to release him, and pulling him to his feet, he swung him around, slamming him into the nearest wall, where he placed a dagger at his throat; the blood trickled down the blade.

'Where are they?' he asked softly, pressing harder.

'They have all gone into the palace to confront the Emperor, but the palace is enormous, and several have more loot than they can carry,' he gasped.

'What did you do with the Varangian guards?' he asked, pointing at the uniform.

'We killed half a dozen out here; the rest are locked in their barracks,' he said, pointing at the hefty oak door from which an occasional muffled thump could be heard.

'Take those axes and get that door open; we need all the help we can get,' he shouted at Gracchus, who picked up the nearest axe and headed for the door.

'Aim for the hinges and the lock, boys!' he shouted. Within a short time, the door was hanging drunkenly, with the Varangians attacking at the same time from the other side. They burst out with a roar of rage, ready to kill anyone in sight, but Georgio bravely stood before them, holding up his hands and shouting they were from John Doukas. They then moved forward as a large group towards the huge main doors, which were slightly ajar, and dragged them open, surging into the large, inner courtyard. Georgio had not been inside before, but at the far side, he could see the wide marble steps that led to the famous audience chamber; the Varangians surged ahead, axes raised. Not for a second had any of them glanced at the archway through to the large stable block where Conn, with a rope around his neck, balanced precariously on a bench, waiting for it to be kicked away and the rope to tighten on his throat.

Having seen to the stabling of the troop's horses, with the help of the inn's grooms, Darius came rushing through the palace gates. He stopped, finding the outer courtyard empty apart from bodies; he noticed the heavy door hanging off its hinges. Georgio and the men had no doubt fought here and moved on. Having spent years on the streets, he knew not to stand out, so he automatically clung to the buildings as he made his way to the left and round to the main doors, expecting rebels to burst through them to escape at any moment, if the Horse Warriors were inside, as it seemed.

As he reached the stone arch on the left, he suddenly heard the laughter, which seemed incongruous, and he went through the arch towards the long stable block. He crept closer, peering around the double doorway into the darkness; the stable was extensive, with enough stalls for at least eighty horses. As his eyes adjusted, he saw that most of the stalls were full of horses, but he recognised the shrill scream of outrage from Diablo, who was repeatedly kicking the sides of a stall on the left, while splinters flew in every direction. The noise the stallion made hid the sound of Darius as he crept, stall by stall, towards the jeering and laughter at the end of the row. Flattening himself against the walls, in the shadows, he could see a handful of men through the half-open door of a box stall; he quietly drew his sword and crept closer but then froze at what he saw.

A bruised and bleeding Malvais with a noose around his neck, hands tied, was on the very edge of a bench that the men were taking turns to kick so it rocked back and forth while Conn's feet scrabbled to keep it still. He saw Fumagalli leaning against the wall laughing and realised with horror that he was on his own and there were too many of them to take on to save Malvais; they would kill him instantly if he attacked. If he ran to get help, he was sure that Malvais would be dead before he returned; he wracked his brains while Diablo stamped, kicked and screamed two stalls away.

Suddenly, he had an idea that may or may not work, but he could not stand there and watch Malvais die without trying something. He crept back along the wall, crossed to the stalls and, taking his life in his hands, he moved alongside the stamping, snorting stallion, who immediately swung all of his body to try and crush him against the partition. It was one of his usual tricks, and Darius used his knuckles to give him a hard jab in the rib cage, which made the horse move and allowed him enough room to get to his head and try to calm him. Conn had removed the bridle and bit from his mouth, but a head collar and rope had been used to tether him. Sheathing his sword and talking softly, he untied and backed him slowly out of the stall.

Higher than the others, Conn noticed the movement and saw what Darius was trying to do, and he prayed as he had never prayed before that Diablo would obey Darius. The men in the box stall, most of them drunk and preoccupied with what they were doing, did not realise the massive war horse was backing out of its stall, and within seconds, Darius swung himself up and lay forward along Diablo's bare back to await the right moment, whilst praying that the stallion would not try to buck him off - as he often did. At that moment, Fumagalli pushed himself off the wall and stepped towards Conn.

'Time to end this, boys; we need to make our escape,' he ordered whilst aiming a hard kick at the bench, which toppled backwards, leaving Conn gasping and choking on the end of the rope.

Seeing this, Darius sat up, drew his sword and kicked Diablo forward; the huge horse burst into the box stall, striking out with his hooves and tearing at the men with his teeth. Fumagalli, avoiding the lethal hooves and expecting more Horse Warriors to arrive, ran past, while Darius stabbed down at any man that came within range. Then, standing in his stirrups, he slashed at the rope holding Conn, and the Horse Warrior crashed to the ground with a coughing cry of pain as his bound hands tore at the rope around his neck to loosen it. Darius leapt to the ground while keeping an eye on the two men still in the corner of the stall, held there by a stamping Diablo; using his dagger, he cut the ropes at Conn's wrists and feet. Conn, having pulled the noose off his neck, rubbed his wrists and then grunted with pain as he reached for his sword. The two drunken men, seeing a vengeful armed warrior, braved the teeth and hooves to get out, but as they burst into the courtyard, the men of Captain Orontes arrived, and they were cut down immediately. Conn, ignoring the shouts from Orontes, ran through the main doors hoping to find Fumagalli, for he had no doubt he would be going to find his master, Altasparta.

The fighting inside the silver and gold audience chamber was intense; the noise of clashing blades, screams and grunts of pain was clamorous, but as trained warriors, Georgio, his men and the Varangians were winning against large numbers of poorly trained rebels. The floor was slippery with blood as Fumagalli managed to avoid their blades, skirting the edges, sword drawn, to reach the door to the spiral staircase. When Conn and Darius came running in, there was no sign of him, so despite his injuries, Conn threw himself into the fray, thinking the weasel-faced traitor was somewhere in the middle of the throng. All fear gone, Darius followed him, hacking left and right but determined to have the Horse Warriors back.

Meanwhile, Altasparta had not found another entrance to the apartments, and he realised with frustration that he would not have his chance to confront Alexios, but he smiled at the thought of the message he had delivered. With his two men, he walked along the paved edge of one of the large stone terraces when suddenly, one of the men pushed his way through a bush and stepped out into nothing. Falling forward, he grabbed a branch of the large bush and swung out; with his feet scrabbling, he tried to get any purchase on the wall to push and pull himself up. Even more so when he heard a noise from below, and glancing down, he realised he was hanging over the Emperor's lion enclosure. They had all heard the stories of the wild animals Emperor Alexios kept, but none of them had ever seen a lion. There were five of them; one was a very large male who lay on his side and regarded the dangling man with sleepy eyes.

Altasparta was delighted, 'I have it; we will kill his lions. They threatened to feed me to them, and so we will kill them all. You have a sword in your belt; drop in, kill the big one,

CHAPTER EIGHTEEN

and the others will run away; then we will find the entrance door, join you and kill the rest of them,' he ordered.

The man hanging had realised that he could not get back up. They could not reach him, and the branch he was clinging to was too supple and bending too much, so he drew his sword and dropped, shouting at them to hurry down. Clinging close to the wall, he made his way around to the big male who did not move a muscle; the lionesses and younger male prowled restlessly back and forth, watching his every step. He moved as close as he could to the lion, who raised a paw in playfulness as the man, both hands on his sword, plunged it into its heart. The lion now gave a roar of agony, matched by one above him. Altasparta whirled at the cry and stared in shock at the terrace on the opposite side of the lion enclosure, for there stood Emperor Alexios, his son and John Doukas, swords drawn as dozens of men poured out behind them.

Alexios was incandescent with rage at the slaying of his pet; he had raised him from a cub, and he was completely tame. As Altasparta turned to run, he saw the remaining lions attack the man below. His high-pitched screams followed them as they raced back along the corridors down the side of the Emperor's chambers. Otto was still wearing his mask and prayed he had not been recognised. Seeing a door, he yanked it open to reveal a narrow staircase; he told the other men to keep running to the other exit, to draw them off while he ran down the stairs two at a time, praying it would take him to the postern gate that Fumagalli had found. He reached another door and then more stairs going downward, and suddenly, he emerged into a church at the bottom. He looked around for an exit or somewhere to hide, for this was much bigger than a family chapel and then, walking to the nave, he stepped up onto the marble dais, crawled under the back of the altar and pulled the cloth back down; he hid and waited. Trying to run further with the Emperor's troops searching everywhere would be suicide; they would never find him there.

Conn, meanwhile, could see no sign of Fumagalli; he must have escaped, and he caught the eye of Darius and gave an angry shrug. The young squire stood on a chest against the wall and scanned the room while Conn watched him; then, Darius excitedly pointed out the door on the far side of the chamber. Conn ran across the chamber, pushing people from both sides out of the way and, pulling the door open, saw that steep, narrow stairs went down a spiral staircase. He followed them down, followed by Darius and came to a long landing on which two doorways existed. The one on the right was open, and they ran down more stairs until they levelled into a long, narrow corridor lit with torches. At the end was a door standing slightly ajar. Conn gently opened it, expecting Fumagalli to be here, and he realised it was a postern gate in the eastern wall; there was no sign of the weasel-faced captain who had ordered him kicked and beaten.

As they stood on the wide terrace, Darius quietly pointed out the steep, narrow steps on the left, and they ran swiftly down them, the young man in the lead; they found Fumagalli at the other end, standing with two horses. Hearing the sound of footsteps, he breathed a sigh of relief; he had convinced himself that Altasparta was not coming and was now considering escaping somehow on his own. His face changed as Darius appeared.

'You! I tell you, street rat, that you are dead for coming after me. I will gut you, boy!' he yelled as he stepped forward, sword drawn.

CHAPTER EIGHTEEN

But then he stopped and stepped backwards, his face registering his shock as the beaten Horse Warrior appeared, someone he never thought to see alive again. Conn stood leaning on his sword, getting his breath back through the pain from his broken ribs, as Darius moved towards the nervous captain.

'Finish him off, Darius; he is no swordsman. I will take his head when you have killed him and stick it on a spike outside the walls.'

Conn was right; Darius had rarely missed sword training on the beach each morning, Fumagalli, although a captain had never taken part. It was soon over as the young squire, seeing an opening, thrust his blade deep into Fumagalli's chest. Almost before Darius had time to pull out his blade, Conn had stepped forward and taken the Lombard's head from his shoulders with one swipe of his heavy double-edged sword.

'There is no doubt that he was waiting here for Altasparta with two horses, which means he is either dead or still in the palace, waiting for a chance to get down here,' said Darius. Conn nodded in agreement.

'I was never one to stand and wait, so you stay here; let me see if I can find Altasparta, as he is undoubtedly the architect of this attack. However, Altasparta is a trained knight and a far better swordsman than Fumagalli; if you try to take him alone, you may find him too much of a challenge, Darius. I suggest you stay hidden in the trees and bushes, but first cut the girth on both saddles almost all the way through; when he tries to mount, he'll be off the ground when it snaps, then attack him as he falls backwards. Give no quarter, Darius, and move Fumagalli's remains out of sight and quickly sweep soil over the blood with a branch.'

He clasped arms with the young man, thinking it was a good day indeed when Georgio found him; then he re-entered the palace, running back up the long torch-lit passageway to the landing. Seeing the door opposite, he paused and tried the handle; he opened it slowly and was surprised to find himself in a church with a high-arched ceiling. It was far bigger than any chapel, and the smell of dozens of candles and incense filled the air. He realised that this must be the Holy Church of St. Mary of Blachernae; he had heard of it and remembered Orontes saying the palace had literally been built around it.

He began to search the church on the off chance that Altasparta was hiding there; sword drawn, he walked to the back. There were several small wooden doors, but they only contained priest's vestments hung on hooks and other church ephemera on shelves. He headed for the chancel, stepping up onto the raised marble dais; the back of the altar was decorated in gold leaf and lapis lazuli and would take anyone's breath away. Again, there was a door at the side, which he pulled open, but the room was a small sacristy with several locked chests, no doubt containing the gold chalices used for mass. He was surprised that these had not been smashed open and looted yet. This suggested that the rebels had not made it down here.

Underneath the altar table, Altasparta, sword and dagger ready, waited to spring on whoever searched the church. He heard them pulling doors open and twitched the altar cloth aside by a sliver. He saw the crossed swords and the back of Conn Fitz Malvais and gave a sharp intake of breath whilst praying he would not find him. He weighed up the possibility of running, but the Horse Warrior would be difficult to outrun despite his beating. He heard Conn close the sacristy door and walk towards him, crouched under the altar. He tensed every muscle to spring out and prayed that the element of surprise would give him an advantage.

The sound of footsteps saved him, and he hoped it was Fumagalli and his men; with a few of them, they might have a chance against the Horse Warrior.

Chapter Nineteen

John Doukas had finally managed to calm his raging brother-in-law. However, the Emperor was still pacing up and down, fists clenched, making bloodthirsty threats against the Lombard counts, whom he was convinced had orchestrated the attack to force his hand to allow them to stay on this side of the Bosphorus. John Doukas was not convinced that they would be that rash; they would know the consequences; they had seen the power and might of Alexios and knew that his forces could obliterate their whole camp in a day.

In this, he had an ally, Raymond of Toulouse, who had returned to be at the Emperor's court. After the success of the First Crusade, Raymond opted to stay in the Emperor's service in Byzantium; he had been away visiting his family in France but had arrived today in time to see the aftermath of the attack. The palace was littered with bodies; the rebels had been slaughtered where they stood by the Horse Warriors and the Emperor's troops. Some were lucky and had escaped, but any wounded found had been given no quarter.

Count Raymond tried to reason with Alexios.

'I cannot believe that Count Albert or the Archbishop would ever sanction, or have any knowledge, of such a raid. Your Horse Warrior tells me,' pausing and pointing at Georgio. 'that

CHAPTER NINETEEN

these attackers are men from the slums of Milan, are only here on the crusade to get loot and rich pickings. I will ride out to the camp, inform the nobles of what has happened here, and ascertain what they know of this.' The Emperor, though, was not so easily assuaged.

'I want him found, do you hear? I want him found and ripped apart in front of me!' he shouted.

Raymond, not sure whom he meant, looked at John Doukas for enlightenment.

'The leader of this rabble, the man in the Greek mask, ordered the Emperor's pet lion killed; he ran, and we gave chase. We have not found him yet, but we will; no corner is small enough to hide him in the whole Empire.'

'I know they set a trap for Malvais; he could be dead or injured for all we know,' said Georgio, his voice breaking with emotion.

John Doukas put a hand on the Horse Warrior's shoulder.

'I know he is like a brother to you, but from what I have seen and heard, he is a hard man to kill. Send your Horse Warriors to search every inch of the palace and outbuildings; we'll find him.'

But Georgio was not done yet.

'This leader, the man in the mask, is Otto Altasparta; we know it is him; he is here with his captain, Fumagalli. We have had men watching him; he has been in the city for days with his men. I would lay money he is your man in the mask, as this is his last throw of the dice, and he would not chance being recognised. He will have had an escape route planned out of the palace, for he is the type of craven coward we would expect,' he shouted.

Georgio now had the attention of all three great men, and

he coloured slightly, realising that he shouldn't have spoken in such a way in front of the Emperor, but he held his head high. However, he had given John Doukas food for thought.

'The eastern postern gate, they may be trying to escape from there; if so, my horsemen will scour the countryside and hunt them down with dogs, like the scum they are. Georgio, bring three of your men and come with me. Let us see if I'm right.'

The Megas Doux led the way through several rooms, back to the top of the lion enclosure and into the long corridor that led to the private audience chamber.

'They ran this way, and my men chased and killed two of them, but neither wore a mask. They may have split up, and he could have gone down here; this door is usually locked, but as we see, it is now open,' he said as Georgio looked down at a narrow staircase, which they descended.

Conn was bending to lift the altar cloth in the church when he heard a door opening and footsteps. Altasparta realised that he was saved by that sound, whoever it was. Conn straightened and placed himself behind a pillar on the left of the altar. By the sound of the footsteps, there were several of them, and he presumed they were escaping rebels as he raised his sword.

John Doukas reached the last step at the bottom and glanced around the empty church before walking further in.

'Use your men and search every inch of this place,' he ordered Georgio.

Recognising the voice, with some relief, Conn stepped out behind them.

'I think you will find that I have already done that, Sire,' he said as John Doukas whirled around in alarm.

'God's blood, Malvais, don't creep up on me like that in the middle of a rebellion; my hand was on my sword. However, I am glad to see you are still alive and almost in one piece,' he said as Conn stepped into the light from the high windows. Georgio felt almost faint with relief and clasped arms with his friend, tutting at the cuts and bruises and the blood stain down his shirt from the gash in his forehead, which was still bleeding.

'They gave me a kicking and even tried to hang me, but Darius came to my rescue just in time.'

'Darius?' said Georgio in surprise, realising that he had not seen the young squire since they arrived.

'He was exceedingly brave and even rode Diablo at them to rescue me, but we caught up with Fumagalli and made him pay; we have his head for the Emperor to place on a spike.'

'We think Altasparta is still hiding in the palace, but we have not found him yet. The Emperor is screaming for him to be found; he plans to have him torn apart by four horses in the main square. He killed the Emperor's favourite lion; he has had it for twenty years since it was a cub,' he explained to Conn's questioning look.

'There is no doubt that Altasparta planned to leave by the postern gate. Are there only the two staircases down to it?' asked Conn.

'Yes, and I will put men at the top of each; he'll not escape that way. I have promised the Emperor we will find him, and by the Face of Lucca, we will. I suggest you get the worst of those wounds seen to, and then we'll continue the search together,' declared John Doukas as he slapped Georgio on the shoulder.

'I told you Malvais would be alive; he takes some killing.'

Georgio grinned as they made their way up the staircase.

Altasparta was frozen with fear under the altar cloth. He had been within seconds of being found, and then they stood only feet away from him. He was sure they would be able to hear his heart beating; it was so loud as they discussed him being torn apart. He had to escape, do everything he could to get away and ride for Milan; he would be safe there. Fumagalli was dead, and he had to do this on his own. He waited for some time to ensure they had left the church, and then he lifted the edge of the heavily embroidered cloth and stared into the dim interior of the church. The coast was clear, so he crept along the side of the chancel down into the transept and over to the door. This was going to be the dangerous part. If the Megas Doux had put guards on the staircase, they might hear him emerging at the top.

He opened the door as quietly as possible and listened; he heard nothing except the neigh of a horse from the tunnel opposite. He breathed a sigh of relief and sent a prayer up to Fumagalli for putting the horses out there. Then he silently laughed at himself, for he was sure Fumagalli would be in hell. He took the risk of peering up the spiral staircase; there was no sound, so he leapt across to the door opposite, taking the stairs two at a time. He raced along the tunnel to the postern gate that led to freedom; he could see the sunlight streaming through it, and the relief he felt was overwhelming.

Having initially been apprehensive about being left alone, Darius was becoming bored. He had followed the instructions to the letter. He had dragged Fumagalli's headless body behind the bushes and then stood just inside them, sword drawn, waiting for anything to happen. He noticed the loud clash of swords and screams echoing from above had almost stopped, so he presumed the rebel crusaders had been dealt with. Suddenly, he could hear feet pounding; someone was running at speed along the tunnel towards him, and he knew Malvais would not run like that.

He moved back into the trees and bushes of the Emperor's garden and waited in anticipation; only an escaping rebel would run like that, whoever it was, emerged from the postern gate. He heard the feet sliding on the rough rock of the steps as they ran down the narrow stone staircase to the bottom gate and the horses; then he saw one man walking towards them, his face covered in a Greek tragic mask. Darius parted the branches and peered behind him to see if the man was alone; he could not take on several rebels. No one else was there, and the man was now gathering the reins and placing his left foot in the stirrup. From the back, he could see that it was Altasparta; from the auburn curly hair, his right hand gripped the saddle's high pommel, and he swung himself up.

As Conn had predicted, hanging by a few threads, the girth snapped, and the saddle came off. Altasparta landed on the rocky ground, the heavy saddle coming with him and hitting him in the groin. He squealed in pain and swore; ripping his mask off, he made to get up but froze as he saw the sword above his head. With his feet planted firmly, Darius held his sword with both hands and plunged it into the knight's chest. Altasparta screamed, both hands going to the blade as if he could pull it out. Darius stood still, holding the sword firmly in the rebel's chest, frightened to let it go in case the Lombard would try to get back up.

'This was a far quicker death than you deserve, but I was not going to give you the chance to escape.' Gripping it tightly, he twisted his sword as he had seen other knights do. Altasparta screamed again, and blood bubbled from his mouth and nose.

At that instant, there were loud cheers and the sound of fists being thumped on leather doublets in respect. Darius looked up, and on the top terrace, he saw Conn, Georgio and half a dozen of the Horse Warriors; he flushed with embarrassment but was inwardly pleased. Even more so when he realised that John Doukas and Emperor Alexios were there as well, and they saluted him.

'Bring me his head, young man. Doukas, make sure his body is fed to the lions; I want no grave marker for this traitor,' declared Alexios.

John Doukas bowed to the Emperor, who left to go to his family; they were being escorted back from the caves.

'It is to be hoped that these so-called pet lions do not get a taste for human flesh, or it might not end well for the servants,' he whispered to Conn as he sent two men for Altasparta's body, and they left the terrace.

Conn laughed, relieved it was over, but as the physician strapped up his broken ribs, he wondered what Alexios would now do to the Lombard camp. Would there be retribution? Would he expel them?

Conn and Georgio rode slowly back to Hebdomon the next morning, escorting Raymond of Toulouse. Georgio told the Count he was convinced that Guibert knew of the attack and the plan to trap Conn, but there was no proof now that Altasparta was dead.

The fame and success of Raymond of Toulouse was well

known; he had built up a significant power base in southern France, ruling over thirteen counties. Just as importantly, he had helped Robert, Duke of Normandy, in the capture of Jerusalem. The Lombard counts were awestruck and welcomed him to the camp.

'We are grateful, Sire, that a man of your eminence would come out and act as our intermediary with the Emperor in our dire predicament,' acknowledged Albert pleadingly.

Watching Guibert, Conn could not help adding,

'He might also act as judge and jury if we find any evidence that you colluded in, or encouraged the attack,' he said, his eyes never leaving Guibert's face.

Both men paled, but it was Count Albert who pleaded.

'I swear, Malvais, we had no idea what was afoot. You know what our nephew was like. I'm convinced there was madness there, like his father, volatile and unpredictable. We had little or no control over him and have hardly seen him since he was told he was returning to Milan.'

'No, that was because he was in the city with hundreds of men preparing to attack and loot the Emperor's Palace at Blachernae,' spat Georgio as Raymond held up a hand before it became heated.

'I am prepared to take your word, Count Albert, as I know you to be a man of honour, but you now have no choice but to move across the Bosphorus in two days. The Emperor will no longer tolerate you in this camp. Your nephew is dead; he was beheaded, and his body was fed to the Emperor's lions.' Both men looked shocked, but Conn saw the anger on Guibert's face as he dropped his eyes and clenched his fists, and like Georgio, he did not doubt that Guibert was involved.

Now, however, he was responsible for getting all of them

over the Bosphorus in the shortest possible time. An immense task. Once assembled on the other side in Anatolia, he had to escort them through hostile territory to Nicomedia, as the Seljuk Turks were known to stalk that route. He was to attend John Doukas in the city the following morning, who had hinted that he was getting another cohort of men, so he was interested in finding out who it would be. He prayed they were mounted archers or less than half of the Lombard Crusaders would reach the Emperor's military base at Nicomedia.

Chapter Twenty

Early April 1101 – Hebdomon

Georgio sat with Darius and watched as another ninety people were herded onto the ships. It was day three of the evacuation, but the weather had been poor with wind and rain, which did not help as the captains refused to overload their ships because of the sudden squalls. Several shiploads of horses and animals had been tagged and had gone together with shepherds and grooms to the other side.

'At this rate, it will take another week. Have you seen much of Malvais?' asked Darius.

Georgio glanced over his shoulder, 'He is up there, chivvying the nobility and their retinues. As you know, Orontes and his men are over there organising them into groups and setting out tents in any shade they can find. I have hardly had a word with Conn since we left the palace. I wait up for him, but he does not appear; he has been across to the other side twice. I saw him getting off the ship yesterday morning.'

Darius shouted at a few stragglers overburdened with sacks and bags and then turned back to Georgio. 'He is never easy to talk to but seems more remote than ever.' Georgio gave a brief nod of agreement.

'I think the events at the palace brought back some of last

year's trauma. We stayed at the inn the night before we escorted Raymond to the camp, and it was just as I was drifting off I heard him say, *'Now I know what Finian Ui Neil meant when you have a noose around your neck, and you think you are going to die, you think on your life and what you have done. You realise that you never really told people how much you care, and then it is too late.'*

'Ui Neill was the great Irish warrior; we had heard of him even here in the city; his name was known to my father and brothers,' said Darius.

'Yes, but like Conn, he had a noose around his neck in England and was rescued with only minutes to spare. When something like that happens, it leaves a mark. I'm not concerned about Conn; he'll think it through in his own way, and if he is going to talk, it will be on his terms and only when he is ready,' he said before leaping up to stop two men carrying a wooden table on board.

'You think you will carry that through the heat of the desert? You will be on your knees by the end of the first league,' he shouted at them.

On the hillside, overlooking the chaotic scene below, Conn sat on a restless Diablo and surveyed the long line of people making their way with their bags, boxes, dogs and mules down to the new temporary wooden wharves they had built. The Lombard nobles were below them; the men were dismantling the huge pavilions, which they insisted on taking with them on one of their five carts. Whenever he encountered Guibert, the Lombard count stared at him with ill-concealed hatred. Conn decided he had now had enough of him and rode down to where they were sat in camp chairs, watching the bustle and chaos around them.

CHAPTER TWENTY

'Your ship will be here at midday; it will pull in at that end of the bay where they have built the wooden ramps for the carts. I suggest you begin to move soon as that ship is needed again to move several thousand pilgrims once you disembark.

Count Albert stood at once and moved to ensure his personal belongings, weapons, and accoutrements were on the first cart. Guibert stayed where he was and stared into the distance.

'I would be extremely happy to leave you behind, Count Guibert, for I am more convinced than ever that you were behind, or even arranged, the treasonous attack on the Blachernae Palace. If I find even one scrap of evidence, one man willing to talk, I will take it to John Doukas and ride to watch them take you in front of Alexios.'

He turned Diablo away as Guibert sprang to his feet, the camp chair flying to the rocky ground behind him.

'I will see you dead, Malvais, because of you, we do not even have a body to bury for my sister. You were lucky in that stable this time, but you won't be next time, I swear,' he spat and stomped off to join his brother.

Conn watched him go, satisfied that he had been right in his suspicions and shown his true colours, but without evidence, he could do little but keep a watch on him.

Two days later, the camp was empty, apart from the scavengers taking anything left behind and the dozens of pilgrims who had decided not to go any further. Some were ill or injured, some disillusioned and had decided the price was too high now that the dangers and conditions of a march to Jerusalem had become apparent. Conn left these people to the Emperor's men to deal with as he led a snorting and stamping Diablo up the ramp onto the last ship. Orontes and his men had worked tirelessly to organise the disembarking crusaders and pilgrims. He had used the cohorts from the camps to organise their groups and had set up food and water stations along the route of the three-day trek across Anatolia to safety in Nicomedia.

On Conn's orders, Georgio had sent scouts ahead on either side of the hills to scan for enemy movement. At the same time, vedettes and Horse Warriors constantly rode up and down the column to keep the thousands of people moving. Learning from their experience in Spain, they wore their all-enveloping Berber headdress as the cloud of dust the long column raised was immense and covered everything in its wake. Conn had shown all his Horse Warriors the nose covering he used for his horses, for a horse with its lungs full of dust and sand was useless and would not last long.

Orontes, riding back to check in, covered from head to foot in dust, was impressed by their garb.

'You look like a ghost,' laughed Darius and received a glare.

'So will you in another few hours, my friend; my biggest worry, however, is the size and height of the dust cloud. It is a clear day and will be seen for miles, telling the Seljuks we are here.'

Conn nodded, 'I have twenty scouts out, north and south, on the top of the hills. They are riding in pairs for safety; they will give us warning if the Seljuks attack.'

Satisfied, Orontes fell back to ride alongside Conn for a while.

'I believe congratulations are in order for your promotion, Malvais. I hear you are to become a topoteretes.'

Conn could hear a small amount of envy in his friend's voice.

'I am as surprised as you are, Orontes; my remit was

originally to double and then treble the number of trained Horse Warriors. I was not prepared for anything more. Now I am to become Topoteretes or Deputy to the Commander of Nicomedia and in charge of four thousand men.'

'The Megas Doux is impressed by your organisation and handling of the camp, as are we all. You are a natural leader, Malvais; these four thousand are not infantry; they are mounted Pechenegs, the archers you wanted. They are under the command of one of the most impressive Byzantine commanders, General Tzitas. So the Megas Doux is putting his two most successful commanders together in Nicomedia; the Seljuks will be shaking in their boots,' he laughed.

Conn, however, was thoughtful; he knew of the General's reputation, but the name Pecheneg often produced a sharp intake of breath and a shaking of heads when mentioned. Almost unmanageable, one captain had said; he needed to know far more about them and no doubt General Tzitas would do that when he reported to him in Nicomedia.

It was late afternoon on the third day, the daily temperatures had risen, and the Lombard nobles were clamouring to stop when two of Conn's scouts rode up to report a dust cloud following them a league or so back. Conn sent his vedettes down the column to tell them to pick up the pace. Food, water and shelter for the second night awaited them only a league away, ahead of them in a shady valley. Conn also sent Darius ahead to tell Orontes the news with the order to get them into the valley and set up a defensive line across it with men up on the hills and archers on the eastern slopes.

The news of a possible enemy pursuing them certainly quickened the pace while Conn gathered forty of his men and rode back to wait for, and assess the size of, the attack correctly.

His scouts came back with information. The group behind them was mounted and coming at speed. They assessed it as seventy or eighty strong, but it was difficult because of the dust cloud. There may be as many as a hundred. Conn would confidently pitch his Horse Warriors against that number, but he sent fifteen of his men up onto the right flank to attack on his signal and slam into the sides of the enemy. Then, they waited as the scouts reported that the enemy was slowing.

'Shields up!' Conn shouted to his men, aware that the Seljuks were expert archers at speed on their fleet horses. However, as the group slowed and the dust began to disperse, Conn realised that he could see pennants flying; he knew that the Turks would not use the twin-tailed gonfalons, so he shouted the order to stand down. *Was this the vanguard of the French?* he wondered, as they came closer.

The leader held up a hand in greeting and unwrapped the long scarf from his face. Conn recognised him immediately, Count Raymond of Toulouse, who had acted as the intermediary for the Lombards. *Was he out here checking on them?* he wondered. To his surprise, Raymond rode alongside him and clasped arms in a warrior salute.

'Well met, Malvais; you are progressing faster than I expected.'

'Yes, my Lord Count, we hope to be in Nicomedia by late afternoon tomorrow.'

'Excellent, I will join you tonight and return to Constantinople tomorrow. I wanted to ensure that our Lombard nobles were keeping their word.'

Conn realised it was as he thought; Raymond was nothing if not thorough, and his reputation was on the line this time if they rebelled again and broke their word, for he had made pledges for them. Conn shared his concerns about Guibert and related their last conversation.

'Guibert of Parma has always been a snake, a cunning and avaricious man; I own I'm surprised he came on the crusade; keep a close eye on him, Malvais. I'm returning to the city so soon because we expect the French contingent to arrive any day, and I must be there to greet them. Alexios has decided I should take charge of the whole expedition as I have completed the journey to Jerusalem twice.'

'Relief will no doubt be felt in several quarters to hear that news, Sire,' he said, and Raymond laughed.

The Lombards, aware that they had already burnt their bridges, acceded to the Emperor's wish, not that they were given much choice, thought Conn as he stood by the fire and watched Raymond easily bend the nobles to his will.

'An impressive man, full of knowledge, but also with such presence and charisma,' whispered Georgio beside him.

'Yes, the experience of the terrain, the enemy and the cities they will reach, that will be invaluable,' added Conn.

'He must be in his late fifties now, but he looks younger and fitter. You can see why Alexios and the Megas Doux have so much confidence in him,' whispered Georgio.

An hour or so later, to their surprise and that of the Lombard nobles, Raymond came over to sit at their campfire.

'I knew your father, Luc De Malvais, well; I fought beside him for King William, a truly inspiring warrior and your uncle, Morvan De Malvais. You come from one of the greatest Breton families.' Conn inclined his head in thanks.

'Alexios is very impressed with your abilities; your men stopped the rebellion and probably saved the Emperor and his family.'

'I think that was down to Georgio and Darius here, who rode hell for leather and alerted the Megas Doux while I was still tied and bound in a stable, courtesy of Guibert's nephew and his men.'

Raymond smiled. 'One sign of a great leader, Malvais, is when he gives praise where it is due to the men and officers he commands. I hear you have just been appointed as Topoteretes, an honour indeed for one so young. With the Emperor's permission, I wondered if you would consider joining us on the crusade to Jerusalem with five hundred, or even better, a thousand of your Pecheneg warriors.'

Conn was taken aback, 'That decision is not mine to take and will it not look like ingratitude if I leave Nicomedia so soon?'

'You have no doubt heard that they call this the 'Crusade of the Faint Hearted.' I assure you that isn't an accolade; it is a derisory title for the nobles who ran away from the First Crusade and broke their vows. You can see why we need as many great leaders as possible to join us.'

Georgio had listened to this with growing concern, but this was too much, and he could not help himself as he blurted out,

'No! That is impossible, as we are committed to joining Chatillon in the summer.'

Raymond looked at the young curly-haired Horse Warrior in astonishment, narrowing his eyes, but then addressed Malvais.

'Piers De Chatillon, the Papal Envoy? Amongst other things, of course, how is that so? In what way are you committed to him?' he asked in a puzzled tone.

Conn sent Georgio an angry look, for Chatillon never liked

his business or plans known, but he also had to protect his friend from Raymond's wrath.

'Forgive Georgio, my lord; he is somewhat impulsive but has the right of it. We, both of us, owe Piers de Chatillon a great debt. We are only here alive and free to follow our calling because of him, he saved our lives. Since our return from Spain, he has been our mentor and our patron; he needs us later in the summer and has requested our return.'

This was news to Raymond, and it gave him a dilemma.

'I know Chatillon; he is a powerful and dangerous man who does not take people under his wing lightly, his uncle, Pope Urban, I called a friend. But surely, if he knew, he would see the importance of what I ask you to do. He supported his friend, Duke Robert of Normandy, on the First Crusade and even travelled with us as far as Lucca to meet with the Pope. Leave it with me. I will send him a missive and explain our need for your extraordinary talents.'

At that, he left them and made for his bed, leaving a highly perturbed Georgio behind him.

'We cannot commit ourselves to this, Conn; if you agree to join this rag-tag of a crusade, it will take a year or probably more from our lives. That is, if we survive, given the disastrous odds of the last crusade, that is unlikely, and they had ten times the knights and warriors of this one.'

Conn shrugged and stood to head for his bed.

'Let us see what we find at Nicomedia; my orders will come from General Tzitas, and his come directly from the Megas Doux. You may be worrying about something that will never happen. The Pechenegs are based in Nicomedia to patrol Anatolia to prevent the Seljuk Turks from threatening Constantinople. I cannot see us being used to guard a group of crusaders to Jerusalem while leaving Constantinople more vulnerable.'

At that, he left, leaving Georgio staring disconsolately into the fire.

'Surely we are not going on this crusade?' asked Darius in a worried tone.

'My fear, Darius, is that Raymond of Toulouse holds so much sway with the Emperor that he may override the wishes and concerns of the Megas Doux. I will send another pigeon to Chatillon; tell him what is afoot; if anyone can prevent this, he can!'

Chapter Twenty-One

Late April 1101 – Rouen

Chatillon sat at the end of the Council table. Robert Belleme, Earl of Shrewsbury, was by his side, and Flambard had now wormed a place there too. Piers smiled as he listened to the ploys and flattery that Flambard was using to impress Robert.

'Sire, you have ten times the support of the usurper, Henry; some of the wealthiest and most powerful names in England and Normandy are sitting here, around this table, ready to do your bidding. You need to invade this summer; with your expertise in battle and the experience of those in this room, you cannot fail.'

'I think I'm going to be physically sick if I have to listen to any more of this mealy-mouthed flattery,' said Belleme in a loud whisper designed to reach everyone around the table. Several smirked, and even the Duke smiled while Flambard darted a poisonous glance at a man he had always detested.

'God's blood, Robert, we must sail and land your armies. The ships are gathering already, and young Mortimer has his troops and the fyrd waiting to join you as soon as you reach England. Flambard, I hate to say it, is right in one regard; nothing is stopping us,' stated Belleme.

Duke Robert stood; his wife, Sibylla, did not have a seat

at the table but sat slightly behind him and smiled at him in reassurance.

'The plans are already in place, my Lord Earl. Chatillon and I put the finishing touches on them last night. I will share with you all the preparations so far, but only three people in this room will ever know where we intend to make the landing. I have half a dozen suitable places, from Hull to Cornwall. I will not share our destination until the ships set sail. I do not intend this to degenerate into the last disastrous invasion.'

For the next hour, the Duke explained the preparations and logistics of the operation already in place; ships, horses, weapons, supplies and troops were all catered for.

Again, Belleme nodded in congratulation to the Papal Envoy. At the same time, Flambard gritted his teeth in frustration and anger at being kept away from something he knew he was good at, but it was to be expected, as few people trusted him yet. He intended to work hard at rebuilding that trust and creating a niche for himself, but he had bigger plans that would have to wait.

As he left the chamber, Chatillon found Edvard waiting for him with a message.

'This has arrived via Rome and Marseilles, Sire,' he said, handing him a thin strip of vellum.

As Chatillon took it, he hoped it would say that Conn and Georgio would be returning. He read its contents and swore softly.

'Trouble?' asked Edvard, concerned.

'Nothing that cannot be sorted, but damn the man for interfering!' he spat. Edvard quietly walked beside him as he knew the explanation would be forthcoming.

'Raymond of Toulouse has requested of Alexios that Conn,

CHAPTER TWENTY-ONE

Georgio and the Horse Warriors be released from his service to be assigned to him on the crusade to Jerusalem.'

Edvard tutted, 'Surely Conn would not be that stupid; that crusade is just a quick way to an unmarked grave in the sands.'

'It depends on his state of mind. I had hoped that he had come to terms with things, but there is a chance that he may still be running from her death last year.'

'Do you want Count Raymond removed, Sire?'

Chatillon smiled at his friend in amusement.

'Assassinate Raymond of Toulouse, one of the heroes of Jerusalem? I think not, for I feel he will not survive this 'Crusade of the Faint Hearted'. No, I will just put a spoke in the wheel of his plans. Come to my room; I need to send a message to John Doukas immediately, before Raymond can do any more damage.'

For the second night in a row, Conn Fitz Malvais woke in a sweat with tears on his cheeks. He rubbed them away and chastised himself for his weakness. It was not quite dawn, and he prayed that he had not cried out in his sleep. But, all the men wrapped tightly in their blankets around the campfire seemed fast asleep. He put his hands behind his head and took a shuddering breath; Marietta, the dreams were always of Marietta, beginning with her laughing in his arms and ending with her blood soaking his clothes. He threw his blanket off in disgust, then shivered. The heat during the day may be rising, but here in the higher valleys of Anatolia, the nights were cold.

However, today, they would finally reach their destination, Nicomedia. Once the most senior city of the Roman Eastern Empire, it was now a large military base for Emperor Alexios with many thousands of troops and four thousand of those would be under his command. It was rare that he ever felt any self-doubt about his ability, but this was a huge number of men, and it felt a little overwhelming; the Emperor and John Doukas must have had a lot of faith in him. He had seen the surprise on both Raymond's face and that of Orontes. As always, he would break the number down into manageable sections.

The yawning Darius went to get them some breakfast from the supply carts, and a short time later, they were ready to begin the last stretch. Raymond of Toulouse rode by to bid them farewell.

'Think about what I said, Malvais, helping me to lead this crusade; you could make a name for yourself across Christendom.'

Conn raised a fist in salute and ignored Georgio's scowl as he mounted and rode along the road ahead to check the long caravan was ready to move. He locked away Raymond's demands; for now, he had more important things to think about as Orontes told him the next valley was notorious for Seljuk ambushes, and he needed his scouts up and over the high, rugged hills on either side.

At the end of another hot and weary day, they finally reached the outskirts of Nicomedia without incident. Conn felt as if he had ridden twice the distance as he had ridden back and forth and up and down the hills to get advance warning of any attacks. Looking west towards the ancient city, Conn saw it sat on the side of a hill in a wide, lush coastal plain that ran down to the Sea of Marmara. The tired and dusty pilgrims were delighted to enter a green valley that led to Nicomedia. They were thankful that Malvais had not lied, and orchards and crops in terraces covered the slopes. The tree-covered camp they were shown into outside the city provided ample shade, and large cisterns fed by Roman aqueducts, still in use, were full of fresh water. It did not take long for the children to be splashing and laughing in the River Kumla while the women began to wash their dust ingrained clothes in the shallows.

Sitting on his horse, watching them play in the river, Georgio felt sad.

'Would you risk taking your children on a journey with little water or food across inhospitable enemy territory? How many of them will survive? I pray that many of them decide to stay here in Nicomedia,' he said to Darius before shaking his head in dismay and turning away to oversee the setting up of the tents.

Conn rode to find Orontes to check that cohorts of guards had been allocated camp areas to patrol. As he rode up the side of the hill, he found Archbishop Anselm of Milan and his clerics on their knees in one of the orchards. The apple trees were covered in late blossom, a beautiful spot. He waited until the Archbishop got to his feet and hailed him.

'I'm going to report to General Tzitas, the base commander; I can request accommodation in the town for you and your senior clerics if you wish.'

The archbishop was approaching sixty, but nothing was wrong with the keen, bright eyes that surveyed him.

'Yes, I will accept your kind offer, but I also want to thank you for your patience and fair handling of our little problems,

Malvais. I know you have had a difficult and trying time of it, but you have brought us safely to a veritable Garden of Eden while we wait for our French and German compatriots to arrive, and I will ensure there are no more incidents.'

Conn inclined his head in thanks and rode on, he would not have called the murder and rape of the villagers or the attack on the palace as little problems, but this summed up the attitude of the arrogant and ungrateful Lombard leadership. He hoped the arrival of the significant French leaders of higher rank would change this. He reined in and looked down across the beautiful valley; another forty thousand crusaders and pilgrims would arrive soon. That would certainly leave its mark on this valley, and no doubt decimate the food stocks of the local inhabitants as well. He shook his head at the number of crusaders and pilgrims and rode up the hill towards the walled town and recently fortified fortress at the top.

Looking west, he could now look down on the overgrown ruins of the ancient Roman city and harbour on the shores of the sea. It had been abandoned hundreds of years ago for a more defensive position on the hillside. This had been reinforced and rebuilt by Alexios to defend the routes to the city of Constantinople. There was now a large military base to the east of the original city, and John Doukas had told him that there were at least fifteen thousand men here at any one time. Looking at the dozens of square barrack blocks and stables, Conn could well believe that. Above him on the slopes were meadows full of horses, hundreds of them grazing.

As he rode through the gates, he realised the town was deceptive, much bigger than he originally thought because it was also built on terraces, but with tall, thin houses, two and three stories high. It was also very busy, with dozens of

CHAPTER TWENTY-ONE

traders carrying their wares back and forth or dismantling their stalls for the day. Finally, he reached the walls of the large stone keep and dismounted; half a dozen guards were on the gate led by a grizzled serjeant who looked like he had spent a lifetime at war.

'Commander Conn Fitz Malvais, reporting to General Tzitas,' he announced. The serjeant nodded and signalled one of his men to take the horse. Diablo immediately snapped at the man's face, and he jumped back in alarm. Conn tapped Diablo on the nose and shook his head while he showed the man how to grasp the bridle under his head to avoid the teeth.

'He is often very playful,' smiled Conn while the man rolled his eyes and tried to persuade the horse across the courtyard into the stable block.

'That is some warhorse you have there, the biggest Destrier I have ever seen; he is a beauty,' commented the serjeant whilst leading Conn into the cool corridors across a large hall and then up a spiral staircase that seemed never-ending. At the top was a heavy wooden door studded with iron, on which the serjeant knocked, and they entered. The room was at the top of one of the two towers he had seen from a distance; it was octagonal, and shuttered windows looked out on four sides. On the fifth, there was a large fireplace. It was plainly furnished as befitted a military outpost, but the carved wooden furniture was solid and good quality. On one wall were maps of the surrounding area; on the other, several rectangular, colourful silk hangings with tassels at the bottom. Horses were the subject of these unusual tapestries, rearing and racing at speed with a rider hanging over the side with a bow. But Conn's eyes were drawn to the figure standing at the window. Hands resting on the sill, he stared out in the twilight at the growing camp spreading below, then turned.

'I have heard much of you, Conn Fitz Malvais. You certainly have a reputation to live up to, but John Doukas speaks highly of you; he is an excellent judge of men, which is enough for me.'

He waved Conn to a chair while he settled himself behind the document-strewn table. Conn was unsure what to expect, but he had presumed that such a high-ranking general would have the usual Greek patrician features. In this, he was wrong. General Tzitas was a big, solid, stocky man with dark, almost silky black hair. His features were wide, and his eyes had a slight eastern slant. Conn suddenly realised he was staring and glanced away, but the general laughed.

'Not what you expected, Malvais? I'm afraid I'm somewhat of a mix, which has advantages and disadvantages. A patrician Greek warrior for a father and a beautiful Pecheneg girl for a mother.'

Conn could not help grinning back at this genial, self-effacing man.

'I hear you have had several problems with this particular group of crusaders.'

'Yes, but most of the troublemakers, several hundred of them, are now dead. Reprisals were swift, and I do not expect any more incidents, although I am keeping a close watch on Count Guibert of Parma as I'm convinced he was involved.'

'I own myself astounded that Alexios did not expel them all; he is not known for his leniency.'

'Raymond of Toulouse intervened for the Lombards and pleaded for clemency.'

'Ah! Of course, I hear he has the ear of the Emperor now, a dangerous and ambitious man; be wary of him. I tend to

CHAPTER TWENTY-ONE

believe only half of what he tells me. However, you did well, Malvais, to get such numbers onto the ships and here in one piece. We were involved in escorting the First Crusade part of the way. My serjeant said it was like trying to herd weasels.'

Both men laughed.

'I was surprised you had no trouble in the final pass with such rich pickings on show; the number of mounted warriors must have scared them off,' he said, suddenly, serious.

'I sent dozens of scouts out. They saw small marauding groups of riders following us, but they did not attack or worry the scouts unduly.'

The general nodded, 'They will wait until the next stage when the pilgrims are strung out over many miles, attacking at dawn or dusk, slaughtering the weak, seizing horses, mules and livestock. Night after night, they will come attacking different points. Their horses are so fast it is almost impossible to stop them.'

'You paint a bleak picture, Sire. I have twenty-five well-trained Horse Warriors with me, and I am now under your command; I have been instructed to hand command of the camp over to Captain Orontes.

The general looked at the Horse Warrior before him; he was certainly a prepossessing sight, tall, broad and confident. He had no doubt he would be an efficient second in command, but more importantly, he was intelligent and sensible enough to act independently. He might be young for such a post, but he knew he had years of experience fighting against the Berber forces in Spain, which would stand him in good stead.

'When did you leave home?' he asked.

Conn frowned, trying to find the right answer.

'If you mean my home in Brittany, we left when we were

sixteen. My captain, Georgio and I left to go to Spain to fight for El Cid.'

Tzitas nodded, 'That explains a great deal, and of course, you were trained as Horse Warriors before that by the best Horse Warrior of them all.'

Conn smiled at the words; he knew what was coming, but to his surprise, the General said no more; he just nodded and smiled.

'As well as the Emperor's usual forces, I have a large tagma of about four thousand Pechenegs now allied to the Emperor Alexios after he defeated them in battle. I have scattered two thousand of them over several of our smaller military bases in Anatolia as I endeavoured to put a steel ring around Constantinople on the orders of the Megas Doux. The other two thousand Pechenegs are here; I'm putting you in command of them; you will have to earn their respect, or they will not follow your orders.'

Conn nodded, as he had come across this before, 'What can you tell me of them?'

'They are a Turkic, semi-nomadic race, mercenaries who will fight for whoever pays the most, even for former enemies such as Alexios. Now, they live mainly in Anatolia, although there are still hundreds of families out on the steppes of Asia, breeding the fastest ponies you will ever see. The Pecheneg are brutal in battle; they fought off the Magyars of Hungary for the Bulgars and are still at war with the land-grabbing Rus, whom they despise. They are also valiant, noble, fiercely proud and independent.'

He paused while he stood, poured two cups of wine, and handed one to Conn before raising it in a welcome toast.

'You need to know they are not one large conglomerate

mass. Within the tagma, they have their tribes, customs and religions. Each tribe also has its own colour of ponies; they may only reach fourteen hands in height, but their ability to manoeuvre is astounding; they can turn on a coin. There are five main tribes.' So saying he reached behind him, picked up an old sheet of vellum and handed it to Conn. It was a list, but he noticed it only had four names on it.

The Cur – Bluish-toned horses

The Khabuzi –light bark-coloured horses

The Qara Bay – Black horses

The Yazi – Dark brown bays

He watched Conn with a slight smile, waiting for the question, but then took pity on him.

'This sheet was given to me by the leader of the last tribe, The Bula Copan; he considers himself the ruler of the rest and he does not like the written word, so he refuses to write the name of his own tribe.

They ride piebalds and are the most difficult and aggressive of the tribes. The bloodshed we had last year because a piebald stallion covered a Khabuzi mare without permission went on for months. Volatile! Did I mention how volatile they all are? They never forgive or forget an insult, and fights between them are not infrequent and usually to the death, but we do not interfere; the tribes rule their own and have their own laws.'

Conn suddenly laughed; he could not help himself, and the General joined in with him.

'I'm sorry, Sire, but you are beginning to make the Lombards look attractive. I cannot wait to relate all of this to my men.'

'You have an advantage, Malvais. Your reputation as a Breton Horse Warrior is known to them, as is that of your family, so the foundation of that respect is there. One other thing, I always found it easier to work with the tribal leaders and not try to impose my will upon them. I tend to ask rather than order the Pechenegs. Except in the heat of battle, when they do everything, I tell them. It is an unspoken tacit understanding that warfare is different. You have been allocated a room here in the fortress for your use, but I suggest you use that for business and raise your pavilion near the Pecheneg lines so they feel your presence. I hear that the morning training for your Horse Warriors is something to behold; let the Pechenegs see that, and I may even come to watch myself.'

With that, Conn was dismissed, and he left to find his men, his head filled with a whirl of thoughts. This might be the most challenging task he had ever undertaken; he thought as he rode Diablo back through the town's winding streets.

Chapter Twenty-Two

Conn took the General's advice, and after completing a nighttime circuit of the camp with his friend, he informed Captain Orontes that he, too, had a promotion and that he was now Commander of the camp; it was all his. Orontes pulled his horse alongside, skillfully avoiding Diablo's teeth and laughing.

'No doubt you are heartbroken to lose the Lombard nobles, and I promise to follow your lead and keep a watchful eye on Guibert.'

'I still expect to see you at our campfire regularly, Orontes,' he grinned; he greatly respected the hard-working Byzantine captain, now a commander.

'Of course, try not to get yourselves killed on your daily patrols into Anatolia. I have lost over a dozen men to the Seljuks in the past,' he said as he raised a fist in salute to Conn and rode off.

Conn headed for the training ground the next morning, where he had ordered his men together. He called them into a tight circle around him and relayed the information from the General. A few smiled, and a few looked shocked at what they were taking on.

'The best advice I can give you all is do nothing to cause

or give offence. Do not start anything with the Pechenegs that you cannot finish, or by the sound of it, they will finish it! They are our allies and outstanding warriors in battle, as are we, so we give them the respect they deserve. Now, let us show them what we can do.'

They moved their great Destriers into battle formation and moved straight into a full gallop charge, the sound of their hooves resounding around the camp. They formed in line, and, moving in perfect unison and timing, their horses struck out with their front hooves, and then they reared and all turned on command to gallop back. They engaged in mock battles that looked so real that Darius, even though he had seen them dozens of times, wondered how on earth they would emerge unscathed. Conn and Georgio then took on a group of six, and it was breathtaking to watch as, using two swords, they unhorsed or drove off their men.

A small crowd had gathered around the edge when they started, but over a hundred Pechenegs were watching when they finished. Darius examined them with interest; he had seen a few before in the city; their garb was distinctive. Baggy, voluminous, colourful trousers tucked into knee-high boots, a belted overtunic split up the front and back for riding; most of the men had the front of their hair braided. All wore conical caps or gold-decorated metal conical helmets with a large plume that dropped to their shoulders. They carried swords, but many also carried a spear and a bow. They watched the Horse Warriors with interest, and there was much chatter and gesticulating at different manoeuvres.

Ultimately, Malvais ordered his men to dismount and fight hand-to-hand. The noise of clashing blades filled the air, and the crowd went silent when Malvais took on three at once,

CHAPTER TWENTY-TWO

using all his skill and several tricks he learned from Chatillon to disarm his opponents. As he stood leaning on his sword, wiping the sweat from his brow, spears banging on shields filled the air. The Pechenegs liked and appreciated a good performance.

An hour later, Conn summoned the tribal chiefs to a meeting; they all came, some of them bringing their sons or second in command, so Conn faced over twenty of them in the large room of his pavilion. He offered the tribal leaders camp stools to sit on; the others stood behind. He introduced himself, making sure he took the right track.

'I have heard much of the skills and bravery of the Pechenegs, and I'm honoured to be given the command of you and your warriors. However, I'm new here, and you are the ones with the experience; you know this land, you know our enemy, the Seljuk Turks, you know how to defeat them. I'm here to learn from you, as are my men.'

There was much nodding and smiles at this.

'Previously, you have sorted out any issues within or between the tribes. I intend to leave that in place. However, if anything escalates that affects our patrols or damages the morale of our force, then I will step in and deal with it.'

Again, they nodded in agreement that this was fair.

'Tomorrow, the patrols begin again, and either Georgio or I will be riding with you almost daily,' he said, indicating the tall, curly-haired warrior beside him.

There was a buzz of chatter at this and much slapping of hands against chests in approval. He then gave them a chance to ask questions, which threw them for a few moments. Then, a few inconsequential things were raised about supplies and equipment. Until one broad, scar-faced Pecheneg warrior sat forward, his hands on his knees, all the others were immediately silent.

'I am Banadir Timur, leader of the Bula Copan.'

Conn bowed his head in recognition of his status as the man continued.

'Is it true that you beheaded murderers and rapists on the beach at Hebdomon and even branded and flogged a noble?'

For a second, Malvais wondered whether to say he was carrying out the Emperor's orders, but then he decided he needed to establish his reputation amongst these tribes.

'Yes, Banadir, for no man should be beyond the laws of the Emperor. That way chaos and corruption lies. I wanted to execute Altasparta, but the Archbishop of Milan begged for his life. However, justice prevailed for my young squire here ran him through, and I put his head on a spike outside the Emperor's palace at Blachernae.'

There were some in-drawn breaths at this and exclamations of approval while several looked at young Darius with respect. He then dismissed them until only Banadir and another warrior remained. Conn waited as the silence lengthened, but there was obviously something they wanted to say.

'This is my son, Mengu Timur. He asks if he can ride out with you on your first patrols; he'll be your guide and answer any questions you may have.'

Conn glanced at the well-built young man, probably a few years older than him and smiled.

'I would consider myself honoured and lucky to have his company,' he answered.

Both men looked pleased as they bowed and left.

'Raising their status?' asked Georgio.

'I think they are probably reinforcing or maintaining it as

CHAPTER TWENTY-TWO

the General implied; they are at the top of the tree in the tribal hierarchy, one of the oldest and most powerful groups but often the most trouble,' he explained.

That afternoon, Mengu Timur returned to invite Malvais and Georgio to their camp before dusk, where there would be competitions, food, and drink to welcome the great Horse Warriors to Nicomedia. Conn accepted with pleasure.

The Bula Copan camp was immense; it was easily the largest Pecheneg tribe, with over five hundred warriors who had their extended families and a string of horses. However, the leaders of the other tribes and their retinues were present, which swelled the numbers, so it seemed as if over a thousand encircled the large central training ground. At first, they were taken into Banadir's cavernous tent, which was round but had several tunnels and rooms running off it. Thick wool rugs covered the floor, there were low silk-covered divans, and bright, colourful tapestries hung on the walls. They sat cross-legged on the divans while his wife and daughters brought a large silver tray with silver cups and presented them as their welcome drink to the guests. Conn took a mouthful and was not surprised, nor was Georgio, but Darius, who had accompanied them, was taken aback, for it was warm creamy milk with a tang of something in the background.

'Koumiss,' whispered Georgio. 'with nutmeg and some kind of fermented spirit, I think.'

'Mares milk, a rare treat, so show your enjoyment,' suggested Conn as he drained the cup and smacked his lips to show his appreciation.

Talk then turned to several things, but especially the foolishness of this crusade.

'They ride or walk to their deaths; if the Seljuks do not kill them, the Fatimids further south will, or they will die on the bleak stone-covered hills and sands of the deserts. They left thousands of bodies behind in the wilderness last time. Their bones are still scattered there,' growled Banadir.

Conn tried to explain the concept of pilgrimage and the washing away of sins on the soul if completed and reached Jerusalem, but Banadir just shook his head, not convinced it was worth it.

Shortly afterwards, the blowing of horns summoned them outside. It was darker now, but the training area was lit by dozens of high flaming torches planted in the ground.

'This is not only the training ground for the tribes which we own and oversee, but it is also our Jereed field,' explained Mengu to Conn, who still looked puzzled.

'It is a game our ancestors have played for centuries, two teams at either end of the field; the first man charges his horse towards the enemy line but pulls his horse into a rear at the last minute and issues the challenge. One of their best riders then chases him back, and at speed, he throws a Jereed at him, a blunt but heavy wooden javelin. If it hits the rider, it is one point to us; if it only hits the horse, a point is deducted. The riders can use any tactics they wish to try and avoid being hit by the Jereed.'

A raised platform had been set out at the side for the leaders to watch; besides this was a man with four baskets, one full of small white stones, one full of black ones and two empty baskets.

'He must be keeping a tally,' hissed Darius, excited at the prospect of watching the game.

All at once, the crowd parted, and flute-like instruments began to play a regular quick beat accompanied by several

CHAPTER TWENTY-TWO

drums. The two teams of six players entered side by side, but to the delight of Darius, who clapped his hands in time to the music, the horses danced, high-stepping a circuit around the field first, to finally take up their positions facing each other.

The ones on Conn's left were all piebald horses of the Bula Copan tribe; they were well built but short-backed for speed, large enough for him to call them horses rather than the ponies the General mentioned. The challengers at the far end were mixed colours from the other tribes, but a horse with an unusual shining golden coat was in the centre.

'That is a very beautiful horse; I have never seen a horse with a coat that shines like that,' murmured Georgio.

'It is one of the rare Turkoman horses; it is called an Akhal-Teke and is bred to withstand the harshest conditions of cold and heat and be highly intelligent and fast. However, the rider was not permitted to ride in this competition and has earned my displeasure!' said Banadir, while Conn saw Mengu shake his head and frown at his father.

Moments later, the horns blew, and the game began. Conn received many impressions from the game; it was fast, almost relentless, the galloping swerving horses, the wooden javelins flying through the air, and he was engrossed by the end and convinced that these were some of the best riders he had ever seen. The rider of the golden horse was an acrobat; there was no other way to describe him. The aim was to avoid the javelin hitting you while ensuring they hit your horse and lost a point. And at that, he was an expert. Conn watched in astonishment as he hung under the stomach of his horse, which swerved left and right before reaching its lines again. Was this why Banadir would not let him ride, he wondered, because he was outstandingly good.

However, the result was very close when the stones were counted; the challengers had won by only one point. The rider on the golden horse danced his horse around the field to the scowls of Banadir, whose team rarely lost.

'Father, you have to stop this, that win was deserved and listen to the crowd, they think so,' said Mengu.

'You may present the prize, Malvais,' said the leader, reaching behind to take the fresh carcass of a young goat from a servant.

Conn stepped forward as the winning team rode up to much cheering from the crowd, and the rider of the golden horse came to take the forelegs of the goat and hold it aloft in triumph. For a few seconds, he got the flash of unusual dark blue eyes ringed with dark kohl, and he heard her laugh ring out as she rode back to her team, who did another lap of honour.

'The rider is a girl?' he asked in astonishment, for his own Horse Warriors could not equal her skills on a horse.

Mengu nodded, 'She is a Cambazi, a horse daredevil, and some say that, like her mother, she was born in the saddle.'

'She is not of the tribes, however, not a full-blood Pecheneg, and we should not allow her to take part; she can do her stunts and tricks before the game, but she should not have tricked us by appearing tonight. Tell her of my displeasure, Mengu. If she does this again, I will ban her from our camp,' growled Banadir.

'That will not please the General, Father; it may well sour your good relationship with him.'

'Why is General Tzitas involved in a tribal matter?' asked Conn, perplexed.

Banadir spat on the ground in disgust before he answered.

CHAPTER TWENTY-TWO

'Because she is his daughter, he knows how wild she is, but he has little control over her,' he answered.

It was a pleasant evening with more music and dancing, and they thanked Banadir for his hospitality before walking back to their pavilion.

'Interesting people, their customs, their music and traditions are all so different, and there were very few women there apart from the leaders' wives,' commented Georgio.

Conn laughed and slapped his friend on the shoulder.

'Were you disappointed, Georgio? Do you want me to find you a beautiful silken-haired Pecheneg girl to warm your bed,' he taunted.

'Any girl to warm my bed would be welcome, Conn,' he muttered.

Sleep was a long time coming that night as Conn mulled over the events of the past few days; it all seemed to have happened so fast. The promotion and meeting with the famous General Tzitas, the tribal leaders, the atmosphere of the Bula Copan camp, strange smells, sounds and entertainment. He looked forward to the patrol at dawn tomorrow with his men and fifty Pecheneg warriors. He pulled his blanket tighter around him against the chill of the night as he drifted off, but he could still see the dancing golden horse and its daredevil rider.

Chapter Twenty-Three

April 1101 – Nicomedia
It was an interesting ensemble that set off the next morning; the contrast between the eighteen-hand high War Destriers and the Pecheneg horses was stark. Diablo took exception to the new riders, snorting, sidling left and right, rolling his eyes, or snapping if they came near. But once out of the camp, Conn put him straight into a gallop south across the plain towards the hills in the distance. Mengu Timur eventually caught up and pulled alongside Conn,

'The distance these great horses cover is impressive; they seem to eat up the miles,' he shouted to Conn as the rest of his men galloped to join them.

'My family bred them for strength, intelligence and endurance. Most have been bred from large Arab dams and Frisian or Belgian stallions. They respond to training very well. Where are you taking us today?'

'We are heading up to the high lake of Kirazdere in the hills above. We have found in the past that the Seljuks sometimes use it as a base to water their horses before sweeping down to attack travellers on the coastal route or from the local villages,' explained Mengu.

Conn pulled up and allowed his men to gather, repeating

CHAPTER TWENTY-THREE

what Mengu had told him.

'Mengu and his men will lead the way as they know the route.' The Pecheneg leader nodded in satisfaction,

'We will be following the Kiraz stream. The slopes are steep in places, but there is a manageable path we use,' he added with a grin.

It took several hours for them to pick their way up the narrow valley to the lake; although scrub covered the sides, several chestnut trees grew on the sheltered banks of the Kiraz stream, which gave them all welcome shade as the sun rose. As they neared their destination, Mengu called a halt to send some of his scouts ahead. Conn noticed he sent two members of the Cur tribe on their less noticeable bluish-coated horses. While they waited, they dismounted and watered the horses in the shade; however, before long, the two scouts came back, their ponies sliding down the scree slopes to the east. Conn could see immediately that they had found something; they leapt from their horses and ran to Mengu, chattering excitedly in their language. Conn and Georgio walked over to join them.

'They have found a Seljuk camp, possibly ten to twelve men. They are about a quarter of the way down the lake, where there is a wide inlet on the eastern side. It is thickly forested on both sides, but at the very end, there is a clearing, a small beach often used by travelling peddlers and the local men who trap for eels. They are camped there and are becoming careless, for Dolchuk here smelt the smoke from their fires; the scouts think they are getting ready to leave, so we must attack now. I will send half of my men back over the top to come from behind them while we follow the coastal path. I would lay odds that they have already attacked the hilltop villages of Astacus and Camaduzo. The snow is almost gone now, and it makes them more accessible. They usually take livestock, and women and children for the slave markets.'

Conn nodded in understanding, 'Let us go!' he said to his men, mounting and following Mengu and the remainder of the patrol along the path, which was precarious as it climbed up the side of the steeper cliffs. Suddenly, they emerged at a small plateau beside a waterfall which was in full spate with the melting snow. This made the path they were using impassable. Mengu tutted and shook his head as they were forced to return to a steep scree-covered slope, which Diablo took exception to, but Conn pushed him on, moving sideways across it. Finally, they emerged into the thinly wooded area at the top, and the large lake spread along the valley in front of them. It was colder up there, and a reasonable amount of snow remained on the heights. However, this was no time to admire the scenery as Mengu had already pushed on ahead.

A short time later, the sound of shouts and clashing blades filled the air; Mengu gave a shout to his men and with a grin at Conn, he and his men abruptly turned and hurtled their ponies at the trees, weaving them right and left and ducking to avoid the low branches. Georgio watched them in dismay.

'We cannot follow through there; the trees are far too close together and the branches too low for our horses.'

Conn grimaced in annoyance and pulled Diablo back onto the track.

'Why do I suspect that Mengu did that on purpose to show his ponies could go where we couldn't?' he exclaimed, pushing his horse into a canter on the narrow path at the side of the lake.

There were now screams and yells with the sound of blades as Conn and his men splashed through the shallows and into

CHAPTER TWENTY-THREE

the clearing. The Pechenegs were swarming over the Seljuk Turks, who never stood a chance. There was nothing for the Horse Warriors to do as they sat and watched the slaughter. With some alarm and dismay, Conn watched Mengu standing over a wounded Seljuk. The man was face down, several arrows in his back, and he was pulling himself along the ground, his fingers clawing at the earth. Conn waited for the death blow to fall, but instead, several Pechenegs dismounted to watch as Mengu began to chop from the feet up. The man's screams of agony echoed across the cliffs and valley until finally, the man lay still, the grass and leaves around covered in his blood, but still, Mengu did not stop as he took his arms and head.

His sword dripping with blood, Mengu raised it with a roar of triumph that his men joined in with, banging their spears and swords on their shields. He wiped his blade and walked over to where Conn was sitting silently.

'That is one group that will not attack our villages again,' he grinned.

Conn shook his head. 'We do things differently in Europe; it is rare that we ever mutilate the wounded. We tend to make a quick ending, for, after all, they are warriors as well.'

'You have a lot to learn, Horse Warrior, for we learnt how to do this from the Seljuk Turks who did this to our men,' he said, annoyance clear on his face.

'You have your methods, Mengu; we will keep to ours, as I like to be able to sleep at night,' said Conn, turning away and leading his men back down the valley.

Mengu stood, his anger building while his men watched and waited; bewilderment was clear on their faces, for they had expected their leader to get an accolade for this attack. They could not hear the conversation, but they could see Mengu Timur was unhappy with Conn's reaction.

'Take the weapons and any plunder as well as their horses,' he shouted, his face grim.

On returning to the camp, Conn handed Diablo to Darius, and he made for the fortress to report to General Tzitas. He put the words together carefully in his head; after all, the Pechenegs were now his command, and he did not want to run to the General with issues. The grizzled serjeant greeted him with a salute and waved him to the staircase. However, as Conn reached the door, he could hear raised voices, so he waited until there was a lull before raising his hand to knock. However, the door was abruptly pulled open, and to his surprise, the rider from the Jereed was standing there. She was obviously angry, and her skin was flushed, but she was also thrown by the Horse Warrior filling the door frame, and she stepped back. The General, also red-faced, was on his feet behind her.

'I'm sorry, I did not wish to intrude,' murmured Conn, looking from one to the other.

'I believe you have already had the pleasure of seeing my daughter, Rhea, perform her tricks in front of a crowd.'

The General's voice was now cold and calm, but his eyes were angry.

'I am honoured to meet you in person, my lady; I cannot begin to say how impressed I was with your riding skills.'

Rhea was taken aback by this as she had not expected praise, and the visitor sounded cultured and intelligent, unlike the people she was forced to mix with on her father's postings.

'Rhea, may I introduce my new deputy, Sir Conn Fitz Malvais, late of the Reconquista wars in Spain, part of the

CHAPTER TWENTY-THREE

Emperor's guard and now commanding our Pecheneg troops.'

Rhea took a step back and looked him up and down as he resisted the urge to laugh at being assessed in this way. Then she held out a hand in greeting and smiling; he bowed and took it.

'You may go, Rhea, as we have business to discuss, but I expect you after dinner in the hall tonight; we have about twenty guests, so liaise with the Steward and ensure that things go smoothly. Do not appear in those clothes; I expect you to be dressed as befits a daughter of the House of Tzitas,' he said in a tone that encouraged no discussion.

She nodded, flashed another glance at Conn and left, pulling the door shut with a distinctive thump behind her. The General sighed as he dropped into his chair.

'I'm afraid that my impetuous daughter is one of the crosses I must bear for all I love her. She seems to have inherited her headstrong traits from the Pecheneg side and the pig-headed stubbornness from her mother. I should never have brought her here after her mother's death; I should have left her with her grandparents in Constantinople, for she is nineteen now and should be married to a boy from a good Greek family. She is only a quarter Pecheneg, but she embraces that quarter for some reason, wearing the clothes, immersing herself in the culture and traditions and doing everything she can to defy me.'

Conn smiled, 'No doubt the problems of many fathers the world over, Sire.'

The General laughed and settled himself while waving Conn to a chair.

'Now, tell me how your first patrol went?' he asked. Noticing the frown that descended on Conn's face that perhaps things had not gone smoothly, he was surprised by the next words.

'It was very successful, Sire; we tracked and found a camp of Seljuk raiders on the shores of Lake Kirazdere. We wiped them out, taking their horses and weapons.'

'A good start, Malvais, so why the concern I can see in your face?'

'I'm afraid that the methods the Pechenegs use to dispose of the wounded are not something that we would ever do.'

It was silent for some time as the General walked to the open window and leaned on the sill.

'I agree. I have seen this several times, and it does give you somewhat of a dilemma. They have fought the Seljuks for decades, with much barbarity on both sides, so there is history there and memories of atrocities, but what do you do? Do you alienate our allies, or do you look for a compromise? I told them to burn the bodies, thinking I had found a solution, but then found them throwing the lightly wounded onto the flames as well; now I ride away; it was the smoother path if I wanted them to fight by our side. I suggest you go and find Mengu and congratulate him on today's success. He is the heir to the Bula Copan, and no matter what he has done, you need him on your side.'

Conn thanked him for his advice but was never sure he would get used to such tactics.

'I expect you and Georgio to be at the dinner tonight. I give you warning that the Lombard nobles will be there, although I will try to seat them as far away from you as possible,' he added as Conn reached the door. Conn smiled and bowed his thanks.

Conn had managed to avoid formal dinners with the

CHAPTER TWENTY-THREE

Lombard nobility, but he dressed with care in a belted blue velvet tunic and only a dagger at his belt. He was surprised at how crowded the hall was when they entered; there seemed to be several local knights and their ladies, as well as Banadir and his son Mengu, to represent the Pecheneg contingent. Conn made straight for them, and bowing to Banadir, he turned to Mengu.

'Can I thank you for your advice and experience today, Mengu? That was a very successful patrol and will undoubtedly send a message to our enemies. You and I will sit down with a map tomorrow as I would like two or three patrols to go out simultaneously.'

Mengu looked somewhat taken aback, but Banadir beamed at the praise heaped on his son. At that point, the Steward was at Conn's side waving him to his seat on the top table. He was pleased to see he was on the General's left whilst the Lombard nobles and the Archbishop of Milan were on his right. He made a point of punctiliously bowing to them and received the usual glare from Guibert. The General's daughter, Rhea, was sat on Conn's right, unrecognisable in a deep blue overgown, a golden band holding back her long, silky black hair. He bowed and sat in the chair beside her, thinking how different and beautiful she looked.

Rhea was delighted the handsome Horse Warrior was sitting beside her, a man from a different world; he had seen and done things she could only dream of stuck in this backwater. Before long, they were deep in conversation as she plied him with questions about his experiences. Everyone had heard of El Cid, but she wanted to know more about the man himself. Conn found himself pleasantly surprised, for her questions were not just small talk and superficial; they showed insight and intelligence, and she listened.

Soon, they were laughing as he recounted various exploits. She hung on his every word as he told of the burning of the Sheikhs ships in Tunisia, for even here in Nicomedia, they knew the dreaded name of Sheikh Ishmael. At that point, the music began, and several couples began to dance; the General encouraged Conn to take Rhea into the round dance, which he happily did.

Georgio, on a side table, watched with interest, for Conn had shown little interest in women apart from whores, which he could pay and leave. But now, Conn was smiling as he lifted Rhea and swung her around. Georgio sat back, glancing across at the side table opposite; he saw Banadir enjoying himself, quaffing wine and laughing at Captain Orontes beside him. However, Mengu drew his attention, white-faced, fists clenched, lips thin with anger. He watched Conn and Rhea dance together. The music ended, and Conn swung her around again before they both returned to their seats with flushed faces and bright eyes. Georgio's gaze went back to Mengu, who looked as if he could commit murder.

Was there some understanding between Mengu and Rhea? Was she handfasted to him? he wondered. He needed to find out and warn Conn.

Meanwhile, after several heady glasses of wine, Rhea was enjoying herself. She was very aware of Mengu's jealousy in the same way she knew most men's eyes followed her. She had learnt of the power she had at an early age. Now, she set out to keep Conn amused, refilling his wine goblet, placing her hand on his arm, and hanging on his every word. Mengu had kept her amused for several months. Still, he would only ever be the leader of the Bula Copan tribe; he had no ambition to be more than that. He could not compete with a famous Breton Horse Warrior who would go far and take her away from here; he was her future. However, she would keep Mengu dangling for now, as she enjoyed his lovemaking in the stolen moments they found.

She knew that to captivate Conn, she needed to display her chaste and demure side; her father was about to see a new side of her, and she smiled at the thought. She placed her long, elegant fingers on his arm.

'You have no idea how refreshing it is to have a conversation with an interesting man who has been to the courts of Europe; tell me more,' she whispered as Conn smiled into her almond-shaped, dark blue eyes and placed his fingers over hers.

Chapter Twenty-Four

A few days later, a messenger arrived from John Doukas to say that the French and German cohorts had arrived and they were beginning to ship them over the Bosphorus. They had lost several thousand on the long journey to Constantinople in cold and difficult weather, but there were still nearly twenty-five thousand. John Doukas wanted them to stay in Nicomedia for no more than a month at the latest. He intended to join them there in a few weeks to hurry them on their way. General Tzitas decided to leave Conn in charge to ride out and meet them in Anatolia.

Meanwhile, Conn's days moved into a pattern; patrols took place daily, and sometimes they were away overnight. Conn found that he saw less and less of Mengu, who volunteered to lead the other patrols; there was no doubt in Conn's mind that the young Pecheneg had not forgiven him yet for his words at the lake whenever they met; he was cool and offhand. They had several skirmishes with the Seljuks, usually swift attacks by their mounted bowmen who would purposefully aim for the Pecheneg horses that pursued them. Several times, a pony's throat had to be cut in the desert due to serious wounds. Conn empathised with the tears these hardened warriors shed, for they were all attached to their horses. They

CHAPTER TWENTY-FOUR

captured several wounded Seljuks whom Conn rescued from a brutal death to imprison and extract information about the movement of their troops.

At night, he often found that he and Georgio were invited by various tribal leaders and to dinner by the General and his daughter. Georgio watched the performance she put on with interest; there was no doubt that she had Conn in her sights, and her vivaciousness and her beauty attracted Conn. Georgio thought how different she was from Marietta, who, while lively, had been a pure and lovely soul. Georgio shared his concerns with Darius, who had also been watching the developing friendship as she had taken to riding out with Conn, sometimes in Western clothing, sometimes in her Pecheneg clothes. They seemed to be spending a great deal of time together, which the General watched with a benevolent eye as he thought a great deal of Malvais.

However, time was running out for Rhea, lying naked in the arms of Mengu above the stables; she reassured him that she was only following her father's instructions to make their guest feel welcome; she swore it was him whom she loved. In reality, she intended to bed Conn as soon as possible, she was determined to have him, and the opportunity came at the Jereed game in the Khabuzi camp. She persuaded Conn to take part. He was initially dubious, for he had never ridden a Pecheneg horse, but she took him out on one of hers, weaving through the forests. He found the horses unbelievably responsive to the lightest touch and supple. Being much shorter backed and only fourteen hands or less they were supple and could turn back on themselves in seconds.

It was a warm spring evening as they gathered under a clear sky with the promise of a rising full moon. Rhea had her servants lace the Koumiss heavily with spirit as they raised toast after toast. Her orders to the servants were to keep his cup filled with wine before and after the game. Conn found he was excited, as were Georgio and Darius, and numerous bets were changing hands as all his men came to watch. Conn prayed he did not make a fool of himself and fall off, which would lose the challenging team several points.

He need not have worried, for although nowhere as good as the Pecheneg riders who had spent their lives weaving in and out on these horses, he still acquitted himself well, scoring several points and only losing one. There were gasps of awe and shouts of encouragement as he made his horse swerve, turn on the spot, and even rear and turn at one point to avoid the wooden javelin that whistled past his face. However, the home Khabuzi team won, which everyone cheered, except for Banadir, who was still smarting from his previous defeat.

Afterwards, Rhea joined Conn and Georgio to toast his success, and it was late as they walked and swayed back towards the town. Georgio and Darius turned towards their pavilion while Conn and Rhea walked towards the fortress. The moon had risen in a clear star-studded sky, and it was light.

'It is too beautiful a night to go to bed yet; come with me,' she said, leading him on a path she knew through the ancient ruins towards the beach.

'Come, let us go for a swim to get the sweat from our bodies,' she whispered, moving close and placing her hands on his chest.

Conn blinked; he had imbibed a lot of wine, more than usual, but was still cautious.

'Surely that would not be seemly,' he murmured.

CHAPTER TWENTY-FOUR

'I come here all the time to swim. There is a sheltered cove, and no one will see us. Unless Horse Warriors are afraid of the sea? Can you even swim?' she asked, laughing while taking him by the hand and leading him over a rocky outcrop to a small sandy cove.

Once there, she helped him to remove his clothes, but his hands stopped her when she tried to remove his thin linen shirt.

'I always leave this on,' he murmured.

She nodded in acceptance, and within moments, she was naked and laughing, and she ran into the sea. She was beautiful; the moon shone on her perfect body, and her long, black, silky hair fell to her waist. He stood and watched her entranced as she stood in the shallows, arms raised, breasts standing proud, as she tied up her hair in a ribbon. Then she plunged into the water, and Conn followed her. It seemed a long time since he had swum in the sea, but in moments, he was striking out with powerful strokes to join her. She was a strong swimmer, and they played in the moonlit water for a while as she dived below the surface and came up, running her hands up his thighs and onto his chest under the linen shirt. Without warning, she then wrapped her arms and legs around him, and for a few seconds, he went under with the weight of her and came up spluttering and laughing, but her naked body was still wrapped tightly around him, and he felt his own body responding.

'Let us go back; I'm getting cold,' she said, turning and swimming back to the cove, but once there, she clung to him again and lifted her face to be kissed.

Conn could not help himself, the feel of her soft, pliant body against his. Yet again, she jumped, wrapping her arms around his neck and her legs around his waist. He carried her up the sand and then fell to his knees between her legs as she whispered.

'Make love to me, Conn, do not fear, for I lost my virginity as a foolish girl to a handsome captain, but there has been no one since.'

Her hands seemed to caress him everywhere as she pulled him closer. When he thought about it afterwards, he did not know what possessed him, but he knew he needed to bury himself deep inside her. He plunged into her, making her cry out as she arched to meet him. She ripped the shirt from his back to feel his naked body touching hers, and suddenly, he didn't care if she saw that tattoo that was such an abomination on his flesh. He had always intended to withdraw, but the moment was too intense as she clasped his buttocks and pulled him deeper.

Afterwards, he lay on top of her and, kissing her face, he murmured, 'I should not have done that; I do not know how I will face your father.'

'He is away for three or four days, meeting the French and German nobility from the ships. I will meet you here again for the next two nights, for I want you to do that again and again, Malvais. We will be lovers for a while, but when he returns, we'll be friends again, and he will suspect nothing,' she whispered.

Conn found himself agreeing, and he dropped his head onto her breasts; he felt content in a way he had not for some time, and soon afterwards, he was asleep. She lay beside him, smiling at the moon above while her hands ran over him.

'You are mine now, Conn Fitz Malvais,' she whispered before gently untangling herself from his arms and pulling on her clothes. She could not afford to go missing all night, or it would be reported, and her father would be furious. She stood to leave and then stared in the moonlight at the coloured tattoo that covered him from his neck to the base of his spine. Her mouth dropped open in awe; she had never seen anything like it. She immediately realised that the sword was a cross; this warrior wore his religion and his faith on his body. She hoped the Seljuks never captured him, for they would flay him alive to have this as a trophy. She bent forward, and her fingers followed the outline from top to the flaming tip of the sword; then, she tore herself away and raced back to the fortress, an excuse ready on her lips for the serjeant.

They met again for the next two nights; Conn could not stay away from her; she was all he thought about, and the pleasure and almost relief he felt when he took her was something he had never felt before. On the third night, he led her naked to the sand and pulled her on top to mount him; she threw her head back in pleasure as she held his hands on her breasts; his eyes never leaving her face, he realised he had never felt such ecstasy as he once again exploded inside her.

However, they had a spectator this time; Georgio, worried by Conn's nights out and preoccupation, had Darius follow him. Hiding in the ruins, he had seen the liaison and the beginning of the lovemaking before leaving them to their privacy and returning to the pavilion to report to Georgio, who had suspected as much.

'I suppose I should see this as a good thing, as it means he is finally recovering from the death of Marietta. But I'm worried, as I saw Mengu's face when Conn danced with her; I dread to think what would happen if he discovered this was happening.'

Darius looked thoughtful for a moment because, on his

frequent foraging expeditions, he had seen a laughing Rhea leading Mengu by the hand into the stables, and he was sure they were lovers as well. However, he decided to keep that to himself, for this dalliance may not last. He did add one piece of information.

'He takes his shirt off when they make love; she knows about the tattoo,' he said, making for his bed while Georgio stood there with a shocked expression.

Was this dalliance more serious than he thought, that Conn would trust her? he wondered. He shook his head as he had far more important things to think about. He had been assigned to Orontes to help build the new camp for the French and Germans, and they had worked tirelessly to bring in provisions, erect tents, and dig more latrines. The contingent would arrive tomorrow afternoon, and they still had much to do. However, despite aching everywhere and his eyes feeling full of grit from tiredness, sleep would not come as he waited for Conn's return. This did not happen as it was their last night on the beach. Rhea had brought blankets, lit a fire, and they drank wine and then curled up in each other's arms.

Chapter Twenty-Five

Early May 1101 – Nicomedia
Riding back into camp after several days patrolling the route to Doryleum, the first person Conn saw was Raymond de Toulouse, with General Tzitas; they were on horseback on a slight hill looking down on the considerable camp that covered half of the valley. Conn pulled up alongside and waved his men towards the town.

'Well met, Malvais, a tough patrol, I see. Did you lose any?' asked the General, watching several wounded men with makeshift bandages slumped in their saddles.

'No, mainly arrow injuries. They will recover, but the attacking Seljuk groups are becoming larger and bolder; there were at least fifty in the group that attacked us on the road to Doryleum. We were close to the village of the Thebasion when suddenly, without warning, they came down seemingly impossible steep scree slopes at speed to attack us. Mengu was with me; he said a new Seljuk tribe, the Kayi, had moved into the area. They train their horses to lie down flat on the slopes so there are no silhouettes against the skyline.'

'Very clever; no doubt the numbers are increasing in that area because the spies in the camp have told them we will be following that main road to Doryleum very soon,' suggested

Raymond.

The General nodded. 'I am sure of it; I will send a large group of Pechenegs with you for protection as far as Doryleum. After that, you are on your own, Count Raymond, for the rest of the forces are needed to keep Anatolia and the capital safe from attack. Their numbers are increasing, and because the Seljuks are becoming more daring, we'll need every man we can get.'

Raymond nodded in reluctant understanding, but at least the French and German contingents had more troops with them.

'And what of you, Malvais? Have you decided to accept my offer to come with us?' he asked.

The General who had been watching the camp suddenly turned and gave Conn a hard look as this was the first he had heard of this; he faced them both.....

'I was under the impression that the Megas Doux had plans for you here, Malvais. I was told not to mention it until he arrived, but he hopes you will take over this command from me; I intend to return to a post in Constantinople.'

Conn was shocked at this news. He had considered Raymond's offer, but after weighing up the pros and cons, he had concluded that the risk was too great, and he still had a debt to pay to Chatillon. However, there was now a lucrative position on offer, one beyond his imagining here in Nicomedia, and of course, there was Rhea, who still occupied too many of his thoughts.

'John Doukas must think a great deal of you indeed to consider you for such a prestigious post, Malvais, at such a young age, but I still offer you more; I offer you fame and fortune,' countered Raymond.

CHAPTER TWENTY-FIVE

General Tzitas gave a snort of disgust and disbelief at Raymond's claim.

'John Doukas was given a similar opening to this at a young age, and look at him now, to be Megas Doux of the armies and navies of the Byzantine Empire while not yet forty. This crusade is madness, Raymond, and you know it, for despite your experienced leadership, there are simply too many civilians, and then you have squabbling leaders pulling in different directions. Have you talked to the Lombards yet? They are the largest group, yet I heard today that they refuse to go south to Doryleum. Their hero, Behemond, King of Antioch, has been captured, and they have now decided to go hundreds of leagues east into dangerous Seljuk territory to rescue him from the castle of Niksar. I tell you, none of them will survive.'

Conn saw the shock on Raymond's face. Although he had heard of the capture of King Behemond, he had forgotten what a hero he was to the Lombards. He swore long and loudly and kicked his horse into a canter as he headed down into the camp to try and talk them out of such a disastrous move. They could not take tens of thousands of pilgrims to lay siege to a castle; feeding them would be impossible. The General shortened his reins and looked into Conn's face momentarily.

'Think long and hard about any decision you are about to make, Malvais, for it is not only your future; the lives of your men and your friends are also at stake.' With that, he raised a hand in farewell and rode back into Nicomedia.

The arguments between the Lombards, the French and the Germans over which route to take lasted for days. Stephen, Count of Blois, agreed with Raymond that they should head south for Jerusalem and not take a detour that could cost them six months and include the siege of a castle to rescue Behemond. The problem was that Stephens's reputation had been damaged by his cowardice when he fled during the First Crusade, and the Lombards also knew about Raymond's jealousy and hatred of King Behemond. The arguments continued, and the temperatures rose with the days that went by.

A few nights later, Conn, Georgio and Orontes were dining with General Tzitas and his daughter when Banadir arrived to have speech with the General, alone. Instead, he had to join the guests for dinner and wait. The crusade was still the topic of conversation.

'The journey south to Jerusalem alone would have claimed tens of thousands of lives, but now they are heading east into the territory of the great Seljuk Sultan, Kilij Arslan. He will be rubbing his hands in delight at the thought of the damage he can do, the loot, the horses, the slaves he can take. They are mad to consider going down this route!' exclaimed the General.

'And yet you have pledged to send five hundred of our Pecheneg men with them, probably to their deaths,' growled Banadir.

'I have little choice, Banadir; the Emperor feels he must protect them as significant nobles are now with them, not only Raymond of Toulouse but the French King's brother, Hugh of Vermandois, along with the Count of Burgundy and Conrad, the High Constable of the Holy Roman Empire.'

Conn listened but did not contribute much; he raised his eyes constantly to glance at Rhea, who sat very demurely in a green silk gown beside her father; occasionally, she looked at him surreptitiously under her lashes. The meal finally finished,

CHAPTER TWENTY-FIVE

and Georgio and Captain Orontes left to complete an evening patrol while Banadir glowered, waiting for Conn to leave. Oblivious to this, Conn lingered over his wine until Banadir blurted out,

'I have private business with you, General, with you alone. I cannot wait any longer to discuss this with you.'

Conn looked up in surprise at the red-faced leader of the Bula Copan and made to rise.

'I shall leave,' he said, pushing his chair back.

The General, who was not blind and had watched the relationship developing between his daughter and Malvais, a relationship he had no objection to, insisted he stay as Commander of the Pechenegs, for he had an inkling of what this private business might be. Banadir pushed his chair back, and standing, he took a deep breath.

'I'm here on my son Mengu's behalf; as you know, he'll inherit the Bula Copan on my death, and I'm sure he will become a great and courageous leader of our people for as you know, he has their respect. He now asks for the hand of your daughter, Rhea, in marriage.'

All that could be heard for some time was the rattle of the shutters in the building wind outside as General Tzitas considered the offer and waved Banadir back into his chair. Conn was rigid; every muscle in his body tensed as he raised alarmed eyes to Rhea, who kept hers firmly on the table. However, he could see that she had gone deathly pale as her father sat and worked on the right words to answer, but not offend, the prestigious Pecheneg leader.

'My family is honoured, Banadir, that you could consider aligning your great family name with mine. As you know, at times, I have despaired of my daughter's wild and unpredictable behaviour, which has shamed my family name. Mengu must love her very much to be prepared to take such a stubborn, willful and disobedient girl to wife.'

Banadir nodded, 'I cannot lie, General. I have tried to talk him out of this for many months, but her beauty bewitches him, and he refuses to take any of the tribal girls. I told him he would have to beat her regularly.'

The General laughed before answering.

'However, my family are from Greek nobility, leaders in their own right and in our society, we believe in free choice, so I will ask my daughter what her wishes are on hearing this handsome offer. Mengu is a wealthy warrior with a fearsome reputation; any woman would be honoured to accept him and become the first lady of the Bula Copan, ruling over all of the Pecheneg tribes. Rhea, I have watched you spend more time at his side and with the tribes this year, but do you reciprocate his feelings?'

Conn found he was holding his breath. He had just found her; surely, he could not lose her too soon. He had to admit, he had been so wrapped up in her that he had not once thought of marriage, yet she was no servant or doxy; she was a famous General's daughter. He berated himself for what he had done to her; he glanced left and found the General staring at him intently as if he expected him to say something. He swallowed and loosened his fingers, which had been gripping the arm of the chair while they waited for what seemed an interminable time for Rhea's answer.

'I also feel highly honoured by this proposal from Mengu. It is true that over the last year, we have become friends and riding companions, but although he may have stolen the odd kiss as many warriors try to do, I made him no promises.

Unfortunately, I cannot accept his proposal as I am in love with someone else.'

For the first time, she looked Conn full in the face; her blue eyes were filled with tears as she turned to her father to finish the sentence. 'I'm carrying his child!'

The shock in the room was almost tangible as, at first, their mouths dropped open, and they sat stunned and then reacted in their own way. The faces of the General and Banadir flushed red with anger, and they shot to their feet. Banadir turned on Rhea.

'You have sat there and watched me make a fool of myself, girl; I came in good faith, but my son has had a lucky escape, for you are nothing but a whore!' With that, he stormed out, knocking over a chair and throwing the heavy door back with both hands to bang and rebound on the wall.

General Tzitas leaned his hands on the table; at first, he closed his eyes, but then, opening them, he gave them both a hard, cold stare. He could see at once that Conn was as shocked as he was. He had not known.

'Is this true? Or is it yet another one of your ploys to escape from something you do not want to do, Rhea?' His voice resonating with anger.

'It is true, we are deeply in love, Father; I could not help myself,' she said, her voice breaking with emotion.

The General closed his eyes again, and his head dropped forward as he groaned at the implications of this on the Pechenegs.

'Malvais, leave us; I wish to talk to my daughter alone. I dread to think about the repercussions of this; I will send for you in the morning,' he growled.

Conn gave Rhea a long, searching look, the conflicting

emotions clear on his face as he stood; pushing the chair back, he bowed his head to the General and left. He heard the storm above break over Rhea's head as he went through the large inner doors. He stopped and almost turned back, guilty at leaving her to face this alone when he was as much, if not more, to blame. Caught up in pure passion and excitement, he had been thoughtless. Something he had never done before. Banadir was right; she was bewitching, but that was no excuse.

Holding the door, the old serjeant put a hand on his arm.

'I wouldn't, if I were you, let him ring a peel over her head; it will go on for a while. This sounds worse than usual, but he always forgives her.'

'Maybe not this time,' Conn muttered as he walked down the steps and back to his pavilion in the dark.

He expected Darius to be there, but he must have gone with Georgio, and he was glad, for he needed time on his own to think. He wrapped himself firmly in his blanket and faced the tent wall, staring at it, flapping and straining in the rising wind. He knew he had no option but to marry her; he had fallen in love with her but had not expected to take on the responsibility of a wife and child. In a few months, he would be twenty-four, and his career path had been laid out before him. His stomach knotted at the thought of the damage he had now done to his career. He dreaded seeing John Doukas in a few days; he could imagine the conversation and the disappointment in his face. He groaned aloud and pulled the blanket over his head, cursing himself for his foolishness and, worse, his carelessness.

Chapter Twenty-Six

He was summoned early the next morning. His heart was in his mouth as he mounted the steps to the keep; the serjeant was grim-faced and shook his head as he waved him towards the stairs. It had gone around the fortress and would soon be around the camp. He took a deep breath and opened the door; the General was alone; his face was strained, his clothes crumpled, and he looked as if he had not slept. Conn stood before the table and was not told to sit while the General stared at him and sighed.

'In one fell swoop, you have taken your sword to your career, Malvais. You have certainly burnt your boats with the ruling Bula Copan tribe, which makes your position here in Anatolia untenable. There is no way you can command them; they will despise you for your underhand and immoral actions of swiving the chosen bride of their heir. I admit to some of the fault, for I saw the attraction growing between you and my daughter and did nothing. Also, because I had passed command of the Pechenegs to you, I had not sat around their campfires for the last few months; I had not seen or guessed Mengu's intentions.'

General Tzitas folded his arms, his lips tight with anger and sat back in his chair, waiting for Conn to say his piece. He took a deep breath.

'I can make no excuses for my behaviour. I fell in love with your daughter and was so bewitched by her that my normal caution and restraint went out of the window. I know it will be no consolation, but I'm ashamed of my actions as I wanted to earn your respect, and I know I have lost that. I ask you now for your daughter's hand in marriage, and I swear I will love and protect her, and my child.'

The General stared at the Horse Warrior before him; he had such hopes for him, but now they were gone. Malvais was a natural-born leader who acted much older and more mature than his years. He became angry at the thought of losing such talent.

'I must warn you it is probable that your life is in danger; I told you months ago that the Pechenegs never forgive or forget. They will see this as a major insult to the ruling tribe. You cannot ride out on any more patrols, for I know you will not return. I will promote Orontes and put him in charge of them, and you can return to policing the Crusader camp, as few alternatives are now left open to you. I suggest you accept the offer of Raymond of Toulouse and escort them to Niksar to help free King Behemond, then take what's left of them on to Jerusalem. Rhea will stay here initially; you will be married before you go, and I will immediately send her to her grandparents in Constantinople. Also, I only give you a thirty per cent chance of returning, so at least as a beautiful widow, she can start a new life with a new husband in the city where her past will be unknown. You are dismissed.'

Conn left and, closing the door behind him, leaned against the cold stone walls of the spiral staircase. The General was right; he had destroyed his career, and to make it worse, he

CHAPTER TWENTY-SIX

would have a wife he would not see for years and a child who would not know him if he returned.

Rhea was confined to her room with only her maid, Priscilla, for company. She was not unhappy with the outcome, for she had achieved her aim of being taken away from this godforsaken place and having a handsome Horse Warrior in her bed.

'Lady Rhea Fitz Malvais,' she murmured to herself, it sounded good.

Her maid looked up from her needlework and gave her mistress a speculative glance. She had only been there for a year after the dismissal of the last maid, but she was a bright girl and had got the measure of her young mistress quite quickly.

'Are you going to take me with you, mistress?' she asked, a hopeful note in her voice.

'We shall have to see; after all, I may need a much smarter maidservant in my new position, not someone from the city's back streets,' she said with a slight sneer before continuing. 'I hope to persuade him to live in Paris, Rome or even London; I intend to be someone in those cities, Priscilla. More importantly, are you still flirting with that squire of his?' she asked, pinning the thin-lipped Priscilla with a sharp stare.

'Darius? Yes, I allow him to see me occasionally,' she said, trying to keep the anger and contempt for her mistress out of her voice.

'Well, do not be stupid and allow him under your skirts. I want you to find him and take a message for Malvais; I must see him urgently as we have to make plans.'

The atmosphere in Conn's pavilion was equally tense as

Georgio and Darius stared at Conn in disbelief.

'Rhea is carrying your child? How could you be so stupid, Malvais? From what you tell me, you have now destroyed our chances of advancement here due to carelessly swiving a pretty girl, not any girl, but the General's daughter, with no thought about the consequences. So what happens to us now?' yelled Georgio.

Conn dipped his head in his hands, 'I know, you don't have to criticise me; I have berated myself enough already. I can only say it was like a madness; I had to have her, and she was the same.'

'I bet she was; she saw you coming,' declared Darius.

Conn shot to his feet, 'What did you say?'

Behind Conn, Georgio shook his head at Darius, for he could see the anger building in Malvais. But Darius, never one to hold back, kept digging the hole.

'Everyone knows that she hates this place; she was desperate for a chance to leave, and she behaved the way she did so her father would send her back to Constantinople. She saw you as that chance, and suddenly, she is with child. That was very convenient,' he stated, making it worse by shaking his head in disbelief.

Georgio closed his eyes, and Darius did not see the blow coming as Conn lashed out and knocked him clear over to the other side of the tent. Darius lay stunned for a few moments in the middle of spare saddles and shields, and then, wiping the blood from his mouth on his sleeve, he got shakily to his feet, but he would still not be silenced.

'It's true!' he exclaimed as Georgio stood before Conn, hands raised to stop him from hitting their young squire again.

'Get out!' yelled Conn.

CHAPTER TWENTY-SIX

Darius made for the door, tearing the flap open, equally angry because an intelligent man like Conn Fitz Malvais could not see when he was being used. Meanwhile, in the tent, Conn's anger disappeared as quickly as it had come as he flung himself back into the camp chair, disappointed in himself that he had lost control; he could see the surprise and disgust on Georgio's face as he stared down at him before pulling up a chair to face him.

'That was not well done, Conn. The boy saved your life and sees far more of what is happening in the camp and what is being said. So what for us now?'

'We are to patrol the camp and get them ready to leave by the end of the week. We escort them north to the castle of Niksar, where King Behemond is being held prisoner. We are to assist them in laying siege to it and freeing him.'

Georgio put a hand over his eyes and groaned, 'And the Pechenegs?'

'Orontes has been promoted; he'll ride with us, commanding five hundred of them. None from the Bula Copan tribe.'

'You know we are all going to die, and you will never see this child of yours. I am going to find Darius, and I hope I can persuade him to stay with us,' snapped Georgio as he stood and swept out.

Conn ran his hands through his hair in frustration and anger at himself as he could see no way out of the mess he had created.

Darius, meanwhile, was in the stable brushing Diablo with such vigour that the huge horse turned and snapped at him. Darius leaned his forehead on Diablo's flank and gently ran his hand over the great haunches as he murmured, 'Sorry, it isn't your fault, but what a mess this is; everything has been swept away.'

He was still angry at Conn for treating him the way he did; he felt tears suddenly come, and he impatiently brushed them away when a pleasant voice broke in on his thoughts.

'Oh, so this is where you are hiding; I have looked everywhere for you,' said Priscilla, bravely moving in beside him and Diablo. She raised a hand to his cheek as she could see his eyes were full of tears, and standing on tiptoe, she softly kissed his lips. He pulled her into his arms, which Diablo took exception to, so they moved out of the stall, but he kept hold of her hand.

'She wants to see him; she'll meet him here tonight,' she announced.

'How will she do that when her father has her under lock and key?' asked Darius.

Priscilla scoffed, 'There is no gaol made that could contain that one; she has gone out numerous times in my clothes, even dressed as a kitchen boy to keep an assignment with a handsome warrior. I tell you, she is insatiable,' she whispered.

Darius froze at her words. 'Numerous? How numerous and who?'

'Well, I have only been here for a year, and it's a miracle I have stayed here that long, for she is an absolute termagant, I tell you. But I can remember three or four before Mengu, then it was nothing but him, for she enjoyed the danger of the liaison, keeping the top Pecheneg warrior on a string at her beck and call. That was until your Horse Warrior came along, and he was a better catch.'

Darius felt the first stirrings of hope, and he swung her round and round before he kissed her soundly. She looked up at him breathlessly.

CHAPTER TWENTY-SIX

'Names, Priscilla. Can you remember any of their names?' he said, releasing her.

She nodded; 'One or two of them, the monks here, taught me my letters so I could help my mistress. I will write them down when I get inside; I will find you tomorrow morning.'

He kissed her again in thanks, and she went on her way.

Conn did not get to meet Rhea as a fracas kicked off in the camp again that evening, and a few of the nobles came to blows over their route. Raymond, now the anointed leader of the crusade, helped Conn to resolve the situation, but it took several hours. He had heard of Conn's tribulations and demotion and was delighted, slapping him on the back in greeting.

'Forget this backwater, Malvais; I swear you will win fame and fortune by my side; you would have just stagnated here in Nicomedia.'

The next day, two things happened that made Conn's stomach knot. The horns blew along the valley, announcing the arrival of the Emperor's Megas Doux, John Doukas. He arrived at the head of a hundred of the Emperor's elite troops in full formation, galloping five abreast, their burnished metal breastplates shining in the sun. It was an awe-inspiring sight that resulted in a tremendous crowd outside the fortress, sitting and standing on walls and rooves to get a view of the famous Megas Doux, the Emperor's right-hand man. Then Banadir appeared at the fortress as John Doukas mounted the top step to greet a grim-faced General Tzitas. The General watched in alarm as the leader of the Bula Copan, flanked by half a dozen heavily armed Pecheneg warriors, pushed his way through the crowd, cheering the arrival of the Megas Doux. Silence came over the crowd as Banadir mounted the steps.

Conn, who was stood to one side, stared in consternation. He had an idea of what was coming.

'I am here to issue a challenge to Sir Conn Fitz Malvais on behalf of my son Mengu Timur. He has been grievously insulted and wronged by this Horse Warrior, so as is our right, we demand he meet in a fight to the death to restore Mengu's honour and that of the Bula Copan.' Banadir folded his massive arms, and with an angry scowl, stood waiting for the reply.

John Doukas, who had met the leader of the Bula Copan several times, looked at him in annoyance and then turned his glare on Conn and then General Tzitas, who had expected this to happen but had hoped to avert it before the arrival of the Megas Doux.

'Would someone like to enlighten me as to what the hell is going on?' he snapped, as the General wearily waved Conn over.

'Do you accept the challenge, Malvais?' he asked in a booming voice that carried over the large crowd.

'I do!' exclaimed Conn, bowing to Banadir.

The General waved an angry John Doukas inside, beckoning Conn to follow.

Chapter Twenty-Seven

General Tzitas took John Doukas to his business room, leaving Conn to stride restlessly around the Great Hall until he was called. He was ashamed that he had let both of these men down. As he respected both of them, they had shown their confidence and faith in him as a leader, and he had proved them wrong in the worst possible way.

On the balcony above, Rhea stood and watched him. She could see his torment, and she did care for him, but it suited her plans that he could no longer stay and take up the prestigious post here. She could even be happy going back to Constantinople, for as a wife, she would have the freedom to do as she wished with whom she wished once this child was born. She thought about calling his name but thought better of it as his fate was undoubtedly in the hands of John Doukas. So she would wait and see what happened; she made her way back to her room, where she found Priscilla in a state of some excitement.

'Have you heard about the challenge, my lady? They are fighting over you to the death.'

Rhea paled; this was not part of her plan, and if Conn was killed, her father might force her to marry Mengu. That would be a fate worse than death, for she could never leave

Nicomedia; she would be trapped in that tribe forever. She knew her father would be deaf to her pleas to go to her grandparents, for she would have to admit the shame of bringing a bastard child into the world, disgracing the proud family name. She paced back and forth and realised there was only one solution: to persuade her father to let her marry Conn Fitz Malvais before the fight.

In the hall, Conn had finally been summoned, and with some trepidation, he mounted the stairs. Both men met him tight-lipped with glares until John Doukas turned on him.

'You stupid young fool, not only have you finished your career in Nicomedia, you have seriously damaged relations with the Pechenegs and forced General Tzitas to stay here for another year, as he embeds Orontes into the role you should have had, which has disrupted my plans for the General. I never thought of you as someone who would be thinking with his prick rather than his brain. You have thrown everything away for a roll in the hay with a wild girl who offered herself on a platter.'

The General coughed and sat forward, 'That is my daughter we are talking about, Sire. I admit she is complicit in this, but I do not expect to hear her abused in my presence.'

However, Doukas was not in the mood to temper his language.

'Do you not think I know what goes on in every one of my military bases in the empire, Tzitas? I'm aware she has run rings around you since her mother died. She seduced my Captain of the Guard the last time I was here. The question is, what do we do now?' The General bowed his head and stared at the table in embarrassment before wearily dropping his face into his hands as the silence continued. Finally, he sat back with a sigh.

'Malvais has no choice; he has to face Mengu or be branded a coward. This is important if we are to rebuild trust with them. We cannot intervene and simply send him away.'

'I'm aware of that, Tzitas, but we know both are outstanding, fierce fighters who give no quarter. If Malvais kills Mengu, do you think the Bula Copan will calmly accept that as justice? I think not! We could have a rebellion on our hands, or they will leave, return to the steppes, and probably take the other tribes north with them. How do I explain to Alexios that he has lost four or five thousand much-needed troops from Anatolia, one of our main defensive borders? So if either of you have a solution, come up with it now,' he growled.

'I could negotiate with Banadir, offer Mengu my daughter's hand,' suggested Tzitas.

Conn's eyes widened in horror at this suggestion. 'No! You cannot do that; she is carrying my child. Mengu would probably drown it at birth or expose it on the hillside. I have to fight this challenge; I have no choice as it is now a matter of honour for both of us.'

John Doukas shook his head in frustration at the situation, then stood, as did the other two men.

'I have to meet Stephen de Blois and Raymond of Toulouse to discuss this sudden change of plan to go east; another foolish decision,' he said. Making for the door, he stopped beside Conn and looked down at him.

'You could have gone so far, so fast, Malvais,' he exclaimed and descended the stairs. Conn closed his eyes for a second as he experienced guilt, shame and remorse for his actions and then bowing his head to Tzitas, he followed John Doukas out. Surprisingly, he found the Megas Doux waiting at the bottom of the stairs.

'Make sure you kill him, Malvais. We will deal with the fallout, and I can threaten the Pecheneg or take a few leaders hostage if I need to. A lot is riding on this challenge, and winning it is the only way you will rescue any shred of your reputation.'

To Rhea's astonishment, her father would not see her or listen to any of her requests from her servants. She had always been able to talk him around, but this time, she had gone too far; there was no coming back from this, and her pleas were to no avail. There was now an extra, new guard on her door, one she could not talk around and could only pace her room in anger.

Georgio waited for Conn outside the fortress and walked with him to the stables. He knew about the challenge but was just as concerned about the disappearance of Darius.

'He has not been seen since you hit him; I fear he may have returned to Constantinople,' he exclaimed in annoyance.

'If that's the case, then he does not have the resilience and grit I expect as a squire, so good riddance. When I think of the regular beatings you and I took from the knights as young squires, one blow from me was nothing,' he growled.

Georgio shook his head and turned away; it was pointless talking to Conn when he was like this; he determined to keep looking for Darius, who had taken a horse and ridden out.

Darius had not gone to the city; he was still in Anatolia but searching for people. He was on a mission to save Conn; his anger at the Horse Warrior had abated. It was not the blow that had angered him as he had suffered far worse working in the inns; it was the unfairness of it, for he knew he was right

CHAPTER TWENTY-SEVEN

about Rhea.

John Doukas had insisted that the challenge take place on the large training ground, as he knew that hundreds would want to watch. He ordered Orontes to bring five hundred of the Emperor's spear-carrying troops to ring the area, placing them within a spear length of each other to hold back the crowd in case of trouble. He was right to be concerned, for most of the men of the Bula Copan tribe were there from dawn. When they arrived, John Doukas made a point of going to Banadir.

'The General will ensure that this is a fair fight, but I promise you, Banadir, if Mengu loses and there is any bloodshed by your men, I will bring five thousand men over from the city and hang every one of those responsible. As you have found in the past, I always keep my word. I hope it will not come to that. Despite this annoying incident, Emperor Alexios values our alliance with the Pechenegs.'

So saying, he turned on his heel, leaving Banadir to thoughtfully chew on the end of his long moustache before calling his senior men over to repeat the words of the Megas Doux. They were grim-faced when they went to pass on warnings to the assembled warriors; they knew the power and brutality of the Megas Doux; in his war against them, he had wiped out whole villages without a backward glance. They were also highly paid as allied warriors of the Emperor, and no one wanted to risk that, so the senior men picked out their men who they knew could be volatile and threatened them.

Conn arrived with Georgio and his men, who looked apprehensively at the crowds of Pechenegs. They stood in the shade and waited for Mengu to arrive. Tradition had it that he would issue the challenge again in public, as the man who had been wronged, he had the choice of weapons, and then the fight would begin.

'You do know that this is to the death and not first blood,' whispered a pale-faced and worried Georgio. A stern-faced Conn did not reply; he just nodded.

'I have said little on this, for you made your choices and are now paying the price for them, but I am surprised and saddened that you would risk, and throw away, everything you have achieved for a woman such as this'

Again, Conn said nothing. He continued to stare over the heads of the immense crowd at the mountains encircling Nicomedia, but Georgio saw the flush on his face, and he knew his words had struck home.

Georgio continued, 'The men have their instructions; if Mengu delivers the killing blow, the Horse Warriors will immediately run to protect your body. I refuse to stand and let them dismember you piece by piece; I will ensure you are embalmed and sent whole back to our family in Morlaix. That is what your father would expect.'

Conn inclined his head in thanks, but his stomach knotted at those words, not in fear, as he was rarely afraid, but at the realisation that Georgio thought he might lose, and at the mention of his family. Suddenly, the faces of his family came to him: his father, and his uncle, Luc De Malvais; what would they say if he died, not in battle as expected, but over something like this? Then, his stepmother, Ette, small, pretty and elfin, there would be tears and even more from his aunt, Merewyn, who had brought him up as a baby until he was kidnapped five years later. He took a deep breath, realising it was far too long since he had seen them or been home to Morlaix. He could suddenly see the castle on the cliffs in

CHAPTER TWENTY-SEVEN

Brittany, the fields and meadows below full of horses, and he berated himself for not returning sooner, as now, there was a chance that he may never return.

Mengu arrived to tremendous cheers and the almost deafening sound of hundreds of warriors banging weapons on their shields. He walked into the centre and raised his arms to the crowd to recognise their acclaim. Conn saw that he was naked to the waist, his baggy trousers tucked into high boots, a long curved dagger at his waist. He unlaced his own leather doublet and let it drop to the ground at Georgio's feet and tucked his linen shirt into his braies, tying them tightly in a double knot. Then he stepped forward to the raucous whoops and cheers from his men, the Emperor's troops, and the few hundred Lombard soldiers who had secured a space.

Both men gathered before the long dais erected under a large awning to give Rhea, her father, the nobles, and tribal leaders shade while the crowd sweltered in the heat. It was almost noon, and the heat of the Anatolian sun was beginning to be felt. Conn noticed that the Lombard nobles were also seated there; Guibert of Parma sneered and raised his goblet mockingly to Conn, which he ignored.

General Tzitas stood and asked Mengu to issue his challenge and choose his weapons. It was no surprise to Conn or Georgio that he chose spears and daggers once he had repeated the challenge; he had watched Conn with a sword and knew he would have no chance.

'Hold the spear halfway down, short jabs,' whispered Georgio as he took Conn's sword away and handed him the spear. For the first time, Conn smiled.

'I do know what to do with a spear, Georgio, but I will not take the curved dagger; I fight far better with a good, straight

Breton one,' he murmured as he clasped arms with him.

Unexpectedly, Georgio's eyes became wet at this, as it was like a last farewell, and he found he had to look down and turn away quickly so no one would notice or see his weakness.

Mengu had moved into the centre of the arena, his feet apart, his spear firmly planted, and his hand on the long curved dagger. Conn strode firmly forward to face him; he could see the hatred on the Pecheneg warrior's face as Conn purposefully moved closer to him.

'Before we begin, I have to say truthfully that I had no idea she was your chosen bride. She gave no indication of that, or I swear I would not have impugned your honour in this way, Mengu. I have a lot of respect for you. I am saddened that it has come to this between us.'

There was confusion on the young Pecheneg's face for a few moments as the Horse Warrior's words resonated, but then the anger returned.

'The whole camp now knows what you did to her. You swived her night after night, and for that alone, I promise that I will gut you and then cut out your heart to drop in her lap.'

Conn gave Mengu a calm, amused smile and bowed his head before moving away to pick up a handful of grit to rub on his hands as he waited for the horns to be blown.

The two men circled warily, spears poised and daggers drawn, each determined that they alone would emerge alive and triumphant.

A league away, Darius and two others galloped towards Nicomedia. Darius was hot and sweating; it ran down his temples and dripped onto his chest as he narrowed his eyes to gaze at the sun's position. He also knew that their horses were nearly blown as they had galloped at speed for several leagues; he kicked his horse harder, praying it would not collapse before they reached the training ground. He knew it was now afternoon; he was afraid they had left it too late to set off, and it would be all over before they arrived. If so, Conn or Mengu would be dead, and he would have had a wasted journey.

Chapter Twenty-Eight

The sun beat down on the two men as Conn, after several feints and grapples, realised that he was truly fighting for his life. Mengu was good, very good. The choice of weapons had given him an advantage; he had spent his life with a spear in his hand. He was also very quick on his feet as the spear whirled above his head and delivered several lightning wounds to Conn in his upper arms and thighs, and the splotches of blood now stained his white linen shirt, to the delight of the Pecheneg crowd.

Conn wracked his brain for the skills that Edvard had taught him with a staff as he realised that those same skills could be applied to this long javelin-style weapon. Mengu was now enjoying playing to the crowd. By inflicting early wounds, he became overconfident and basked in the acclaim from his supporters, which made him careless. Conn decided to play to that, and he began to limp on the leg that was injured, and there was a gasp from his supporters; the blood had now impressively stained his white braies. He purposefully moved more slowly and made wild jabs with the spear and swipes with the dagger that would never connect with Mengu, who danced away, laughing. The shock was clear on Georgio's face as he watched what was being enacted before him. He never

CHAPTER TWENTY-EIGHT

truly thought Conn would lose; he had never seen him beaten in this type of combat. He was usually proficient with most weapons, but like Conn, he realised that Mengu was an expert with the light Pecheneg spear.

At one point, Conn even stopped, and he leaned his hands on his thighs; he bent forward as if he was catching his breath, or as if the pain from half a dozen wounds was becoming too much. Mengu saw this as his chance and charged at Conn with a roar, but he found nothing there. Conn, anticipating and hoping for this, had moved swiftly to one side and then stabbed hard with his dagger into the back of Mengu's right shoulder, above the arm holding the spear. As Mengu cried out and tried to turn, Conn twisted the dagger in the wound before leaping back out of range. The blood flowed freely and dripped onto the ground, and it was Conn's turn to laugh aloud before an enraged Mengu charged at him. Conn dropped his spear so that he could grab both of his enemy's wrists, which he did in an iron grip, then moved to crush the Pecheneg warrior's fingers, so he also dropped his spear. Conn's years of sword practice had given him immense strength in his hands and forearms, so now, at close quarters, he had the advantage over Mengu.

They grappled back and forth, neither releasing, but Mengu was also a practised wrestler with strong thighs and calves, solid from a lifetime in the saddle. As they turned, he managed to sweep Conn's legs from beneath him. They both fell to the ground, but Conn rolled aside as he fell; Mengu grabbed the linen shirt to hold him, which was now proving to be a disadvantage to Conn, who pulled away; fortunately, the shirt ripped, and Conn sprang to his feet, pulling the shirt off. There was an audible gasp from the huge crowd behind

Conn, and then wild cheers as the full glory of the brightly coloured tattoo was revealed. To the crusading crowds, it was an omen that God was indeed on the side of this great warrior, for he wore the sign of Christ on his back, a flaming sword in the shape of a cross and a crown of thorns, and they shouted in triumph. Even John Doukas and Tzitas blinked in surprise, while Raymond of Toulouse was elated as he looked at it. He could imagine the impact of having a warrior with this tattoo on his back at the front of his crusading column as they headed to Niksar or Jerusalem.

The enormous Pecheneg crowd were initially silenced by the tattoo, for three-quarters of them were Christian converts, although the old religion of Shamanism still had its hold over many. Both warriors, naked from the waist up, dripping blood from several wounds, confronted each other, slowly stepping left in a circular movement. Both had daggers, and each man was now wary of the other, realising they were closely matched. Then, Mengu launched himself at his spear, picking it up as Conn quickly did the same, and then he charged at the Pecheneg. Mengu, with a frightening speed, threw his spear with force at the attacking Horse Warrior. Conn quickly swerved, turning sideways, which saved his life, but it embedded itself in his shoulder, and he dropped to his knees from the force of the blow. Mengu sprang forward, and in seconds, he was behind him and had his curved dagger at Conn's throat, and blood trickled. Mengu looked at the crowd with a gloating grin, ready to deliver the final death cut. The cheers from the Pecheneg crowd were tumultuous.

Georgio and the Horse Warriors cried out in dismay and disbelief. But, this pause for acclaim was to be Mengu's downfall, as Conn was a Breton and was not done. He

CHAPTER TWENTY-EIGHT

slammed his heavy dagger through the soft boot of the Pecheneg warrior into his instep, near the ankle, pinning his foot to the ground and breaking through several bones. Mengu screamed in pain while Conn flung his head backwards with force, and Mengu lost his balance and fell backwards, his arms flailing and his dagger still in his hand. Conn sprang from his grip and staggered to his feet; gritting his teeth, he gripped the unbarbed weapon with both hands and groaned loudly as he pulled it from his shoulder. The blood ran down his chest in rivulets, but seconds later, he was astride Mengu, throwing the warrior's dagger away, ready to plunge the spear into the pinned and fallen Pecheneg.

'Do not fear Mengu. I will not mutilate your body as we Bretons are not Barbarians, and I will see that you are buried with honour,' he shouted, holding the spear high to plunge it through Mengu's heart. Considering the thousand or so in the crowd, there was absolute silence as they listened and waited for the death blow, some pleased, some with tears streaming, and some in shock like Banadir, who did not want to believe what he was seeing as he never expected his son to lose.

Were family honour and pride really worth this? Banadir asked himself, closing his eyes at first but then forcing himself to watch Mengu's death in respect for his son.

Suddenly, a lone voice cried out, 'Stop! Stop, Malvais, do not kill him. The child is not yours; it is Mengu's child.'

Conn froze and quickly glanced at the owner of the voice as the crowd gasped. A dust-covered Darius pushed his horse through them to ride into the centre of the arena, followed by several others.

'I have proof, Conn, solid proof that she tricked you! I have here Captain Achemis, who is here to admit he took her virginity, which she gave him after he promised to take her away from here, back to Constantinople, but the Megas Doux found out, and she was foiled. Riding beside him are two young Pecheneg warriors she had bedded before Mengu; they will tell you the truth about her to save Mengu's life. He has been her lover for the last six months, and her maid, Priscilla, told me her courses stopped over two months ago, certainly a month before your affair with her started. She knew she was with child and she knew it was Mengu's, but she saw you as a better chance of escaping from here, to take her to Europe'.

Still holding the spear poised in case Mengu reacted, Conn turned his head towards the dais before him and glared at Rhea, who, white-faced, had risen to her feet and backed away.

'Is this true?' he yelled. 'Is it true, Rhea?' The rage was clear to see on his face.

All eyes turned to her, fists were shaken, and vile abuse was shouted. Realising she had been exposed, with people willing to give evidence, her shoulders sagged, and she nodded. Her father, also white with anger, stood up and slapped her so hard she fell back into the chair.

Conn lowered the spear and shook his head in disbelief at the fool he had been, at how he had been taken in and used by her. Standing, he reached down and pulled the dagger out of Mengu's foot, who groaned at the excruciating pain, but then Conn held out a hand to pull the Pecheneg to his feet. Mengu looked at him in surprise but slowly reached and took the hand. The crowd buzzed with excitement at what had just happened while the two bleeding warriors stood facing each other.

'We can fight on if you wish, probably just to settle our sense of honour, but I think that child needs a father, especially if it is to be a warrior as brave as you,' said Conn. Mengu nodded as Conn put both hands on Mengu's shoulders and bowed in recognition of a great fighter, and Mengu returned it. Then Banadir was there with servants. He gripped his son by the shoulders, his eyes wet with relief; he helped carry him to the physicians. However, he made time to stop to give a quick bow of his head to Conn in thanks and left as Georgio ran up with several of their men and linen strips to bind the shoulder wound, which was bleeding heavily.

'Don't ever do that to me again, Malvais; at one point, I honestly thought you were going to lose,' said a relieved Georgio, padding and tightly binding the wound.

Conn bent his head close to his friends and whispered, 'So did I, Georgio. So did I.'

May 1101 – Rouen

Preparations were going exceptionally well for the planned summer invasion; dozens of ships were assembled in the harbour of Treport, supervised by the Count of Eu.

Robert and his inner circle had ridden north to see the progress being made personally.

'It is a sight to gladden even the coldest of hearts, Sire,' said Belleme as they all gazed over the forests of masts in the bustling harbour, where hundreds of seamen and soldiers were engaged in various tasks.

As they watched, wagon after wagon of supplies arrived and were loaded into the holds or stored in the large wooden warehouses that Henry of Eu had ordered built. Piers De Chatillon cast his eyes over the harbour and beyond to where he could see meadows of horses waiting to be loaded when the day arrived to sail for England. Having watched the disastrous attempted invasion in 1085, when Robert had not even boarded a ship, and several of his ships were lost in the channel, he felt far more confident about this one.

'I presume you are still thinking about a calm period in July as we discussed,' asked Chatillon.

'I see no reason for any delay, Chatillon. Everything is in place, and my support here and with those waiting in England has certainly overwhelmed and reassured me. The only thing that could delay the invasion is the weather, so pray for good weather. This is your doing, you know; you were the one that persuaded me to go on the crusade. You were not sure at first, but then you suggested to Pope Urban that I should be one of the leaders, and you even rode alongside me as far as Lucca. That changed my life. I returned a hero and a changed man, and you enabled me to meet Sibylla; intelligent, wealthy, and the most beautiful wife a man could ever have.'

Belleme rolled his eyes at this sentimental codswallop.

'Very uplifting, Sire, but let us not forget you lost at least fifteen thousand pilgrims and several great nobles; also, you managed to lose your crown by taking too long to come home. Jerusalem is under attack again, and now another death march, derisively called the Crusade of the Faint Hearted, is on its way to lose another fifteen thousand pilgrims and save the city again - supposedly.'

Both men were used to the poisonous remarks that Belleme dripped, so they did not reply.

'How is the Duchess Sibylla? It was wonderful news that she is with child,' asked Chatillon.

Robert smiled, 'She wanted to ride out with us to see the progress we are making, but I refused; she is three months

CHAPTER TWENTY-EIGHT

gone, I believe, still a dangerous time, and she needs to take care. He will be a legitimate son, God willing, an heir to take over the Duchy.'

'An heir to the throne of England as well,' exclaimed Chatillon loudly to a grin and cheer from those in the party around them.

At that moment, Lady Sibylla was indeed resting, lying on a divan in the solar; the early summer sunshine filled the room with warmth, and she was quietly content. She could not wait for this child to be born and wanted several more. She also prayed it was a boy; she would be happy with a girl, but everyone knew it took the pressure off if the first was a healthy boy child. The door opened, and one of her new servants appeared with her favourite small cakes and a drink of warm milk with nutmeg. Sibylla put down the tract she had been reading, The Lives of the Saints, an uplifting volume of stories with prayers at the end of each section. She pushed herself into a sitting position as the girl placed the refreshments on the table beside her.

'I will be as large as a house if I keep eating these, Peggy. They are so irresistible, full of butter and honey.'

Peggy smiled; she was a pleasant young girl with a round, freckled face and a snub nose. Her Italian maid had succumbed to a winter chill, so a replacement was found, an English girl, which Sibylla thought was a good idea if Robert succeeded and she became Queen of England.

'The chef makes a fresh batch for you every day; he is delighted you like them; he is now inventing new ones for you. Puffed up with pride, he is, mistress.'

Sibylla laughed and insisted the girl take one to prevent her from eating them all; the girl did so and went back to her embroidery while Sibylla drank and ate her fill. Several hours later, Sibylla began to sweat and experience an ache that became progressively worse. In another hour, she was vomiting, which continued for most of the night. By dawn, she had miscarried and lost the baby.

Robert arrived back the next day to a castle filled with sadness; he raced to Sibylla's bedside, followed closely by Chatillon, who stood at the door and watched as Robert embraced and reassured his sobbing wife that her recovery and health were of paramount importance; there was plenty of time for more children. Peggy, the maid, sat wide-eyed on her stool, and Chatillon walked to face her.

'What did your mistress have to eat yesterday?' he asked with a penetrating gaze.

He noticed her hands clasped nervously, and her eyes could not meet his.

'The usual, Sire. Bread, cheese, fruit for breaking her fast, and then some sweet honey cakes and warm milk. After that, she was too poorly to eat anything else.'

'So these cakes were the last thing she ate. Who made them?'

'Why the chef, Sire, he makes them fresh every day, honey cakes with a sprinkling of small seeds. My lady insisted that I ate one myself, and I have been fine,' she said, briefly raising her eyes to his before dropping them again.

He moved away and commiserated with Sibylla but reiterated Robert's words that she needed to rest and recuperate. Then he went downstairs to the Great Hall, where many courtiers were gathered, and called Edvard to his side.

'Go to the kitchens. Sibylla ate small cakes and hot milk yesterday, and then the pain started. I want to know how many hands are on those plates and cups before it gets to her,'

CHAPTER TWENTY-EIGHT

he whispered. Edvard understood immediately.

Chatillon went to stand by the window beside Robert De Belleme while his eyes scanned the crowded hall to find what he was looking for. Despite being rejected by Robert, Lady Agness, the Countess of Buckingham, was still here in Rouen, which surprised him. She was holding court with her ladies and acolytes as usual; he watched her for several minutes and noticed how buoyant she was. At one point, she looked up, caught him staring, and gave him a knowing and triumphant smile. Now, he had no doubt.

Belleme followed his gaze and whispered, 'Poisoned?'

'Possibly, Belleme, possibly. I will put more safeguards in place, but keep this quiet until I have any evidence.'

Meanwhile, the maid, Peggy, begged to be excused and walked through the outer bailey and the gates into the town; once there, she met a dark young man who led her into an ally.

'You did very well, Peggy; she is very pleased,' he said, handing her a small purse of silver.

In return, she glanced behind to ensure no one was there and handed him a small stale cake from her pocket with a shaking hand.

'I cannot do it again; I'm terrified of that man, the one with the black eyes. He questioned me, and it was as if could see into my soul and knew exactly what we did.'

'Chatillon,' he spat.

She nodded, turned, and ran back to the castle as if the hellhounds were after her.

Chapter Twenty-nine

May 1101 – Nicomedia

Conn sat in his pavilion in a camp chair; the physician was cleaning and applying a poultice to the deep shoulder wound to draw out any infection, a painful process but now nearly over as he bound it tightly.

'I cannot remember when I ever felt as tired as this; dog tired,' he admitted to Georgio.

'You have had several days of tension, with little or no sleep, followed by a long and vicious fight to the death; your blood will have been raging, and now it is over, it has left you exhausted. Also, you are badly wounded; you lost a lot of blood, and you need to rest,' ordered Georgio.

As he finished the sentence, he was not pleased to see the tent flap thrown aside; as John Doukas swept in with Captain Orontes, Darius followed them, shrugging at Georgio to show that he had tried to keep them out. This made Georgio smile; he could not be expected to keep the Megas Doux of Byzantium out of one of his commander's tents.

'That was some performance you gave out there, Malvais,

and you have no doubt enhanced your reputation, but I came to thank this young man,' he said, turning to Darius, who flushed at the attention.

'Without your squire's intervention, I know you would have killed Mengu. You had no choice, and I admit I wanted his death rather than yours, but with hindsight, that would have ruined everything. This way, the alliance is still intact.'

Conn felt immeasurably weary, not only from the fight but also from finding that he had been duped so easily, and he was ashamed of himself for being so taken in by her. However, John Doukas was right about the role Darius played, and he waved him forward to make his bow.

'The day that Georgio found this young man on the streets of Constantinople was a lucky day for all of us, Sire, and I have no doubt that he'll achieve knighthood as he is already on the way to becoming a competent Horse Warrior.'

Darius blushed, while Georgio smiled, glad that his protégé was receiving some recognition.

John Doukas dropped into a camp chair beside Conn, while turning to Darius again.

'This is for you, a reward for your tenacity and loyalty to your master,' he said, throwing a small purse of silver in the air, which Darius deftly caught.

'Now I need to have words with Malvais and Georgio alone,' he commanded.

The physician and the squire left them, and Georgio poured them wine.

'The outcome of this challenge means that if you wish, you could stay here in Nicomedia. Regain the trust of the Pechenegs; they already hold you in high regard, even more so after the fight. However, you need to be aware that Rhea will be given in marriage to Mengu tomorrow; both fathers have agreed, the General with relief and Banadir with reluctance at accepting such a woman into his tribe. But Mengu is still besotted with her, despite everything she has done, and she is bearing his child. She has now admitted to him that it is his.'

Conn did not answer; he sat forward, winced as he moved his shoulder and stared at the ground beneath his feet until he finally answered.

'I think we both know and accept that relations with the Pechenegs would still be strained. Although I would do my best to rebuild that trust, I have to feel confident in the men who ride beside me into war. I would always be expecting an arrow between my shoulder blades because I dared to swive his woman.'

John Doukas inclined his head in agreement. 'Or he would struggle with the shame that she chose you, despite knowing she was carrying his child because you were the better option to life with the Bula Copan? They are a very proud people, they would take this as an insult and do not easily forgive. It is possible that these thoughts may burn and grow inside him, so he feels that he has to kill you despite you giving him his life back.'

'So that leaves me with the offer from Count Raymond to ride at his side to Niksar, free Behemond and then on to Jerusalem,' stated Conn. Georgio gave a snort of disgust as John Doukas stood and paced back and forth for a while.

'You do not have to take my advice, Malvais, for although you and Georgio signed up to the Emperor's Guard, I can release you in a second, and there are a dozen rulers who would welcome sell-swords such as you two, with open arms. I will say only one thing: this Crusade of the Faint-Hearted is

CHAPTER TWENTY-NINE

riding on a road towards death. To ride blindly east through the territories of the great Seljuk leader, Kilij Arslan, and then lay siege to an inaccessible and fortified castle controlled by the Danishmed Turks, who are equally as barbarous, is pure madness. If a tenth of the Crusaders survive, I will own myself astounded. Do not choose this road, Malvais, for you both know you have a third option.'

Georgio met Conn's eyes and watched him stiffen. They both knew what John Doukas would say next.

'My old enemy and now a good friend, Piers De Chatillon, has been in touch. I do not ever think he has asked me for a favour, although he once saved my life, and in the past, he has removed several enemies for me, so I do owe him. Now he asks me to put forward his plea, for he needs you both to return. There are apparently tasks in England that only you are capable of doing, Malvais, for they are preparing to go to war. Think on it carefully, for what you decide will not only be your fate but the fate of the faithful followers who are at your side.' With that, he turned, and with a salute, he left them to their thoughts.

With a quick glance at Conn's stony countenance, Georgio followed him out, for he found that he suddenly needed some air. He found Darius saying farewell to the maid, Priscilla; he smiled as he saw the young squire kiss her tenderly and then lift her and her bags onto the back of the carrier's cart before waving her off.

'She told the truth, saved a life, and has lost her job because of it,' exclaimed Georgio, shaking his head.

'She wanted to go back to Constantinople; her family are there, and General Tzitas was extremely generous. He even gave her a note of recommendation for other Greek noble families in the city. So what has been decided with the Megas Doux? Do we stay here or do we go, Sire?' he asked.

'Conn is deciding now; I have left him on his own to rest without having to listen to my opinion yet again. I think he is inclined to go with Raymond.'

'What will happen to our troop of Horse Warriors? Malvais may have created and trained them, but they are still the Emperor's men.'

Georgio shrugged, 'I would imagine that if we go with Raymond, then they will be riding with us as part of the protection detail, probably alongside the cohort of men who were with Orontes. I do not know if the five hundred Pecheneg horsemen will still accompany us; I hope so, for despite the risk, they are by far the best horsemen to fight the Seljuk bowmen.'

Conn sat in the pavilion with his eyes closed, turning the alternatives over in his mind. Should they stay here in safety but with numerous problems or risk life and limb on this crusade, which had little chance of success but would add glory and fame to their names? What use was that if they did not survive? They could go on the road to tour the courts of Europe looking for work, or they could finally go to war for Chatillon, to whom he still owed a huge debt. He clenched his fist and let out a strangled cry of frustration, for to be honest with himself, none of these options appealed to him, but he had listened to the warnings from John Doukas and the responsibility he had for those that followed him.

He ran his hands through his dark hair, which had grown much longer during his time in Anatolia. The words of Georgio came back to him. He had to admit that day had resonated far more than he liked to admit at the time.

CHAPTER TWENTY-NINE

I will ensure your body will be returned to our home in Morlaix; it is what our family would expect.

He suddenly had a wave of homesickness, the desire to see his family once more before he risked his life again. He stood up but, feeling slightly dizzy, sat down again; he yelled for Darius, who came running, followed by Georgio.

'Go and get that godforsaken physician back; I need him!'

Darius gave a quick smile and ran off to find him. Georgio stood tentatively by the flap of the pavilion, staring at the angry, bare-chested warrior with blood-soaked bandages covering his shoulder, upper arms and thigh.

'Either come in or get out, but I want no mealy-mouthed comments; I know I have lost blood, and yes, I feel as weak as a kitten, but by tomorrow, with some rest, I will have recovered,' he said, glaring at Georgio in case he dared to challenge that assumption.

Georgio said nothing, but bending forward, he poured him another goblet of strong, rich Syrian red wine.

Conn, seeing the wary expression on his friend's face, stretched out his hand and grasped his wrist as Georgio straightened.

'I have decided,' he exclaimed, but in a low voice as if he didn't really want to put it into words or want anyone else to hear.

Georgio's face took on a concerned, almost frightened look as he waited, fearing the worst as Conn loosened his grip and sat back in the chair, staring down into the goblet of wine in his hand. Finally, he looked up.

'We are going back to the west to honour our debt to Chatillon, Georgio, but first, I want to go home for a short while; I want to go back to Brittany, to Morlaix, to see them all again.' He raised his goblet to take a long draught.

Georgio could feel the tears coming as he grinned down at his friend, who was more like a brother to him. He brushed them away with the back of his hand, but they kept coming as Conn continued.

'Then we are going to war, Georgio. From what Chatillon says, we will probably be on the opposite side to most of our friends, a war for the Crown of England, and we will be fighting *against* Duke Robert and *for* King Henry.'

Georgio hardly heard that last sentence; he could not see, as his eyes were still filled with tears. After everything they had gone through, the hardships, the fear of being unable to find Conn at the palace, the many deaths and finally, the shock of nearly losing him in the fight with Mengu. He was full of relief at Conn's decision and flushed with happiness. He couldn't stop grinning as Darius came through the flap with the physician.

'We are going home, Darius,' he said, punching the air in joy. 'We are going home to Brittany!'

End

You can find out the fate of the Crusade of the Faint Hearted and what happens to Rhea in this bonus chapter (provided through Bookfunnel)

https://dl.bookfunnel.com/c5ap27453w

Author Note

It is always exciting starting to write a new series, albeit a spin-off from the last series, as there are fascinating new characters, both factual and fictional and new places to explore. I remember in my childhood thinking how exotic and thrilling Byzantium sounded, and it still felt the same researching Constantinople and Emperor Alexios in the year 1100 AD.

Being a historian, I love the research entailed in a new project, and I throw myself into it, spending weeks poring over books, journals and sources from the period to find those all-important threads. These threads are what lead you to the hidden but sometimes poignant or gripping stories, hence the tale of Altasparta and the lion.

The disastrous crusade from Lombardy was exactly as described: a nightmare to contain and control both for its leaders and for the Emperor. They not only looted and attacked the local villages, they also attacked the Blachernae Palace and killed the pet lion of Alexios.

I found the Pecheneg tribes intriguing; the more I delved and discovered their lifestyle, customs and laws, the more I understood why they were such a force to be reckoned with. They were fearsome and brutal in battle, and Emperor Alexios only finally managed to defeat them with the sheer numbers he sent against them. He then kept them as allies by paying them well, as he knew they were one of the few people the Seljuk Turks feared.

In London, Ranulf Flambard was, indeed, not only the first prisoner in the Tower but the first to escape, and his mother did cling to the mast and scream at the sky during the crossing to Normandy. The crew wanted to throw her overboard twice, but he talked them around. Flambard is a great historical figure, cunning, manipulative and, most of all, a survivor. In the forthcoming book two of the series, he comes into his own once again when he pulls off an unbelievable coup de grace.

Raymond of Toulouse and Stephen de Blois failed to persuade the Lombards to go south, especially when the German contingent backed them, and so the Crusade of the Faint Hearted headed north to Niksar to attempt to free King Behemond. How this ends and who survives are included in a bonus chapter that will be coming out in the December newsletter. It also covers the fate of Rhea, the wayward daughter of General Tzitas.

Thank you for reading and enjoying this book. I hope to launch book two in early 2024.

S.J. Martin

November 2023

List of Characters

Fictional characters in *italics*

Constantinople
Emperor Alexios Komnenos
John Doukas – The Megas Doux
Raymond of Toulouse
Conn Fitz Malvais
Georgio di Milan
Darius. Squire to Conn and Georgio.
Captain Orontes. A captain of the Emperor's troops.
Gracchus. Milanese soldier.
Lombard Crusade
Albert, Count of Biandrate
Guibert, Count of Parma
Otto Altasparta. Nephew of Albert and Guibert
Archbishop Anselm of Milan
Captain Fumagalli. A captain of the Milanese troops.

Nicomedia
General Tzitas. Leader of the Emperor's troops in Nicomedia.
Stephen of Blois
Rhea Tzitas. Daughter of General Tzitas

Banadir Timur. Leader of the Bula Copan
Mengu Timur. Son of Banadir.
London
King Henry I
Matilda of Scotland (Queen)
Robert de Beaumont, Earl of Leicester
Henry de Beaumont, Earl of Warwick
Anselm, Archbishop of Canterbury.
Ranulf Flambard
Lord William De Mandeville, Constable of the Tower of London
Rouen
Robert, Duke of Normandy
Sibylla of Conversano, Duchess of Normandy
William, Count of Mortain and Earl of Cornwall
Robert De Belleme, Earl of Shrewsbury
Agness, Countess of Buckingham
Henry, Count of Eu
Piers De Chatillon, Papal Envoy
Edvard of Silesia, Chatillon's vavasseur and friend

Glossary

Bailey - A ward or courtyard in a castle, some outer baileys could be huge, encompassing grazing land.

Braies - A type of trouser often used as an undergarment, often to mid-calf and made of light or heavier linen. Usually covered by chausses.

Chausses – Attached by laces to the waist of the braies, these were tighter fitting coverings for the legs.

Dais – A raised platform in a hall for a throne or tables, often for nobles.

Destrier – A knight's large warhorse, often trained to fight, bite and strike out.

Doublet – A close-fitting jacket or jerkin often made from leather, with or without sleeves. Laced at the front and worn either under or over, a chain mail hauberk.

Fyrd – An army raised from a lords manor, freemen and villeins pledged to fight for their lord.

Give no quarter – To give no mercy or show no clemency for the vanquished.

Hand-fasting – A legally binding ceremony for a couple could replace marriage.

Hauberk – A tunic of chain mail, often reaching to mid-thigh.

Holy See – The jurisdiction of the Bishop of Rome – the Pope.

Jereed – A team sport on horseback, scoring points by hitting an opponent with a blunt javelin.

League – A league is equivalent to approx. 3 miles in modern terms.

Liege lord – A feudal lord, such as a count or baron, entitled to allegiance and service from his knights.

Pallet bed – A bed made of straw or hay. Close to the ground, generally covered by a linen sheet and also known as a palliasse.

Patron – An individual who gives financial, political, or social patronage to others.

Pell – A stout wooden post for sword practice.

Pell-Mell – Confused or disorganised action, often in street riots or battles.

Pottage – A staple of the medieval diet, a thick soup made by boiling grains and vegetables and, if available, meat or fish.

Prelate – A high-ranking member of the clergy.

Retainer – A dependent or follower often rewarded or paid for their services.

Rout - A disorderly withdrawal from a battle.

Serjeant – The soldier serjeant was a man who often came from a higher class; most experienced medieval mercenaries fell into this class; they were deemed 'half of the value of a knight' in military terms.

Tagma – A Byzantine military unit of regiment size.

Vedette - An outrider or scout used by cavalry.

Vellum - Finest scraped and treated calfskin, used for writing messages.

Vifgage -A conditional grant of land that allows the grantee to enjoy the fruits of the land for a certain term as security for a loan.

Map

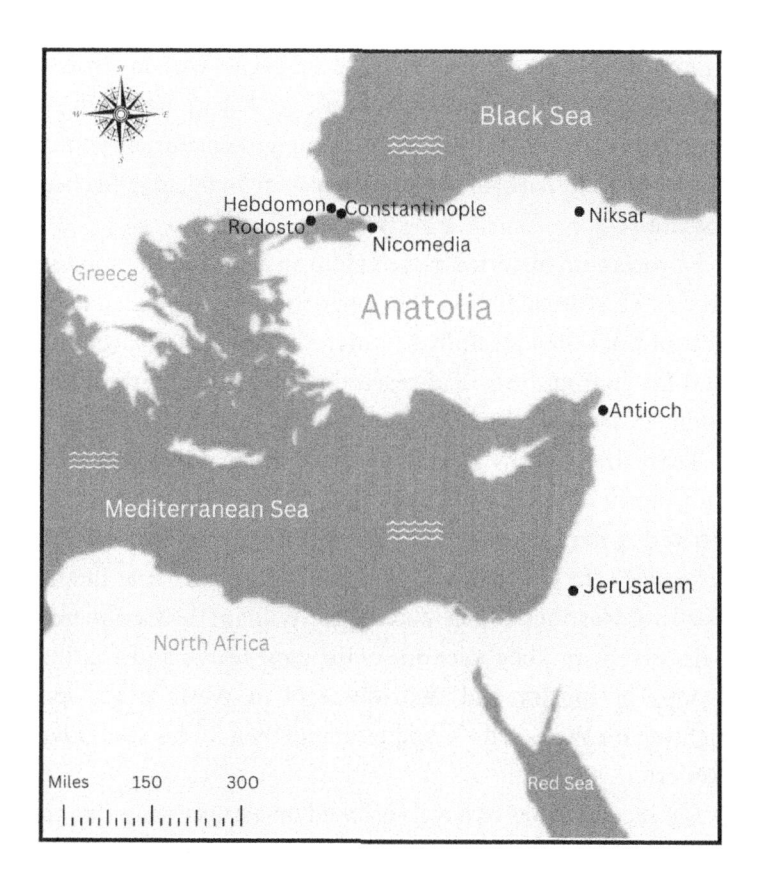

About the Author

I have adored all aspects of history from an early age, but I find the lawlessness, intrigue and danger of medieval times fascinating. This interest in history influenced my choices at university and my career. I spent several years with my trowel in the interesting world of archaeology before becoming a storyteller as a history teacher. I wanted to encourage young people to find that same interest in history that had enlivened my life.

I always read historical novels from an early age and wanted to write historical fiction. The opportunity came when I left education; I then gleefully re-entered the world of engaging and fascinating historical research into the background of some of my favourite historical periods.

There are so many stories out there still waiting to be told, and my first series of books, 'The Breton Horse Warriors' proved to be one of them. The Breton lords, such as my fictional Luc De Malvais, played a significant role in the Battle of Hastings and helped to give William the Conqueror a decisive win. They were one of the most feared and exciting troops of cavalry and swordmasters in Western Europe, fighting for William the Conqueror and then for his son, Duke Robert.

My second series of novels is based on a captivating character from the first series. My readers clamoured for the ruthless

Papal Envoy, Piers De Chatillon, to have his own series, and so the Papal Assassin Series was born. It is amazing how an immoral, murdering, manipulative diplomat and assassin can seize the imagination as he cuts a swathe through Europe. Undoubtedly, he is an enthralling and mesmerising character; I will be sad to let him finally go when the time comes.

I hope you enjoy reading my books as much as I have enjoyed writing them.

You can connect with me on:
- https://www.moonstormbooks.com/sjmartin
- https://twitter.com/SJMarti40719548
- https://www.facebook.com/people/SJ-Martin-Author/100064591194374

Subscribe to my newsletter:
- https://www.moonstormbooks.com/sjmartin

Also by S.J. Martin

The Breton Horse Warriors series

The Breton Horse Warriors series follows the adventures of our hero Luc De Malvais and his brother Morvan. It begins in Saxon England, during the Norman Conquest and travels to war-torn Brittany and then Normandy. Luc De Malvais is a Breton lord, a master swordsman and leader of the famous horse warriors. He faces threatening rebellion, revenge and warfare as he fights to defeat the enemies of King William. However, his duty and loyalty to his king come at a price, as his marriage and family are torn apart. He now has to do everything he can to save his family name, the love of his life and his banished brother…**but at what price?**

https://www.amazon.com/dp/B0921952WQ/

The Papal Assassin series

The Papal Assassin series follows the adventures, life and times of the darkly handsome swordmaster Piers De Chatillon. A wealthy French noble, the young influential Papal Envoy of several popes and a consummate diplomat, he spreads his influence, favours and threats around the courts of Europe.

He is an arch manipulator, desired by women and feared by men; he is also a lethal assassin used by kings and princes alike. His adventures take him back and forth across Europe in the turbulent seas of politics and intrigue in the 11th century.

Meanwhile, an array of enemies plots his downfall and demise. With the help of his close compatriots and friends, he manages to keep them at bay, but time is running out for Piers De Chatillon, and danger draws ever closer to his beautiful wife, Isabella and their children.

https://www.amazon.com/dp/B0BJ7V39RQ/

The Duke, the Girl and the Ermine
A short story.

Following her mother's death, Cecilia Gallerani, a talented and beautiful young musician, had spent most of her life within the cloistered walls of a convent in Florence. However, at the age of sixteen, all of that was to change.

In 1489, at the court of Lorenzo Medici in Florence, whilst taking part in a performance, she came to the notice of Ludovico Sforza, the powerful Duke of Milan, who insisted that her father bring her to his court.

Within only a few months, she was taken from seclusion into the overwhelming splendour and intrigue of the Milanese court. Whilst there, she would be swept into a scandalous and dangerous liaison that would change her life forever.

https://www.amazon.com/dp/B0CMC6R7W7/

Printed in Great Britain
by Amazon